To

The chaos continues.
Thank you for everything.
Enjoy!

Smoke And Stars

Book Two of The Rise of the Phoenix

MICHELLE SCHAD

Smoke and Stars

Copyright © 2022 by Chaos Publications
Copyright © 2022 by Michelle Schad

All rights reserved. Printed in the United States of America. No part of this book may be used or reproduced in any manner whatsoever without written permission except in the case of brief quotations embodied in critical articles or reviews.

This book is a work of fiction. Names, characters, businesses, organizations, places, events and incidents either are the product of the author's imagination or are used fictitiously. Any resemblance to actual persons, living or dead, events, or locales is entirely coincidental.

For information contact :
http://www.tamingchaos.net

Interior design by Chaos Publications
Cover art by Neil Que
Cover design by Black Bird Covers

ISBN: 9 7 8 1 9 5 4 4 4 1 3 1 0 8
1st Edition: April 2023

Dedication

For those that continue to show interest in my world, my characters, and my games.
For Matthew who always indulges me, my kids who always 'nag' (aka encourage) me, and my friends who support me. And for coffee, without which, none of this would have been possible. Wine too. You were instrumental in the creation and completion of this book.

Thank you.

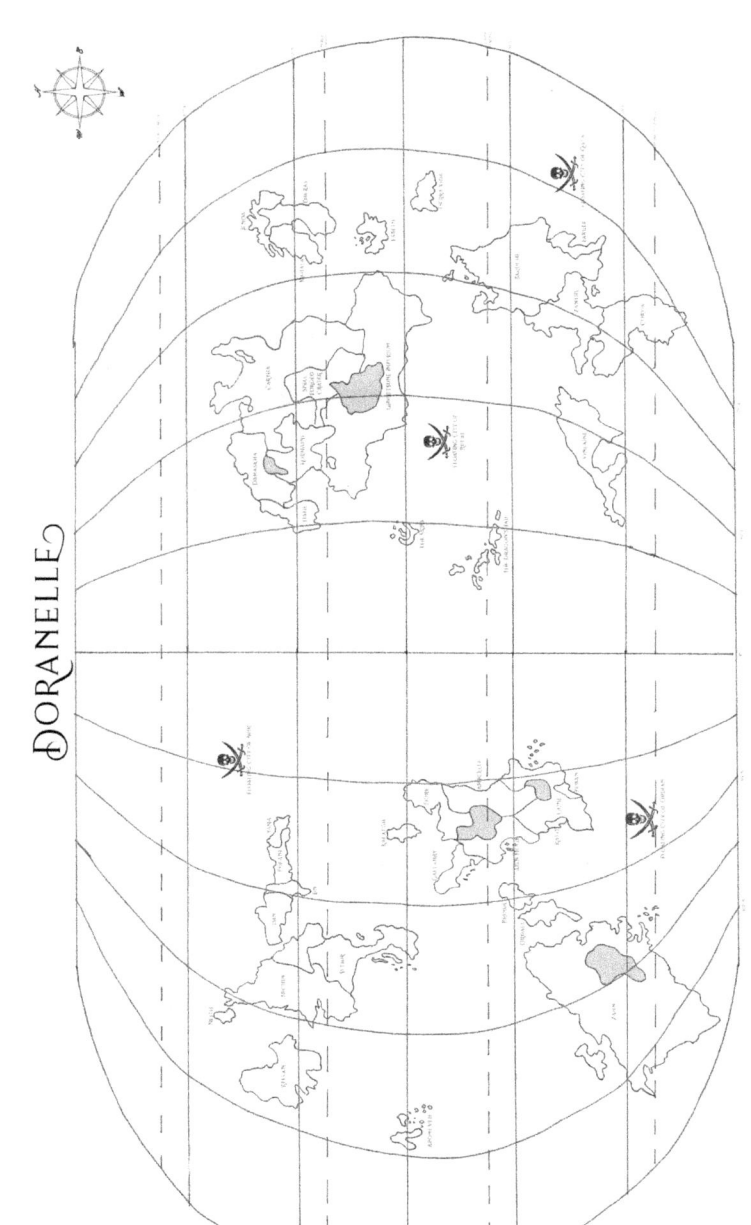

Chapter One

General Tondra Caelestis made a face of disgust as she stared at the empty, decrepit manse before her. Three days searching the densely forested hillsides of the Sierra Alto mountains yielded nothing in her hunt for the traitorous brat who attacked the Amatessa and the Esbethi Anointed One. Not only that, but he freed two prisoners as well. The edifice before her gave the illusion that it might crumble if someone sneezed too loudly and left an odd sensation between her wings, shoulder blades twitching no matter where she stood. It was as if the *building* watched *her*.

  Sitting outside the manse was an elderly gentleman, a human, with a graying goatee and balding head. He'd named himself Sergio, but said little else since they found him. He'd returned to the manse with a wagon full of supplies, surprised to find the building crawling with avian soldiers rather than the home's inhabitants. Tondra narrowed her eyes at the old man, stepping over to where he sat in the filth that *used* to be a shrub.

"I know you understand me," Tondra began, looking down at the man. He looked up with benign, innocent black eyes staring at her. "Where have they gone? People do not just vanish into thin air. Where would they go? Somewhere here? Somewhere else? Tell me, and you can go."

The man offered only a silent grin in response. Tondra's lip curled in anger. There was absolutely no sign of where they could have gone. She *knew* Kaleo did not have the ability to Travel. Perhaps the bard did, but even then, Traveling had limitations. Distance, number of people, familiarity - they were all factors that went into Travel when not using a Port Circle and very few people could do it unguided. It was those limitations that helped create Port Circles to begin with. Travel via Circle was controlled, guided, and focused. Whatever they had done to leave the manse followed none of those rules.

"General!"

Tondra glanced in the direction of the voice that called to her. She looked down at the old man one more time before going to where she was called. One of her soldiers stood near a flat stone buried deep in the muck and mud around the manse. It looked as old as the manse itself, if not older. The surrounding property held another edifice that *might* have been a servant's house at some point, but now was merely a shell of something that had four walls. The fourth wall was actually missing and the lower levels flooded with green, boggy water. The soldiers stood nearby, five of them all staring at a hole in the ground near some buried bricks.

"What is that?" Tondra demanded. She looked down into the hole to see the flat stone that took so much attention. Only part of it showed, the rest still firmly set into the moist earth.

"A Grove Stone, general," the soldier replied. "An old one, but it still radiates."

"Are there others?" Tondra frowned, squatting down to get a closer look. Time had worn some runes away and pocked the stone with holes as if acid had eaten it away. But if it still radiated, that meant it still worked.

"At least one more, general. It's... old. It would take ages to regrow a Grove here."

"But that gives me an idea of where that fool brat has gone."

"Where, general?"

"Tierra Vida."

"From here, ma'am?"

"That brat pulls off the impossible like a roach. Gather the soldiers. And get rid of the old man," Tondra said, rising to her full height. Two soldiers simply nodded, going to the front of the manse while the one near the stone gaped at her, quickly averting his gaze when she frowned at *him* instead of the stone. She would not lose Kaleo again.

***

Kaleo Oenel sat outside Reven's tent. Serai was inside with the bard. Kaleo had argued with the woman for the last three days since their arrival to Tierra Vida that clothing was required, that they were not home, that she could not walk around nude. It was like speaking to a child sometimes; a very Powerful child. He often forgot how much Power the woman had, tempering his annoyance only *after* he noticed her Power radiated off her like heat from an oven.

Lara sat beside him, idly plucking at blades of grass. The *runeli* thief kept her opinions to herself, mostly, but they still found their way to Kaleo's mind. Everyone's opinions did. Three days since their arrival in Tierra Vida was a lot of time to think about how stupid he had been, how reckless. Whether he'd intended to or not, he'd stepped into a hornet's nest of politics and warfare against an enemy he couldn't see. He was trying to remain calm, to not panic, but it was difficult. He had doubts and fears with no outlet to funnel them. He wasn't a leader; he was the bastard son of a fallen prince.

Gannon would have had kittens over what Kaleo had done. *Reven* drank too much and remembered very little. But he also nearly gave his own life to save Aeron, put himself at risk to keep Kaleo and Lara safe in Kormaine, even forgave the jackass thief-taker that betrayed him. *Reven* was a problem solver. *Kaleo* was a problem maker.

"How is he feeling today?" Ajana asked as she and said jackass thief-taker made their way over to where Kaleo and Lara sat. Kaleo harbored no ill-will toward the *cantari* woman. Ajana was just as angry at Liam for his betrayal, but as quick to forgive him as Reven was. Kaleo didn't see how or why, but it was not his place to question their relationship.

"Seems a little off today. Serai's in with him," Kaleo said. It took less time than expected for Reven to wake after his miraculous save of Aeron. However, part of Kaleo wished it had taken a little longer. The bard would simply stare into space for long periods of time now, or had waking nightmares that shook the entire Grove. It was both concerning and terrifying, with little in the way of explanation.

"Takin' his sweet time gettin' back t'what he was, ain't he?" Liam drawled. The man's boorish brogue made Kaleo's ears hurt. He made *everyone's* ears hurt.

"He nearly died, Liam. Leave him alone," Kaleo said.

"An' who's fault is that, eh? Weren't nothin' but a good bard 'fore ya showed up. Shoulda just stayed where ya belonged, 'stead o' gettin' all mixed up in yer da's schite. He ain't even yer da no more."

Kaleo threw a glower at Liam for the comment. While partially true, Kaleo refused to accept that the bard *only* saw him as a mere apprentice. There was more there than that, even if it was not easily expressed. Their relationship was a complicated, ever-evolving study of oddities.

"Let it be, Liam," Ajana said. She took a seat across from Kaleo. The bangles she wore clinked together and the colorful pattern of her oddly cut pants caught glints of the sunlight on small reflective discs that served as decoration on the fabric. Kaleo could see the appeal Liam, and even Reven, saw in Ajana. She was unique, wise, and fierce in her own right. Liam plopped himself down beside her, grumbling about the grass and sand that blended together within the Grove.

"Let wha' be, eh? Let him be a dumb as schite wha' keeps gettin' us in a heap o'trouble? Weren't me wha' run off t'Kormaine like it were a trip down the cuff. Weren't me wha' bring half a nation down on our heads. They prolly still lookin' what where we gone. Won't take 'em but a tic t'figure it out, I'd wager," Liam said. Kaleo nearly snarled, feeling the ire rise one word at a time. It *was* Liam that brought Tondra to Reven's door, *Liam* who betrayed the bard and turned Kaleo in.

"I ought to beat you to Brecken," Kaleo growled. Liam snorted. There were only a few towns near to Yira's Grove. One was Brecken, a small fishing village, and the other was Davenport, a large city state that had quite a few opportunities, according to the two thief-takers who had been on a few occasions in the past. Liam complained non-stop about going into town where he might be recognized, but still came back with a bottomless trunk full of knickknacks and trinkets, only he found useful the day prior. Kaleo had planned to go to Davenport with Lara to find things he needed or even work out a way to get back to the manor. Everything he'd collected in his brief tenure with the bard was left behind when they fled from Tondra's huntsman. Even poor Sergio got left behind. The old caretaker had gone into town to escort Demyan and Kendal to the Port Circle when they'd fled Tondra's hordes. Kaleo hoped the kind old man was alright.

"Ya bat shit?" Liam growled. "I'd end ya 'fore ya even got off yer arse."

"Not likely," Kaleo retorted sharply. His fists balled at his sides enough that Lara noticed and put a steadying hand on his arm.

"Ya watch yer mouth, whelp, got it? Only gonna tewl ya once," Liam threw back. The man's brogue was grating on Kaleo's nerves more than usual. Kaleo's temper got the better of him after Liam's retort. He let his fist fly. It connected solidly with Liam's fool face and cracked his nose in the process. Blood flew down onto the sandy grass. Everyone within earshot stopped what they were doing to stare at them, to watch the drama unfold like it was a play.

Liam didn't take kindly to being hit and tackled Kaleo to the ground, ignoring Ajana and Lara's shouts for them to stop. The thief-taker hit harder than Kaleo gave him credit for, slugging him in the ribs hard enough to bruise. The man fought dirty - like the rogue he actually was. Kaleo gave back what he got, clocking the fool duende in the head again and kneeing him in the groin.

"Stop!" the women continued to holler, vainly trying to pull the brawling men apart.

"ENOUGH!" a new voice bellowed, carrying

out to the ocean and across the Grove. Everyone froze, Liam and Kaleo included. "Get up!"

Reven barked the order, leaning on Serai. The woman with the wild locks of red curls scowled at both of them while making it seem difficult to hold Reven upright. Maybe it was. The bard was heavier than he looked. Kaleo shoved Liam off him, then got to his feet.

"Gonna take the brat's side! He hit me first!" Liam complained.

"Shut up, Liam! You're both acting like infants! Pull your heads out of your asses before I do it for you!" Reven snarled. He groaned after but refused to look away from either of them. Kaleo simply lowered his gaze to the grass.

"You need to rest," Serai said, taking Reven back into the tent. When she came back out, the glower she gave to both Kaleo and Liam could have frightened stones. "I am going to find herbs that will help him. If you two fight again, I will remove your reason for being men."

That was all she said, giving them both a sweet smile afterwards before walking away.

***

"Drink or somethin', ya look … pathetic."

Reven frowned, turning a slow glare up at Liam as the drawling duende plopped down beside him on the sand that evening with two bottles of liquor in hand. He handed one to the bard by way of apology and drank from the other without saying another word. Unwilling to start yet another argument with the thief-taker, Reven kept his mouth shut and drank. Half a bottle later, he looked at Liam and frowned again.

"How long have you known about me?" Reven asked. Liam didn't answer. "Roe?"

"Day one," Liam sighed, then drank. "Weren't no question when I seen what ya got on yer chest.

Anyone what's paid even a hair's attention t'what tha' bloody nation did woulda known it too. Ya just happened t'end up in a place what don't care. Prolly fer th'best anyhow."

Reven remained silent. He felt betrayed and angry all over again, yet oddly grateful. It was for the best. If he'd been found in the state he was in by anyone else, he'd be dead or worse. But the knowledge that his so-called friend had known who he was, known even the smallest fragment of a life he'd been trying so hard to remember and kept it a secret hurt.

"Kaleo," Reven finally croaked out, throat dry. "You didn't want him to take me from you. Did you?"

Liam drank.

"Roe?"

"He's a spoiled whelp. Always has been."

Now Reven's frown deepened further.

"He didn't recognize you," Reven prodded. Liam shrugged.

"Wouldn't expect him to. He weren't but a few months old first time I seen him. People take notice of kids what should be drown at th'bottom of th'bloody river. Ya was always in Damaskha with th'kid. He stands out. Petulant schite. Gets it from his da."

Again, Liam drank. Reven let him, openly gaping at this man who knew so much about his past; at the idiot who *continued* to declare that Kaleo should have been drowned.

"Gonna catch flies leavin' yer mouth hangin' open. Wouldn'ta mattered if I said nothin' or not. Still woulda been all fogged up. Not even Serai can fix it, can she?"

Reven looked at Liam, but finally looked back at the sand and shook his head. She could not give him his memories, only guide him through the turbulent things he saw. So Reven looked back down at the sand instead, the bottle nestled in the natural divots and grooves within the grain. He wanted to be angry, but the anger leaked into something else, something closer to despair. He *wanted* to know who he'd been, to *remember* it, not just see it in flashes or know that it existed. The people in the Grove all looked at him with a silent plea to remember; Kaleo did too.

"Don't. S'not werf it," Liam said. Reven glanced at him again, knowing that the thief-taker could catch surface thoughts from time to time. "Ya keep stickin' yer foot in it an' eventually somethin's gonna snap it right off or yank ya all the way down. Ain't no comin' back from somethin' like that. "

"He has a point, my love," Ajana said as she glided down to the sand beside Liam, looking over the thief-taker to the bard. "Perhaps it is best that you simply move forward with what is presented instead of trying to dig for what has been lost. Some acquisitions are simply not worth the payout."

Both men looked at the radiantly flawed cantari woman sitting there in the dwindling sunlight. The bangles she wore on her wrists and neck, on her ears and in her nose caught glints of light when she moved. How Reven loved her. He loved listening to her voice, her oddly clipped accent. Looking at her, listening to her words, made the despair fade. It didn't matter who he had been, only who he chose to be in the future and in the present.

"So we move forward," Reven finally said, looking back out to the sea. "Here. With them."

"Are ya bloody crazy? They's what got ya into this schite fest," Liam practically choked. Reven leveled a cool, but threatening, gaze at him.

"And you sold me and my *son* to the Esbethi," Reven reminded him. "Think of it as a penance for your stupidity."

Liam gaped, looked at Ajana and saw that same cool, threatening gaze in *her* eyes and immediately shrank in defeat. He grumbled something unintelligible and finished off the bottle of liquor in his hand before snatching the other one out of the sand. Reven snatched it back.

"That's mine," the bard said, taking another deep swig of the dark liquid inside. Olven rum. It had a stronger kick to it than normal rum, made from specially grown sugars and heady spices found in the roots of the *sephirot* trees where the duende made their homes. It was exactly what the bard needed. Serai flopped herself down on the sand beside him, grabbed the bottle from his hand and drank deeply. Reven blinked at her, watching with an arched brow. He saw the same reaction from Ajana and Liam out of the corner of his eye and just waited.

"Everything alright?" Reven dared. Serai frowned at him, her freckled face scrunching into something very close to an angry pout blended with a wrinkle of disgust. The wild mop of red, frizzy curls on her head was pulled back into a crest of intricate knots that still did not tame everything. Fly-away strands blew into her face or fell around her neck and shoulders, breaking free of the crest that fell to her mid-back. Having her beside him made Reven feel almost complete. It was he who braided her hair earlier, letting the act soothe his aching soul and bring them a moment of much-needed intimacy. He knew things were missing and broken, but Serai filled most of those holes and put a smile on his face. Except when she pout-glowered at him, as she was doing in that moment.

"There is so much that is wrong," she complained, blowing out a huff of air to move some strands of hair from her face. Reven absently reached over to tuck those offending strands into the braids at the side of her head. She continued as if nothing at all had happened. "All the evil and vileness. The people who have been damaged or killed, and then there is the general of your old nation. The one who attacked you. I was just with him. He was not like this before. He was your friend and protector. The Corruption we see is being *forced*, not just something done by demon wounds. Someone is doing this on purpose!"

Reven blinked again, desperately trying to follow Sera's line of thinking. When he couldn't, he looked at Liam and Ajana for help. Both shrugged.

"I'm... sorry?" Reven offered when his compatriots-in-acquisition had nothing to offer. Serai looked at him again and frowned in earnest.

"You do not understand, do you?" she huffed. Reven's eye squinted slightly in a face of confusion and apathy that she apparently did not care for. Instead of saying anything, she took his hand and mentally fed him some of the atrocities she'd seen in Xandrix's mind or the minds of the refugees; of Jaysen, and Nadya - both witnesses to the horrors wrought by the Red and his demons. The pain was excruciating. He yanked his hand away from her and rubbed his head. "Now do you see? This is *wrong!*"

"You couldn't've used your bloody words instead!" Reven barked through a whimper, rocking slightly to focus on *anything* but what Serai showed him.

"I do not know that many of your words!" she argued. She didn't. Serai spoke many languages, but sometimes the word was not quite right or entirely different from what everyone else knew. She spoke a language that Reven had never heard, something as ancient as she was from a time no one remembered anymore.

Serai slammed the bottle of liquor back against

Reven's middle, making him grunt. Some of it sloshed out over his chest and lap as she got up again, moving away from the group as quickly as she'd come.

"What in the... Serai!" Reven called, absently handing Liam the bottle as he got up to follow the red-haired woman who'd wormed her way into his heart as quickly as Kaleo had. Quicker.

People watched and whispered, but Reven ignored them and continued to follow Serai until the Grove became sand and the fires diminished to tiny spots on the horizon. The only thing he heard was the ocean lapping up against the shore at high tide.

"Serai, please, slow down," Reven continued as he followed her just outside the boundaries of the Grove, coming up short when Malek snarled at him. He stood near her, a fixture that was easily forgotten until he hissed or snapped. Azure claimed it was a drake thing. "Will you please talk to me? Preferably away from the overprotective lizard."

"I cannot fix you," she sighed, on the verge of tears. "I see horrible things of what has been done to your people. If I cannot fix anything, then why am I here? What purpose do I serve if I cannot be the healer I am meant to be?"

Tears rolled down her cheeks. Reven was not accustomed to seeing her so vulnerable. She was always so strong, even when she was first found. She was curious, cautious, but never vulnerable or afraid like she was now. That was his role in things - afraid of his own shadow, of what his mind hid in the dark.

He stepped forward, ignoring the low growls of warning from Malek until he could lift her chin carefully. Her eyes glistened with tears in a way that was not at all beautiful. Legends and stories always described the heroines with glistening tears in beautiful moonlight against stunning, pale skin. Except that wasn't how reality worked. Reven smiled, seeing the blotchy red on her freckled face, eyes swollen. Any confusion or annoyance from earlier lifted away.

"I don't need you to fix me," he began, brushing away her tears with his hands. "I need you to teach me. I need you to be there when I fall apart, so I can be right here when *you* fall apart. You're the only thing in my life that's honest and true. Not even Kaleo does that. He still won't admit to being my son, like he's afraid it'll shatter me all over again. I'm not *that* delicate."

Serai laughed and gave him a look that made him sigh. He *was* that fragile. Liam pointed it out on the hour. Reven sighed, pulling Serai into his chest.

He was aware of Malek's low rumble that seemed pervasive no matter what Reven did or did not do to Serai, but ignored the drake like he did most things. Malek was not important; Serai was.

"Liam thinks we should leave."

"Liam is an idiot," Serai replied into his chest. Reven chortled, squeezing her tighter. "This is important for you and for Kaleo. These people need hope."

"I'm no one's hope, Serai."

"You are," she said, pushing back enough to look up at him. "You are Kaleo's hope, and Liam's. You are mine, too."

He looked at her with an argument on the tip of his tongue that faded the longer he looked at her. Instead, he simply smiled and pulled her close again, kissing the top of her head. Perhaps he could try his hand at hope after all.

Chapter Two

Itahl was like nothing Demyan Ovet ever dreamed of. He'd read stories of the Itahli, heard rumors, and listened to the *youkai* that once enslaved him scoff at their infantile science. But what Demyan saw was not infantile. What he saw was nothing short of miraculous at the hands of man. The science they used differed from what the *youkai* had, but was no less awe-inspiring.

The castle palace was easily twice as big as the one in Kormaine. The rest of the city was divided into four quadrants. The castle was the heart of the city, the central point of Rudia. Next was the Royal School of Alchemy at the center of the merchant's quarter, the Temple to Yira was the center of the small row homes where people lived, the Temple to Adrastaeia sat at the center of their military quarter, and the Royal Theatre was the center of the arts quarter where artisans created things of breathtaking beauty. The entire city of Rudia was one giant clover made of gears and cogs. They used strange technology that allowed communication at great distances or created the great sky ships he'd seen when Kendal first came to Kormaine. It was all awe-inspiring and yet all entirely overwhelming.

"You ok?" Kendal drawled in long, honeyed tones. All Itahli spoke in a sweet drawl that made him feel as if they whispered about him behind his back. Demyan *hoped* his new bride did not do that, but he was not quick to trust either. And, in all honesty, he was not ok. Jax had gone to Itahl with them, accorded a spot as the King's assistant, but even *he* looked ill. The duende man had been quiet since their arrival, glowering at corners or staff as if he expected an attack at any moment. Demyan didn't blame him. There was a sensation between his shoulder blades that made him feel uncomfortable, something present since their arrival in Itahl. But rather than burden Kendal with that knowledge, he simply nodded at her with a small smile. Sadly, she did not look convinced.

"You… do not feel it, do you?" Demyan finally asked, his words slightly garbled and slurred together in a mix of terrible accents that simply butchered the Trade Cant. Jax listened, leaning casually against the apartment wall given to the Kormandi royals.

"Feel what?" Kendal asked.

Demyan shrugged his shoulders, then let them twist back as he tried to think of how to describe the sensation to her in words she would understand. "A tickle. Like… hairs standing up."

"The energy waves," she smiled. Demyan frowned in confusion. He even glanced at Jax, who shrugged with a minor grumble that might have been words, making Kendal giggle. The sound was lovely and better than hearing her scream in terror. The safety of four solid walls was welcoming after what they'd experienced, even if he did not feel entirely 'safe'. "I guess it might feel strange to you. Everyone here's just so used to it we don't even notice it no more, but these lights don't power themselves. Energy comes from the Source kept beneath the city."

"Source?" Demyan asked, looking at the small incandescent bulbs all over the room in which they sat. Tiny mechanical creatures scuttled across the floor with little Shards on their backs, using the Power held within to give them life. The *youkai* did the same by using steam or gems modified by their *renkinjutsushi*. But they still used candles and gas lamps, not these odd bulbs. They communicated via carrier bird and messenger rather than the devices the Itahli called 'voice carriers'.

"The Source is Adrastaeia's heart, surrounded by a strand of stars from Yira. They gave it to us as a gift for following a life of law and devotion," Kendal said, as if speaking it straight from a written text. It made Demyan frown. "Don't believe me? I can show you. It's beautiful to see."

Curiosity and suspicions raised, Demyan simply nodded again with a brief glance at Jax. The man nodded, stretching off the wall like a lazy cat. Kendal smiled, taking Demyan's hand as she guided him through the wide halls of the castle palace. Every turn looked the same, every wall identical with matching artwork and tapestries, lamps at even intervals and decorative tiles every ten feet along the floor.

"This was your home?" Demyan dared, remembering the palace in Risoukyou where he grew up before being taken to the castle keep in Sapphire City.

"No, we lived just outside city bounds when I was a child. My home was Yira's Temple from the day I turned ten until the day I… until the day I met you."

She looked down at her feet as they walked, casting a silent glance in his direction with a minor flush to her mocha-colored cheeks. They did not speak much, given their language barriers, but it was clear to both of them that the arrangement made by their two nations was not an arrangement made for the benefit of the two involved. They hardly knew each other, married only a few weeks before the attack on the mountain pass that killed his uncle and put Demyan on the throne for good. Politics and evacuations of various towns and villages, oversight of resources and desperate pleas for aid took up every second of his time after the wedding. He'd been instructed to 'hold the defenses' once the demons came close to Sapphire City, to maintain stoic concentration for the benefit of the people, and did as he was told without question at the cost of his new bride. He'd ignored her, left her alone with a handful of acolytes and two guards, all dead now. They'd not even shared the same bed since the wedding night with Demyan catching naps in a chair or dozing during a meeting of advisors until Vassily shook him awake. He needed his vassal's guidance now more than ever, feeling very alone and detached from everything he saw. Not even Jax helped with that. And then he saw Kendal.

"*Gomennasai*," he said, apologizing for her discomfort. It was one of the few words she'd learned quickly, just based on how often he used it.

"It's alright. Yira has a higher purpose for us still. And… I *do* like you. You're just… real quiet."

Demyan had nothing to say in that regard, so remained quiet, then snorted out a dry laugh Kendal shared with him when he realized what he was doing. They giggled like that for a few turns and twists of the hallways, descending a flight of narrow stairs into the lower levels of the monstrosity of a building they currently inhabited. Jax followed, idly scratching at the back of his neck or grumbling again. The sensation between Demyan's shoulder blades intensified, making him squeeze Kendal's hand with more strength than he'd intended. She looked at his face again, studying him.

"Does it bother you?" she asked with genuine concern. He shook his head, unwilling to trust his voice to hold any conviction in the answer he might give. Whatever this 'Source' was, it was *not* pleasant. Perhaps the *Itahli* were used to such a sensation, but it made Demyan's skin crawl and his stomach clench. By the way Jax kept scratching at his neck, it did the same to him, too. "We don't gotta keep going if you don't want to."

"It's fine," he said, even if it wasn't. Kendal waited a moment before nodding and continuing on until reaching a well-guarded point in the underbelly of the giant edifice above.

"Sorry, your grace. You can go no further today," one of the guards said, directing his statement at Kendal only. She stood straighter and lifted her chin, unwilling to accept any of this nonsense from them.

"Her majesty, the Queen, has tasked me with teaching my husband our ways. Our ways end and begin at the Source. I would like for him to see it."

"We've been told to allow no entry to the sub levels today, your grace. For any reason," the guard continued.

"Shall I tell the Queen that you've denied the request of the High Priestess, then?" Kendal continued, making Demyan look at her. She spoke little in Kormaine, always in her room where she would be out of the way. Here, however, she commanded as much obedience as the queen with a title to back it. She made Demyan feel suddenly small and insignificant.

"N-no, your grace," the guard said, finally stepping aside with a heavy sigh. His partner did the same, each opening an iron door that led further down.

Demyan and Kendal were allowed entry. Jax was not allowed to pass. The duende snarled at the guards, but waited with a minor nod from Demyan.

The amount of Power that radiated out of those doors struck Demyan like a hammer to the gut that nearly doubled him over. He could only imagine how Jax felt. The man only had a minor gift for fetching, but any Power was still enough to feel what radiated from the iron doors. Demyan barely managed to stay upright, hiding it with a trip that he blamed on clumsy feet. Again, Kendal glanced at him, her facial features asking a silent question he dared not answer with anything but a reassuring smile. It was a gesture he was well-schooled in.

The brick walls were lined in miles and miles of thin, narrow-looking tubes filled with something bright blue. It did not flow quite like water, but it was the closest thing Demyan could equate it to. Whatever they were, they traced the ceiling up into the upper levels through tiny holes drilled into the mortar. Kendal spoke as she walked, explaining to him what everything was and where it went, where the Power originated from, and other things he should have been paying attention to. Instead, however, all he felt was overwhelming pain screaming through his mind and core.

"Demyan? Are you ok? Demyan?" Kendal asked, repeating his name a few times. It was only then he realized they'd stopped. And, while he nodded in the affirmative at her question, he could still feel the screaming pain lance through his mind and a rapid thrumming at his core that made his own heartbeat race.

The surrounding brightness grew from the dim lighting in the hallways to something nearly blinding and warm on his face. His eyes narrowed on reflex as he gazed upon this wondrous 'Source' Kendal and her people were so proud of. What Demyan saw made him want to vomit.

The 'Source' was, in fact, three massively sized Shards, similar to the one that once hovered above the spire in Sapphire City. The difference rested *inside* the Shards. Each Shard was wrapped in what he could only describe as barbs of light, which made it difficult to make out the forms inside. The Itahli were draining *people* of their Power. He could hear them, feel their pain, hear them *beg* for Azrus to take them away. It made him want to weep or scream, or both.

"Demyan?"

Instead of answering, Demyan stumbled away from the Source, running in unwieldy steps until he was as far as he could be from the horrible thing he'd just seen and retched in a corner of the hall.

"Demyan!" Kendal said, coming up behind him, resting her hand on his back. Jax followed shortly thereafter, holding Demyan up when his knees gave way.

"*What's wrong?*" Jax asked in Kormandi. "*Majesty?*"

So much was wrong. Demyan didn't know where to start. He panted, leaning heavily on Jax while trying to sort his thoughts. Rather than give an actual answer, all he groaned out was, "We need help."

He needed someone that might understand him, someone that had an outside perspective. Someone that might tell him he was wrong, because if he was *right,* then the 'Source' of all power for the Itahli were Speakers.

***

I see you, Son of the Flame.

A single voice echoed through the piercing darkness. The voice held Power in its vibrations, rippling across the dark to banish it away, bringing a raging heat along with it like from a furnace or oven. Aeron brought his hand up when the brightness became too much for his eyes to handle, the heat too much for his skin.

Put your hand down, Aeron.

He complied, gasping softly at what he saw. Standing before him was a woman of sorts. She appeared to be a harpy with the legs and arms of a bird but the upper body and face of a stunningly beautiful woman. Her 'hair' was a crest of feathers that fell down her back in vibrant orange. Directly behind her was a figure standing in a pool of deep, dark blue that cast a long, stretching shadow behind it.

"Who is that?" Aeron asked. The feathery woman smiled.

That is for you to decide, my beloved one.

"Me? I don't understand. Who are you?" Aeron continued, looking at the figure again, then at the odd feathery woman.

I am Runya.

Aeron felt like asking more, but stilled his tongue and studied Runya. She watched him curiously in return, waiting for the questions to come. Aeron simply stared, then felt his eyes widen as he suddenly realized *what* Runya was. He'd learned from Demyan and his uncle how things appeared to them, appeared to all Speakers. And then what the figure was suddenly clicked into place too. This Node looked different, but their general appearance was always the same according to his uncle: a person in a bright blue pool. Except this one was not bright blue.

"Is it sick?" Aeron asked. "It's not as bright as I would expect him to be."

Runya smiled. *The Node shares its existence with the Shadow Realm, touching all that is there as well as what is here.*

Aeron remained silent as he processed the answer, walking closer to Runya, to the dark blue figure behind her. She stepped aside so Aeron could regard the figure. It did not have an easily determined gender, garbed in loose clothing that hung like skin. A headscarf hid the 'hair' or other telling features. A sudden rush of memory struck Aeron, bombarding his mind with knowledge as old as the planet itself. Aeron felt himself stumble back until Runya steadied him. His breath would not surface immediately either, but when it did, it was a long, deep inhalation that brought a sense of peace with it.

"Kais," Aeron murmured, eyes closed as the knowledge slowly faded away. "You are Kais."

Runya smiled, looking at the figure in the pool. It still had no gender definition, but that did not bother Aeron. He was happy that *it* was happy with the name. It meant wise, something Aeron had heard Navid say.

You must rest more, my beloved one. Regaining your strength is important. Your people need you.

"My people?" he asked, turning to face Runya. She nodded.

They wait for you. As do your loved ones. A girl with hair like summer straw and a boy with wings.

"Nadya," Aeron said. "She's waiting for me? Is she okay?"

Yes. It is you, my beloved one, who is not. I pulled you from the edge of Azrus's embrace. Nevaeh has been lending you her Power.

Aeron felt his brows furrow. He remembered being in Kormaine with Nadya, remembered all the whirling emotions the girl stirred in him. He remembered a battle beneath the city in the catacombs *with* the dead, with a monster sent to hunt them. He remembered hearing Nadya scream when he pushed Demyan aside, taking the full brunt of the monster's attack somewhere near a church where they'd hoped to find respite. Then nothing.

"Demyan. Is he-"

Not with you, my beloved one. It will be difficult, but it is time for you to wake.

Aeron nodded, looking at Kais with a grin on his face. "We'll talk later?"

The figure nodded, reflecting Aeron's grin with one of its own. Aeron looked at Runya again, then felt as if his body became suddenly weightless. It was a fleeting feeling, as a deep, bone-weary heaviness took over, making every muscle ache. Even breathing was difficult. He felt something on his head, damp and cool, with something else on his body. A blanket, perhaps, or something like it. He pried his eyes open, leaving them as narrow slits to survey his surroundings. No light or noise came to him, suggesting it was evening. All he heard was steady breathing beside him. Despite the ache in his muscles, he turned his head to see Nadya sleeping in a cot beside him and smiled.

Runya?

I'm here, my beloved one. You are safe. Rest and regain your strength.

Chapter Three

Five days following his recovery, Reven looked out to the sea, watching its lavender waves lap up over the sand, creeping toward his bare toes. Kaleo sat to his right and Serai to his left, both of them staring at the setting sun ahead with hands resting on their knees. The wind blew Serai's hair all over her freckled face and shoulders. It needed to be rebraided. Kaleo's wings offered him some respite from the wind, the feathers billowing lightly or blowing off entirely to drift down the shoreline. The boy had had another fight with Liam earlier that morning and now sported a bruise on his cheek for the trouble. The thief-taker wanted to leave, wanted Reven to leave with him and get back to the life they had - *without* Kaleo. Regardless of what Reven decided - *if* he decided anything - it would include his urchin; his *son*.

"How is Aeron?" Reven finally asked. News circulated through the Grove that the boy was showing signs of life. Once the news reached *their* ears, Serai offered what healing she could, and Kaleo sat with

Aeron the day before. The Kormandi princess would not be moved from Aeron's side for any reason. The twins, Eila and Rielle, had taken to bringing her meals so she could stay with the ailing prince.

"Weak but mostly coherent," Kaleo said. "Still a prat."

Reven snorted a dry laugh. Eila and Rielle complained about the same thing, claiming that even abed, Aeron was a force to be reckoned with and arrogant to boot. He was not strong enough to lead yet and had very little experience. It was a concern Kaleo shared with Reven and the same concern that had Liam throwing punches at the young avian that morning. Kaleo didn't want to hold Reven back, but didn't want to abandon his cousin either. Reven agreed with the urchin rather than the thief-taker. Liam did not take it well. Things were still too tumultuous in the Grove to abandon *anyone*. Besides, if Reven was to become the hope of the people, he needed to be around to do so.

"What do you think, love?" Reven asked, looking at Serai. She kept her eyes fastened on the sea. He could hear her thoughts tumbling around in her head. She was considering all options, weighing things against each other. It wasn't surprising in and of itself; Reven often heard and shared her thoughts, intimately speaking mind to mind with her. However, what he heard was *how* she weighed things. She weighed them based on what was best for *him.* That realization nearly knocked the bard flat on his back.

"I think that we should stay," Serai finally said. "Until Aeron is stronger. We are the hope of the people. *You* are their shining star that guides them. Maybe we can bring your broken house here, too."

Her response made Reven snort. He missed his house, spirits and all. "It isn't broken, love, just in need of repair."

"Which is the definition of 'broken'," Kaleo threw in. Outside of fighting with Liam, Kaleo had been very quiet of late; sometimes he was entirely absent. It was an odd change after having the avian under foot for over eight months.

"Urchin, I did not ask for your opinion," the bard smirked. Kaleo smirked back. If they were to remain, some changes would need to be made - starting with their location. Perhaps something that was a little more lively than Tierra Vida. There was *nothing* on the patchwork island but oddities. Desert butted against dense forest that ran into flat plains all in an instant. Literal ridges existed at the point where the land changed, as if someone had taken a giant needle and sewn the land masses together like a patchwork cloak. Azucena was a desert city run by cartel lords, but at least it had *something*. Tierra Vida was... strange. Safe, but strange. Reven frowned slightly when he looked at Kaleo, curious and willing to press a little. "If you could go anywhere, urchin, where would you go?"

"Wherever you are," Kaleo shrugged without putting much thought into the question at all. Reven grinned. The answer was mostly expected and nice to hear, but avoided the point of the question.

"Assume I'm with you then," Reven corrected. "Where would you go?"

Now Kaleo put thought into the question. Having Reven with him altered the boy's entire outlook. It set a small knot in Reven's stomach. He knew why, accepted why, but still felt awkward about it. *Gannon* may have been a decent parent, but *Reven* didn't know the first thing about raising a child. Granted, Kaleo was grown, but still. Whatever their relationship was evolving into, it was beyond mere mentor and apprentice, or even father and son.

"Rellan," Kaleo finally said. "I want to see the

homes the tywyll build in the trees. I imagine they're different from what the duende build."

Reven nodded. He'd never been, but Liam spoke of it often. Thinking of the thief-taker put a small grimace on the bard's face. Liam was going to shit bricks when Reven finally told him what he'd decided. Not that Liam had to stay, but the idiot seemed to follow Reven like a lost puppy and pouted anytime he did not get his way.

Serai took Reven's hand right at that moment, as if sensing his concern. She gave him the support he needed, the strength to ground himself. He gave her hand a small squeeze that she reciprocated. Reven looked at Serai then, took in every part of this wild cave woman, from her mop of red coils to every glorious freckle that covered her body. Kaleo may be content to be wherever Reven was, but looking at Serai, the bard knew his happiness, his safety and security was with Serai. She was *his* hope, his star, his everything.

***

"What is it?" Gannon queried. First-Born Son of the Flame, Speaker of Argento, Delegate to the Eastern Nations - - complete and utter dolt.

Noelani arched a perfectly shaped brow, her silver wings fluffing with irritation. "It is a baby, you dolt head."

Status confirmed. Gannon blinked at his betrothed, then looked at the tiny being once again. It was rather small and frail looking, with soft, downy hair sticking out of the swaddle it was wrapped in. There was a breeze in the air that carried the scent of molten metal and baking bread. They were not far from the Artisan's Walk in Joricho. It was Noelani's favorite place and terribly, horribly public.

"Whose baby is it?" Gannon hazarded. Noelani slapped the back of his head. "Ow!"

Noelani had asked to meet him the day before by

messenger. The Esbethi *amatessa* prided herself on a show of assets – Gannon included. They paraded around the whole of the Phoenix Empire whenever possible just to be obnoxious about their coming nuptials. Finding her with an infant was a little unexpected.

"Noe, really, whose baby is it?" he repeated in a pitch aimed for her ears alone. Despite not being in the Artisan's Walk proper, they were close enough for people to notice as they walked by.

"Well, that's the golden question, isn't it?" she replied with a toss of silver-white hair over a perfectly tanned shoulder. She paused, setting the basket down so she could smooth her skirts and tap her bare toes on the fresh earth. The bangles on her slim ankle jingled with a little cadence of uplifting song. "He's yours, dolt head."

Gannon felt his mouth drop. Noelani remained a pond of cool composure while he wrapped his mind around what was just said. Except, he knew that could not possibly be. There had to be a mistake. Noelani had not been pregnant, and she did not have teal wings. The only avian Gannon knew with teal wings was Inola, a girl that had come once or twice to the ambassador's home to work. He didn't actually know what happened to her and never had reason to give it a second thought.

"Ugh!" Noelani growled, taking him by the ear. "How old are you, idiot?"

"One hundred," he answered through a wince. She knew how old he was, they'd been betrothed since they were children.

"And what do you pointed-eared morons do on your hundredth name-day?"

"Drink," Gannon answered again, still wincing.

"And?" she persisted, foot still tapping with increasing speed. He glanced at her toes, hesitating in his answer lest it be wrong. He was bent at the waist, leaning in towards Noelani's chest while forced to stare at the baby in

the basket.
"Drink more?"
She slapped him again. The answer was wrong.

Reven gasped as he sat up in his tent, sweat rolling down his temples and neck. There was nothing to soak it up, no shirt to stave off the chill that raced down his spine. No one slept beside him, making him frown curiously. He knew *someone* should be there with him, but the dream had him confused and shaking for reasons he could not explain. Everything about it faded in his mind like wisps of smoke on the air, confusing him further.

Azure?

Reven rarely called to the phoenix. Usually, it was the other way around, the small magical beast constantly pestering like a nagging mother.

Hunting, beloved. Are you hungry?

The question made Reven snort out a laugh and shake his head as he drew his knees to his chest so he could drape his arms over them. The dream continued to crash through his mind like the rolling waves of the sea battering at the walls that blocked his memories. Each time he reached for them, they vanished between his fingers like smoke, leaving the faintest trail of soot against his skin.

"No," he said aloud, shaking his head. "Do you know where Kaleo is?"

Sleeping, I think. Isn't that what you should be doing, beloved? It's still very early.

Again, Reven snorted and grinned, looking up at the top of the tent. It was little more than an old fishing boat cover and sticks. He'd lived in practical squalor with his companions, but this was rough, even for them. He understood why Liam complained so much. He didn't approve of the complaints, but he understood them. No one told the thief-taker he had to stay. It was a continual point of contention between Liam and Reven. Liam stayed out of guilt and hated it. Kaleo reminded him of that; often.

"Azure, do you know what happened to Kaleo's mother?" he whispered, needing to ask aloud. The conversation at the shore earlier forced him to ask. He needed to know, to learn, to be better; *wanted* to be better. Kaleo deserved as much; more. Reven was determined to give the boy what he could.

She died, beloved. In child birth, I believe. He was conceived at your hundredth-day celebration. You kept him.

That made Reven frown. "As opposed to?"

I'm not sure, beloved. The tirsai are very strange. But it was notable that you did so.

Reven merely sighed. It would do no good to dwell on it now. He needed sleep. Sleep, however, had other ideas. He tossed and rolled for several minutes before giving up entirely, now pondering why it would have been so notable to keep a child. What else should he have done with it?

"Oh, blast it all," he said, throwing the thin covers aside so he could crawl out of the tent into the crisp, pre-dawn air. The autumn months were coming, though Tierra Vida did not seem to be affected by seasons like other places were. He stood and shook himself, still wondering where Serai had gone. Yes, that was who should be in bed beside him; now he remembered. "I'm going for a walk."

Would you like company, beloved? Azure asked. Reven hadn't meant it as an invitation, merely a general statement.

"No, I don't want to disrupt your hunt. I'm fine."

He stuffed his hands in the shallow pockets of his loose trousers and shuffled along the edge of the Grove until his feet met the sand of the shore. He looked out over the sea, its color a deep violet in the dark of night with the faintest shimmer like glitter kissing the top of it. He caught sight of someone further down the beach, out of the periphery of his vision, but when he turned, the beach stood empty.

"...elp!"

Again, much like seeing the individual on the beach, the voice came to him at the edge of an echo as it faded away into the air. It brought a frown onto Reven's face as he slowly turned in a circle, looking for the source - for *anything*.

"Is someone there?" he asked, feeling a rush of icy cold air blast past him. He sighed, letting his face drop in annoyance. "Is someone there *other* than you?"

Several spirits made their home inside the Grove, though only Reven and Serai seemed able to see them. One had taken a liking to the bard since he woke, always brushing past him so he got chills. She was a pretty ghost, though it was difficult to pinpoint her species. At first, he'd believed her to be human or half-olven but he could never see her bottom half. They'd seen centaur and naga in the areas around the Grove, so it was quite possible she was one of those. Reven never asked.

Another shiver ran down his spine as the cold penetrated him. "Really? If you're going to be around, then be helpful. Something is out here. I saw it."

The spirit exploded out of his chest and pouted, folding her arms across her chest. She wore no clothing that he could tell, giving more weight to the argument that she was demi-human of some flavor. Demi-human tribes were not generally inclined to wear 'civilized' attire.

"Unc...!"

"See!" Reven said, pointing at the spirit. She

turned and looked around. She'd heard it too. "I told you. Something's here. Now help. Please."

She smiled when he said 'please' and dashed away in a ribbon of cold fog. Reven rolled his eyes and sighed. Of all the things he was cursed with, seeing the dead seemed like the one that was the least traumatic for him. With his luck, he'd find a ghost that wanted to take over his body and use it for combat practice somewhere. For now, he followed his little friend, slowly making his way down the beach until he saw another thing on the edge of his vision. This time when he turned, he managed to catch a hand desperately reaching up through the dark of a nearby shadow. Out of instinct, Reven grabbed it, surprised to feel something solid, and tugged.

"Come… on…." he grunted, fighting with the shadow as if it were tar. "Oh, for the love of bloody - let go!"

The command brought a bright light that banished the shadows away as if it were daylight rather than full dark. It didn't last long, only long enough to pull whoever was stuck in the inky darkness out. The pair landed on the sand, the individual on top of Reven, panting and heaving with clear panic that Reven felt as if it were his own. It took a moment for him to shake it off.

"You alright?" Reven managed without moving from his spot beneath the other person. Fingers dug harder into his arms or shoulder, but he received a nod in response. "That's a start, I suppose."

A glance down at his chest told him nothing. The person hid their face and shook from head to toe.

"Don't suppose I can get a name," Reven said, still not moving. "Since you're using me as a pillow." The individual snorted and looked up, making Reven's jaw drop. "Aeron?"

"Hullo, uncle."

***

Aeron winced as Nadya wrapped his forearm in a soft gauze cloth soaked in a healing salve that made the young prince's nose wrinkle. His arm felt as if he'd stuck it in a fire even if he hadn't. Nadya merely glared at him as if he'd done something so offensive as to be unforgiveable. Aeron glanced at his uncle rather than look at Nadya, seeing the smirk on the elder man's face.

The sun rose off in the distance, brightening the grove in the process. Reven sat with him just outside the tent he'd been given to recuperate in. Nadya had sent her friend, Adrian, to Brecken for supplies she felt were important. Aeron didn't question it. Most of the time, he was still too tired to do anything but blink. The wound he'd received still hurt, burning his shoulder or chest. The poison in it had been cleansed away - or so he'd been told - but the wound itself still had an angry red look to it no matter what the woman with the wild hair tried. Nadya got on him any time he did more than lift a cup to his lips and thoroughly disapproved of him dropping into shadows - as if it were something he could control.

"It's nice to see you mending well, highness," his uncle said to break the tense silence. It was strange to hear his *uncle* call him 'highness'. Aeron didn't understand why there were formalities. It must have shown on his face, for the man smiled. "It's complicated. Suffice to say, I'm not who you think I am. Not really."

Now Aeron looked over at Nadya. She did not meet his gaze, slowing her fierce wrapping.

"I don't understand. What do you mean, you're not who I think you are? I'd know you blindfolded," Aeron dared.

"That makes one of us. Like I said, it's complicated. I'm only a simple bard, highness."

"Reven was kind enough to help us," Nadya intervened. The name sounded made up. "He lost his home because Kaleo's mother is crazy."

"Step-mother," Aeron and Reven corrected in unison. They looked at each other and smirked, letting silence fall between them for a time. The girls still called him uncle. Aeron had heard them. Still, he watched his uncle, this so-called bard in the morning light, and noted the differences, the things that were just a little off. Like the way Reven seemed to look at Aeron with concern, but no real familiarity or recognition.

"You don't remember us, do you?" Aeron finally said. "Any of us."

Reven merely shook his head. Aeron felt his gut twist. It wasn't unexpected, but still felt like he was losing something dear. Perhaps he was. His uncle sacrificed so much to get him and his sisters out of Illurian City the night of the attack. It would seem that same selflessness remained. It was a debt Aeron intended to repay.

"How are you able to move through shadow like you do?" Reven queried. Aeron looked at Nadya again with a heavy sigh and shrugged.

"Haven't really figured that out yet, hence I keep falling through them. I wasn't even trying to go anywhere far, just move a round a little to stretch my legs," Aeron said. Nadya gave him a fierce look of disbelief. "What! I wasn't! Ask Adrian!"

The shadow-born mute stopped moving as he approached their small group with wide, surprised eyes. His arms were loaded down with wrapped packages and a few odd-looking fruits. Nadya and Reven both looked at the young man, then at Aeron.

"He doesn't speak," Nadya pointed out. "Sit down, Adrian. Thank you for going."

Adrian nodded, carefully setting the packages down. There was one that he smiled at when he picked it up, handing it to the bard. That package was wrapped in silk cloth. Reven looked at it, then at Adrian.

"What's this?" he asked. The boy signed something back. The boy could hear just fine, but could not speak. Aeron would have to remember to ask Nadya why, but it didn't seem important in the immediate moment.

"He says that it is for you. From Kaleo," Nadya said. Reven grinned at Nadya and thanked the young shadow-born man for the gift. Reven unwrapped the package carefully, jaw going a little slack when he saw the violin cradled inside the silk wrappings.

"Aw, the little suck up got you a gift," Aeron teased. Nadya shoved him gently in the shoulder. "Ow!"

Reven merely smirked at them, but admired the violin all the same. *Aeron* threw a glare at Nadya for her continued need to cause him pain. He was starting to think she didn't like him as much as he'd originally believed.

"Will you play?" Nadya asked Reven, ignoring Aeron completely. Women were too complicated.

Reven looked at Nadya, then Aeron, who nodded his encouragements. He remembered when his uncle would play back home. It was always a grand treat to hear. When the bard put the violin to his chin, tuning it, Aeron's heart swelled. The song that came from it was one of the most beautiful things Aeron had ever heard, full of hope and peace that drifted out to the open sea beyond the Grove.

***

A crude canvas tent sat at the center of a deep marsh tucked safely away from Yira's Grove. Notes of music filtered along the currents of air, stirring up a gentle breeze to the crude tent. Inside of it, Xandrix knelt tied to a wooden post that went far down into the earth, part of a tree swallowed up by the surrounding marshes. The noise made the Corrupted tywyll look up, tilting his head as if to capture more of the soothing sounds coming from the grove.

The people there were worthless. They were cattle. None of them were safe. They'd fallen once; soon enough, they would fall again. Xandrix merely needed a little more time, a little more leverage to escape his prison. It should have been simple, something done days gone by now, but the woman with the wild red hair had done something to him, weakened him and made him feel bone weary. No matter what she did, they could not trap a hunter.

Xandrix twisted his wrists enough to make them raw, to make them slick with blood and work the ropes that bound him until they began to give way. He refused to eat and only drank enough to survive. The woman with the red hair - Serai was her name - asked why he did this when she came to speak. She didn't understand. No one did. She wanted to help Xandrix, to make things right and fix the horrors done to him. Anytime she said so, he scoffed. Xandrix knew what he was, knew there was no way to help him, and accepted his new place in life. More than just his own survival depended on that acceptance.

Unlike Reven, Xandrix remembered everything from the life before he was turned into a monster. He'd been a soldier under the banner of the Phoenix and a personal guard to the imperial family, specifically Gannon and Kaleo. The person who taught him, trained him, made him everything he was didn't trust anyone else with such an important task. Xandrix owed High Lord General Otsawa everything, yet had not been able to repay that favor since the Fall. The general, Xandrix, and their whole battalion were captured while they desperately searched for the missing High Lord Arcanist - the man who now wore the skin of the idiot Roth.

Thinking of the High Lord General made Xandrix snarl. If Jaysen had not intervened, if the boy had just done as he was told...

Xandrix continued to growl, baring teeth as he twisted his hands more and more, feeling the rope cut into flesh without actually registering the pain. He let his mind focus on the music drifting to his prison, ignoring the pain as he worked his wrists, heedless of the damage it caused, until the ropes that bound him grew slick enough to let him wrench an arm free with a smothered cry. Flesh tore off with the movement, but it allowed him to free his other arm without issue. His feet came next, the rope collected as a makeshift weapon. He expected to find a guard or trap or *something* to prevent him from leaving, but when he stepped out of the tent, he found only smelly bog as far as the eye could see. It was bright still, too bright for him to see clearly. It didn't matter where he was. What mattered was returning to where he needed to be.

Xandrix stopped even as he took his first step, turning toward the sound of the music, the stirring of the pathetic handful of refugees that survived the demon's incursion to the Phoenix Empire. Jaysen would be there. He knew they'd brought the fool traitor. Part of Xandrix wanted to finish the job, to be *sure* Jaysen could not interfere again. But that would take time, and there was no guarantee he could stay hidden. It was best to leave it alone. Jaysen would get what was owed in due time. They would not leave him to his own devices for long - they never did.

"They're coming for you," Xandrix snarled as he looked in the direction where the music came from. He said nothing more, loping off away from the refugees in search of a way out of the smelly bog and *out* of the patchwork island of Tierra Vida.

Chapter Four

"Go!" Snarls and growls echoed behind the command, pushing people onward into the deeper forests of Lower Asphondel. Syrus Oenel pushed people ahead, making sure his children got through to the safety of a thick tree line that was defended, protected, warded. A tiny ripple raced across the horizon any time someone passed through it. Evanrae held it. For how long, Syrus was uncertain, but he meant to get as many people through the warding as he could before it fell. Eloiny - his *priod;* his life-partner - assisted, creating walls of brambles and thorns to slow the demons in their chase. The demons did not care who they cut down: men, women, children. It was all the same to the denizens of the Nine Hells, nor did they care how many of their own were lost in the process to eradicate the duende. The horrors Syrus had seen were enough to give anyone nightmares.

He ran with a firm grasp on his son's hand while the other held a sword he'd not had to use in decades. Even when the cities of the Phoenix Empire fell, the duende of the forests simply moved into the deeper holds of the trees or south into the Necropolis at Aenidir. Little by little, the tirsai from the white cities filtered into the forests, seeking refuge. Those same refugees moved again and again with the duende to ships waiting along the rocky shores of Asphondel but the duende remained. The forest tribes held strong to their roots and defended their homes and families fiercely. They survived longer than the tirsai because they worked together instead of throwing each other at the tidal wave of demons like their olven cousins in the white cities. The duende knew what was coming, prepared for it, but even that could not save them. They'd reached the end of their ability to hold the demons off.

"Ettrian! Take your brother!" Syrus commanded, swinging the youngest of his children at his middle son. The duende saw families in a different light than the tirsai. It was an adjustment that had been difficult for Syrus to make, but one that Eloiny finally came to a compromise with. Together, they had four children. Individually, they participated in fertility rites once a year and accepted any child that came of it as part of the tribe, just like everyone else did. Syrus looked around at the fallen faces and forced himself to keep going. He recognized too many, saw them all as brothers and sisters, sons and daughters, lovers, friends, parents. He needed to focus, to keep his family safe or go mad with grief.

"Da!" Gael cried, reaching for Syrus as Ettrian hefted him over a shoulder to run faster. Syrus gave his son one last look and turned to stand his ground with the others that fought to buy them time - his partner and daughter included.

"Don't let them scratch you!" Syrus hollered as a reminder. The demons came at them in howling waves. A wound from a demon killed instantly if you were lucky or festered over time if you weren't. The survivors turned to hell-beasts themselves, twisted monsters of the men and women they once were.

"Tell us somethin' we don't know!"

Syrus looked over at his daughter. Alivae was as strong as any of the men in all the tribes and as beautiful as her mother. She had dirt on her face and scratches along her bare arms from rock and twig that were as unforgiving as the demons. Behind her, Evanrae - the Speaker of Tribes - and Eloiny stood holding the warding. Power radiated off them, stretching for miles in either direction. Syrus did not understand it all; his Power was limited to lighting fires and little else, but he could see it, could feel it thrumming through the roots of the trees and the soil beneath his feet. When the wave of demons hit, Syrus felt the Power waver.

They came on with teeth bared and claws already dripping with blood. The first line fell before they had a chance to raise their weapons. Screams echoed out to Syrus's pointed ears as he pulled his line of fighters back further to the warding. One by one, the fighters were overcome, torn apart by living nightmares.

It won't hold! Syrus!

Eloiny's voice lanced across his mind, making him trip up. He felt someone pulling at him, holding him up by the upper arm. The ringing in his ears would not stop and pain shot up his leg.

"Move! Da!"

Alivae. She pulled him. There were smears of blood on her face and tears in her eyes. He was vaguely aware of moving, of seeing a waver in the air as the warding fell. The demons crashed against that ward until their corpses were piled one on top of the other -

and broke down the barrier that protected the fleeing duende.

Evanrae fell first. The elder duende used the last of his Power to take the demons with him into the next life. Syrus felt his stomach clench and felt his heart seize as he watched his partner run to the Speaker - to her father.

"Eloiny…" he mumbled, even as Alivae continued to pull him away. "Eloiny!"

She fell next. Syrus watched that happen as well, watched the demon tear her in half and bury its maw in her chest. He felt himself pull against his daughter, move toward the demon with rage building inside of him.

"No! Ya can't help her!" Alivae cried. "Ferren! Help me!"

She had an iron grip on Syrus's arm and refused to let go. Someone else tugged his other arm, pulling even as his eyes moved across the bloodied forest. He saw Hayden's corpse next - his son. That was why Alivae cried. She was not one to show emotion, not one to give up; now Syrus knew why. "Da!"

He gave in, energy waning faster than he cared to admit. What few survivors there were ran and took to the high branches of the trees where the demons could not reach. They ran until the frothing waves of the ocean collided against their rubbery legs and sore feet. Two ships waited for them. Syrus heard the sounds of explosions, the sizzle and pop of Power being flung out at the demons that continued to chase them, even to the shore. He wanted to help them, to give them more time, but felt his body grow heavy and his heart weigh him down.

"Weigh anchor!"

Syrus looked around him, vision blurred and head spinning. There were too few. Not enough made it onto the ship. And he did not see Alivae.

"No," he grumbled. "No, we need to wait."

"Syrus, lie back," Ferren said, pushing gently on his chest. He looked at the other man with confusion; at his sons, Ettrian and Gael. The youngest stared back at him with wide, tear-filled eyes and streaks of blood on his face and neck.

"El..." Syrus began, throat clenching as he spoke his partner's name. "We have to wait... for El..."

"She's not comin', my friend. I'm sorry," Ferren said.

"Al... Ali..." Syrus pressed, trying to sit up again. The girl was steadfast and strong, but missing among those he saw on the ship. The motion of it nauseated him, made his eyes roll back into his head.

"I'm truly sorry, Syrus," Ferren continued, even as he began washing Syrus's wounds.

Ali... he thought idly, hoping his daughter would hear.

DA!

Syrus croaked, choking on the breath caught in his lungs when he heard his daughter's scream rip through his mind. Nothing held him to consciousness after that, his head falling to the sanded planks of the ship's deck as they set out to sea away from the demons.

***

"NO!"

The people in the Grove encampment at the edge of the beach skirted away from where Reven slept. They already existed in fear after learning Xandrix had escaped. It worried them, made them fear for their security. Reven merely made that fear worse. Sweat trickled down the back of his neck and stuck the linen cloth of his tunic to his sun-sore skin. Air rushed at him, things toppling over with a gentle rocking motion as a fierce wind settled into a low breeze.

"Hey," someone whispered, while Reven's mind still reeled from the nightmare that tore through him. "Reven, look at me."

The bard shut his eyes tight, bringing hands to his temples as his body rocked back and forth on its own. His lungs compressed inwardly, robbing him of breath and thought; of sanity. Muscles turned to rock, every strand of sinew ready to ricochet back on him in a painful cacophony.

"Papa."

That took his attention. Reven looked up sharply, sucking in breath and holding it as he sought the features of a young boy - an avian - with teal wings and hazel blue eyes. Kaleo. His urchin. His son. The boy offered a grin, hands holding tight to Reven's shoulders. Reven's muscles immediately unwound, leaving him feeling drained and tired despite only just waking from a midday nap. If not for Kaleo's hands, he'd have fallen over.

"Tell me what you saw," Kaleo said, holding on to him until Reven could sit upright on his own. Nothing looked familiar to Reven, even though it *should*. He knew it should. He'd seen it before. They'd been here for a while, but nothing surfaced except that horrid nightmare. He glanced around, noting the destroyed tent behind him, the people that watched him warily or tried to move further away from him.

"Where are we?"

"Tierra Vida," Kaleo answered. "Still having memory lapses?"

Reven scrubbed at his face, but nodded. Kaleo did too, letting it stand as what it was. Reven's memory worked like a sieve. It caught some things and let others go with no rhyme or reason to what it held fast to.

"What did you see? In your dreams."

The information made Reven frown. And, like a boulder to the head, everything rushed his mind; again. Glancing around, he felt shame fill his gut. His Power had lashed out on its own, bringing gods only knew what down on the innocent. It was not the first time.

"Tell me," Kaleo prodded. "Listen to the waves. Let them soothe you."

Reven shook from head to toe, raking a hand through hair that needed a good trim and wash. He did as he was told. He listened to the sea. The waves lapped up in a gentle cadence against white-sand beaches that gave way to stunted little shrubs and wide-frond trees that dropped oddly shaped yellow fruit in large bunches from their tops. Tents filled the surrounding grove with two little rafts anchored to the shore for fishing. The number of people was surprising, yet not entirely unexpected either. But the focus was on the sea, not the people. The people only offered fear, the sea offered serenity.

"There's a forest," Reven began through heavy breaths. "I'm running with others, but it isn't me. It's... I'm watching it from above - why?"

"Sea of Stars," Kaleo explained swiftly. "Keep going."

It was important to speak of what he dreamt before the dream went away. Reven was no Dreamer, but Kaleo was. The boy walked through the World of Dreams as easily as he did the waking world. Somewhere in the back of Reven's mind, he recalled a time when *he* was the one encouraging *Kaleo* to speak of his dreams, but the memory faded as quickly as it came, so he continued with his own.

"We're running," Reven repeated. "There's ... I'm holding someone's hand - a boy. He's young. Nine or ten, maybe. There's another boy and I give the little one to him to keep him safe; tell them to run. I…"

The words get caught in Reven's chest, making it difficult for him to speak. He felt a knot forming in his stomach. "There's a girl; duende. She stands with me, but then… something happens. I don't know what; I can't see it. I hear her screaming for… for…"

He felt his brows furrow down together into a deep frown as he remembered the girl's words. She was not a girl, not really. Perhaps Reven's age or younger, but not as young as Kaleo. Reliving the dream kept the girl fresh in his memory for only a short time before those very important details faded away like smoke in the air, drifting upward until it was no longer distinguishable from anything else around him.

"She's screaming for her father, but she's not-"

"Describe her to me," Kaleo cut in. Tears welled in Reven's eyes. He took several more deep breaths, eyes still closed, then lifted his chin.

"Duende. She's … your height. Red hair tied up in a messy knot like Serai's, but not curly. And darker than Serai's. Auburn. There are scratches on her face and arms. She wears dark brown leathers and carries a bow carved with runes. Her eyes are … hazel green like moss with a center like the sky after a storm. It bleeds into the green. There are markings on her upper arms, but I don't know them. Liam has them too; her tribe, maybe?"

Kaleo merely nodded when Reven opened his eyes to regard him.

"Do you know her?" Reven asked. He needed to know, needed to understand why this girl haunted his dreams, to know what it meant. The look on Kaleo's face only tightened the knot in the bard's stomach further. The boy knew her.

"Alivae," Kaleo nodded, though he spoke in a harsh rasp. "Your other sister. You have a lot of siblings. It's complicated. I'll see what I can find out. I don't like how this triggered you. The point is to rebuild, not tear it all down again."

The others near him looked at him with caution, even though Kaleo smiled at him. Serai was Reven's grounding point, her soothing voice always making its way through the chaos of his mind. But she was not there in that moment — which made the bard frown.

"Where is Serai?" he asked, looking for her. He ached for her, he realized. Reven needed his red-haired wildling more than anything.

"With Aeron, I think. He keeps falling into the bloody shadows," Kaleo shrugged. "Feel a little better now? Are you hungry? I can get you something."

Reven wasn't hungry at all and didn't feel better, but he also didn't want to worry Kaleo. The child had enough to worry over. It was too much for Kaleo to shoulder; too much to burden someone so young with. Aeron was just as young and inexperienced. Children did not need to be saddled with such heavy weights around their necks. Reven was supposed to be the hope of the people, not the source of their concerns.

"A little," Reven lied, feeling some of the knot loosen when Kaleo smiled back. The bard watched the young avian rise, following him through a small hamlet of tents and terrified onlookers with his eyes. He averted his eyes after that, looking at his palms instead. Half moons were pressed into the flesh from where his nails dug in.

Are you alright, beloved?

Reven looked up again at the phoenix that came to land on the sandy grass in front of him. No one thought it odd to see the magical beast nearby, though

Reven noted that Fionn remained scarce. Perhaps the birds were a common sight, for he noted Runya loitering around nearby as well and an absurdly large moth covered in fur. Tierra Vida was a strange place.

"Not really," Reven finally sighed. He got to his feet so he could stretch his tight muscles and sore limbs. The glances thrown his way made his stomach twist up again. He looked down at his bare feet instead. Before he realized he'd moved, he was halfway down the shoreline with his hands stuffed into his shallow pockets and shoulders heavy with worry. Azure followed, circling overhead a few times before landing lightly on his bare shoulder.

Talk to me, beloved. What has you in knots?

"Feel that, can you?" Reven snorted.

Usually. You project a lot more than you might think. Your stress concerns me.

That did not help the bard feel any better. He didn't want to project his tumultuous emotions to anyone.

Reven... Azure prodded.

"I dunno, Azure. It isn't an easy question to answer," Reven sighed. "The people here fear me - and they should. I keep tearing apart the only place they have left, and I don't even remember doing it. Kaleo's taken on a heavy burden."

He gets that stubbornness from you.

Reven turned his head toward the bird on his shoulder, feeling Azure's weight drag him further down and his heart sink into his stomach. He remembered the horrible dream he had in Mahala, remembered seeing broken corpses all over the floor and seeing one that had him screaming and confused at the same time. He remembered the conversation that followed and the line of questioning that came with it. Reven had asked if he'd been a good father and, despite the answer that came back, he didn't *feel* like a good father.

"He has a sister, Azure," Reven started.

I do not know her, beloved. She was not born yet when the Empire fell. You never mentioned knowing Noelani was pregnant.

Reven nodded. That made him feel a little better, even if *knowing* he also had a daughter soured his stomach further. He still liked to hear about her. Kaleo told him stories before the events in Kormaine. The girl sounded like a tiny spitfire with a fighter's spirit and a wisewoman's intuition. Reven wanted to meet her - eventually.

It seems like now would be a bad time to tell you about Idris or Marie then, wouldn't it? Azure said, his mental voice small and weak in Reven's mind, as if trying to soften the coming blow.

"Let's just have it out, Azure," Reven sighed. "I'm tired of *not* knowing."

As you wish, beloved. Idris is yours as well. A request, I think, from Zuri. Marie was all you. A 'revenge child', I believe you called it.

Reven merely groaned as he listened and learned just how large an idiot Gannon Oenel had been.

Chapter Five

The city of Grolly was always loud and bustling with life. So many cultures and races blended together in Damaskha's capital city. Calling it a melting pot felt cheap. It was more than that. The city took what came in and absorbed it, integrating everyone and everything into itself, evolving into something new and better. Idris Onegai loved every part of his city. He was as much a part of it as it was of him.

He waved to vendors and people he knew as he walked through the cobbled streets toward the Chateau d'Souie where his mother worked. She worked in all of Damaskha, but Grolly was her home. She commanded the Companion's Guild like a queen commanded a country. In fact, she was due to sit as reigning leader of Damaskha in a few years - something she was greatly looking forward to. Idris didn't want that much power - or responsibility. He had his own life and reasons for doing what he did, growing and learning from the Maison du Hombre. In fact, he passed his home base as he headed down the hill toward his destination.

"Idris!"

The sound of his name caught the young *aurum's* attention. A young woman at the gates of the Maison waved at him, equal in age to himself. Marie had also grown and learned inside the streets of Grolly, splitting her time between the Chateau where she worked in the kitchens and the Maison where she did other creative things.

"What are you doing loitering here?" Idris teased. "Don't you have tea with your mother on First-day?"

Marie snorted softly and gave Idris a playful push against his arm as she joined him. She looked exactly like her mother. Marie had the fair skin men killed for, large amber eyes edged in soft blue, and deep amethyst-colored hair. The only thing she didn't get from her mother were the horns all runeli held because she was not pure-blooded. She was the opposite of Idris, who had dark black hair and tanned skin. The large, powerful wings at his back were a blend of brown, black, and deep auburn tipped in gold.

"Something has come up," Marie said, the tone of her voice robbing Idris of his mirth. Idris frowned. Marie would say nothing further with so many eyes and ears watching. Idris understood and nodded, throwing his arm around Marie's shoulder so he could drag the young woman to a tavern with a private room. Many members of the Maison used the room. It was kept warded from the very thing the two were trying to avoid. Idris bought Marie a drink for dragging her through the streets of Grolly as was his right to do so, but then listened with patience and concern when she explained what she'd heard.

"Jax Delquire hand-delivered a missive this morning to Preston. He came from Itahl," Marie said, explaining things quietly and quickly to Idris. The war with the demons had reached Kormaine faster than expected, with freedom fighters too overwhelmed with the desperate and the wounded to do any actual *fighting*. While it was important to save the innocent, there would be no innocent left to save if they did not start pushing back. The last missive anyone received declared the nobility lost with too many on the run to know if there were any survivors of Sapphire City.

"And another missive showed up from Esbeth."

"What do *they* want? Pillows for their front row seats to the end of the world?" Idris snorted into his tankard.

"Worse," Marie said, sliding two unfolded missives to Idris. "The Esbethi want a bard - - and Kaleo."

"What?" Idris frowned as he read the first missive. It was written in the king's hand - no one else had beautiful penmanship like that kid did. "What do the Esbethi want Kaleo for?"

"Attacking the Amatessa," Marie snorted. Idris rolled his eyes. The Esbethi were notoriously haughty and easily offended. Breathing wrong turned them against you.

"There has to be more to it. Something that we're missing. *Esbeth* put out a hit on Kaleo? *Our* Kaleo?"

For once, Marie remained infuriatingly silent on the matter, looking into her tankard while randomly scratching at her arm. Idris wanted to reach across the table to slap her. The only reason he didn't was because he didn't believe in hitting a woman without reason.

"Marie!" Idris snarled.

"What do you want me to say! I told you, the job came in this morning! You know our brother likes to get into trouble. Looks like trouble finally caught up to him, *non*? You've warned him before, Idris. We both have! What did you tell him when he came looking for you last? Huh? No one takes contracts out to find the dead."

They stopped speaking when there was a gentle knock at the sliding door that divided the private sitting room from the rest of the tavern. Both buried their faces in their tankards for a moment while a maid from outside came in with fresh bread and hard cheese for them to nibble on while they spoke. Plotting on an empty stomach never set well with either of them, anyway.

Marie watched Idris read the Esbethi missive and dismiss it just as quickly. He was not interested in hunting down their brother. He knew Marie wasn't either. They kept the idiot avian at arm's length but watched every move Kaleo made for his own safety. The fool got a little too far out of their reach this time. However, Idris was interested to know why the Kormandi king was in *Itahl* of all places. The letter was simple enough, wishing them well. Idris cared little for well-wishes, focusing on the hidden plea within the carefully formed letters and words.

*I hope that this reaches you in time. Our people will come to you for aid. Please, I beg you to help them. The Baron and Lord Barth are safe in Tierra Vida. A bard from Mahala graciously helped Kendal and I get to Itahl to be with her people, and now I fear that will be **my** undoing. I've sent Jax to find aid. The things I have seen and learned make me sick and put me in great danger. I do not know this nation well enough, but I cannot stay. They know what I am and have done horrible things to those like me. Please. I need your help. The Baron put a great deal of trust in you and always said to reach out to you and you alone if I needed the assistance. I need it. Please.*

With Great Gratitude

- Demyan Ovet

"The Itahli know what the Kormandi king is," Idris said quietly, while re-reading the letter. "The Baron is in Tierra Vida. He told the king to find me."

"Mikhael trusted you. So did the Baron."

Mikhael Dyalov *should* have been the one to sit on the Kormandi throne, but wild circumstances altered that plan. Idris and Marie heard the wide breadth of the entire situation over several pitchers of mead and ale. The Baron ran the Kormandi thieves' network and often worked with Idris and Marie. Mikhael was the Baron's best friend, wandering with the brigand whenever possible. Losing Mikhael hit the Baron hard. It had hit Idris hard, too.

Idris looked at the paper again, then at Marie. She swallowed a mouthful of ale with a loud gulp.

"You're thinking too much, Idris. I don't like it."

"This," Idris said, raising the Esbethi missive. "Doesn't exist."

Idris tore it up right in front of Marie, making the woman groan.

"Idris, you can't-"

"I just did," Idris barked back. "We don't hunt our own blood."

He then picked up the one from the king and smacked Marie on the brow with it.

"You and me are going to Itahl. Let's go get Jax. We have a king to find."

***

The Baron Karov was well-known throughout Kormaine and Damaskha. His reputation even stretched across the Ione Ocean to some of the western nations and south into the Gingetsune Imperium, where the *youkai* spoke of him like one of their strange *oni*. The groan that escaped Gabriel's lips banished anything his reputation may have built up for him. He sounded like a dying whale and felt equally awful. Everything from his hair to his toes hurt in sharp throbs that matched the slow beat of his heart.

The last thing Gabriel remembered was running through the catacombs near Tatengel Minor. That memory forced his blue eyes to snap open with sudden worry filling his heart. The king and queen had been with him, as well as the Phoenix prince and the Kormandi princess. He forced his head to turn so he could see more of his surroundings, but only saw more pallettes and cots like the one that cradled his aching body. A covered body rested on the cot nearest to Gabriel. The dark coloring of the hand that dropped to the ground told Gabriel all he needed to know. Leighton Barth had been with them too, an Itahli alchemist assigned to Kendal's retinue. They'd been attacked by demons in the catacombs and something else that burned with a black flame that melted marble. It would seem Master Barth had not survived the ordeal.

"Baron Karov?" someone said softly. Gabriel's eyes darted toward the voice that spoke, even if the rest of him was much slower to react. It infuriated him.

"Nadya," Gabriel forced out in a gruff croak made worse by his quirky accent. It blended the rolling roughness of the Kormandi tongue with the more drawling Damaskhan tongue.

"She's not here, m'lord." It was a woman that spoke, her voice maddeningly quiet to Gabriel's ringing ears. "She's with the *amati* and Prince Aeron at Yira's Grove."

The relief Gabriel felt was enough to let his eyes close again. At least Nadya was safe. It was a start.

"The king..." Gabriel pressed.

"I don't know, sire. He's not here or the Grove."

The fury boiled up in him again, making his

lip curl. If it weren't for his ringing ears, he'd swear he actually growled.

"I-I can find out," the woman added quickly. Perhaps he had growled. Rather than speak again, he merely nodded, listening to the woman's retreating steps. He needed to know that Demyan was safe, too. The Kormandi people needed to know that. Most of them *should* be in Damaskha by now, but he had no method of telling how long he'd been unconscious.

Slowly, Gabriel forced himself to sit up, gritting his teeth against the pain that movement caused him. It took even longer for Gabriel to force himself to his feet, moving at a glacier's pace, leaning heavily on anything he could reach until he found something that would support him. There were crutches and sticks long enough for a litter. Gabriel grabbed a crutch, tucking it beneath his arm as he wobbled his way out of the tent he'd been placed in. What he saw made his jaw go slack.

The nearby ruins could barely be called a structure, but that was where the small handful of tirsai congregated. Gabriel was good at quick head counts, barely reaching fifty with what he could immediately see. There were no supplies, no guards, no sense of cohesion to the people at all.

"My lord baron," someone said, making Gabriel twitch. He hated weird honorifics. "You shouldn't be up, my lord."

It was the same woman from earlier, tirsai, with dirty hair and bags beneath her eyes.

"Where am I?" Gabriel gruffed out as she helped him back into the tent he worked so hard to get out of.

"The Temple of Sulis, my lord. In Tierra Vida."

"Where is the Grove you spoke of earlier?" he continued, pulling away from her.

"By the shore, my lord. A few miles to the east of here."

"Then I need to be there," Gabriel continued. He turned away from the tent and hobbled in an easterly direction.

"But, my lord," the woman started.

"What is your name, woman?" Gabriel snarled, still hobbling away from her.

"Halora," she said. "Halora Golvayne."

Gabriel recognized the surname; a noble house. "You have two options, Lady Golvayne: help me get to the Grove, or shoot me. That is the only way I'll end up back in that tent."

To her credit, Halora merely glanced back at the tent once, then shifted to take a good bit of Gabriel's weight onto herself.

***

Maeve Oenel growled as she watched Tondra Caelestis and her coterie of winged beasts walk into the ruins of the Temple of Sulis. The woman was tenacious to a fault. Their eyes locked like repulsing magnets. In a different world, Maeve could see being friends with Tondra, but she was simply too overbearing to be at all likeable.

"You never quit, do you, Tondra?" Maeve said when the avian woman came close enough to hear her speak without shouting. The woman's storm gray wings bristled. "Why do you keep coming back here? Do you think I'd hide him from you? He's causing me as many problems as he's causing you!"

"He's here. I know he is. I can see it in the pathetic number of people you have loitering around like dying flies. Did he finally put you in your place?" Tondra retorted. Maeve had to clench her fists to keep from slapping the blasted woman.

Maeve *refused* to acknowledge the dwindling

number of refugees at the Temple of Sulis. She still had control! Those same 'dying flies' as Tondra termed it, watched the interaction closely, hungry for anything that wasn't the bare minimum needed to survive.

Despite what Tondra might say or think about Kaleo, he was still treated as a member of the Amaterasu. Why the winged fools insisted on giving a bastard any form of title was out of Maeve's capacity to rationalize. It would have never happened in the Empire and should have never happened with Kaleo. It seemed to give Tondra some sick satisfaction to throw that in Maeve's face.

"Aeron is with them," Maeve said, recovering a small sliver of her dignity. Tondra merely smirked.

"Where?" the woman practically purred. She was not as tall as Maeve, yet somehow made herself seem more imposing than the tirsai woman was. It was infuriating.

Maeve knew Tondra would not let Kaleo slip away again and, if Maeve was being honest with herself, she didn't really think *Aeron* was ruling material either. The boy was only twenty-six summers old, with very little life experience, let alone political experience. He didn't fight well, and was believed dead until recently. The crown *should* pass to Maeve. She was the eldest after her sister, the one with the most experience and the one most deserving of the throne. Yet *children* took what should have been hers and hers alone. Or, perhaps they were raising a banner behind the fool named as her dead brother. Too many people returning from the grave for Maeve's liking. Too many people in her way.

"Yira's Grove, a few miles east according to this very helpful woman," someone said in a rough accent that made both women turn to find the source. Gabriel Karov hobbled toward them with Halora beneath his arm. "Do I need to get sticks for you two to measure, or will your imaginary cocks work?"

Maeve bristled. She saw the same in Tondra, the woman's wings absolutely writhing with fury.

"Highness," Halora said to Maeve, unable to bob her customary curtsy because of how she supported Baron Karov's weight.

"Shouldn't you be in a bed?" Maeve said in tight, clipped tones of disapproval for the *human* that stood before her. Despite his injuries and clear weakness, the infuriating man smirked.

"That was not a bed. It was a cot. I am grateful. Now, I am going to find Nadya and your prince, who is *not* here with you. What have you done for five years, Captain? Your people should be preparing to fight back, to take back their lands and homes, not hiding in some glittering rocks. And you," the Baron said while looking Tondra up and down with gross disapproval all over his face. "I know you. You are the Tempest, they call you, yes? Tempest of what? A pond? Where was your fury when your allies were falling? Where? You are both jokes. Move. I am going in that direction. You are in my way. Lady Golvayne, if you please."

"Yes, m'lord," Halora muttered, helping the man move through and past Maeve and Tondra, the soldiers that Tondra brought with her, and everyone else that watched.

"Halora!" Maeve barked. The woman flinched but kept moving lest she trip over the very stubborn and very insulting man that used her as a crutch.

"If you can keep up, maybe I will put in a good word to have you muck out prince's stables!" the Baron called. "It is all you are good for, anyway.!"

Tondra sneered while Maeve fumed, listening to the man chortle as he hobbled away from the ruins, away from Maeve, collecting the last remaining vestiges of tirsai in his wake.

Chapter Six

The girl stared, wide-eyed and trembling. She was young, filthy, human, but soft and quiet. Roth liked that she was soft and quiet. He made the floofs dance for her, hoping she would smile. It worked. It always worked. Everyone loved floofs. They were great fun.

"There, you see! They're fun to play with," Roth said. He was supposed to do something, find someone. He couldn't remember who, however. He even tried to ask Ghost - because Ghost remembered trivial things like that - but the mute idiot was gone by the time Roth thought to ask! It was rude! It was cheating! He would lose the game for certain! He asked the soft child, but she didn't know what he should be doing either, nor where he was. The word she said to him when he asked their location didn't make sense to Roth. It sounded like rocks rolling around in her mouth. Roth hated rocks - shifty assassins. He nearly struck her down for bringing them so close to him, but she was so small and fragile-looking. Tears rolled down her face.

He didn't like it when small things cried. He didn't like it when anything cried but, small things especially. Small things rarely knew more than their names and should never cry.

"Do you have a name? Shall I make one up for you? I can do that. I'm good at naming things. I named my Moppet. He's fragile. I miss him so. I wish I knew where he's gone. May I give you a name?"

The girl stared again, sniffling and scrubbing at her dirty face. "Yulia," she said, in a tiny, meek whisper.

Roth blinked at her. It was an odd sound she made, barely audible, but adorable at the same time. Regardless, he did not like what she'd said. It sounded oddly gruff when it should not have. He handed her a colorful floof, watching as she held it in both hands, letting the silky softness of the fur roll around in her palms.

"Is that your name? I don't think I care for it. I will give you a new one. I think I like Malie better. Yes, that's what I'll call you. My Malie. It rolls off the tongue much better than that other name. Will you help me find my Moppet, Malie? I've lost him. I like you. You're quiet. I promise not to eat you. You're too old, anyway. Do you know where we can find babies? I do so like infants. I know I shouldn't, but they're divine. Am I talking too much? Moppet says I do that sometimes. I enjoy talking. It helps to pass the time."

Roth continued talking as he stood, taking Malie's hand in his clawed one. The name meant something. Roth knew it did. Something calm, like Malie was. It suited her. She looked up at him. He smiled at her, but it didn't seem to soothe her. They walked through the charred remains of whatever meager home she lived in before Roth found her. Phier set it all ablaze while he hunted. Corpses littered the ground, all of them twisted in rictus visages of agony or fear. The girl, Roth decided, was lucky and strong to have survived Phier's hunting patterns. That was why he liked her. And because she was soft. And quiet.

"Phier! We're leaving," Roth declared as the giant phoenix soared overhead, blotting out what little remained of the sunlight above. Smoke filled the air, ash raining down like snow from the sky. Everything at ground level all melted together into each other like glass along the shore, creating things that should not have been. The drivers of a wagon were now part of the wood. Furniture sank into the stone that swallowed it up, becoming one melded unit. It was artwork at its finest.

Why are you holding that thing's hand? Phier queried, circling them over and over with a ravenous gaze at Malie.

"Because she's mine now. I found her. She's soft and quiet and will help me find my Moppet."

Idiot, Phier huffed. Roth ignored the black phoenix. He was so cranky after finishing a meal. Not that Roth blamed him. Roth was often cranky after a meal, too. His belly always felt too full, and he never wanted to move much. Phier had to *fly* after eating. Roth could understand the crankiness. *Just kill her and be done with it.*

"No. I like her. You will too, Phier. You'll see. Just like Moppet. You like Moppet, don't you?"

Phier merely groaned. Roth grinned. He knew Phier liked his Moppet as much as Roth did. So Roth kept his new friend Malie. He held her tiny hand and lifted her over the few corpses they passed, so she did not have to jump over them. She remained silent, big blue eyes taking everything in, absorbing it like a tiny sponge.

Roth recalled someone else that absorbed

knowledge in that fashion, learning by proximity alone. He couldn't recall who or when, only that he'd known the person. Young, like Malie. No, not that young, but young-ish.

"Phier, why am I thinking of this? When was it? Who was it?" Roth asked as they left the burnt town in the snow and ash.

How should I know? You think of strange things at random. You're not even wearing pants today.

"I never wear pants. They're far too confining. Malie doesn't either. She knows. Don't you?" Roth asked, looking down at the little girl that held his clawed hand. She looked up with a face so innocent and fearful, shrugging in response. Her dress was torn and as dirty as her tear-streaked face. She would need clean garments, eventually. "Where shall we go, Malie? Shall we go home? Or to a beach? Or a festival! I love festivals!"

Aren't you supposed to be looking for Jaysen? Phier finally said, still soaring in circles above them. Roth stopped.

"Am I? Is that why he's not here with me? Because I'm meant to find him?" Roth said, looking up to the sky, trying to turn in circles to keep track of the black phoenix, dragging Malie with him.

Madhavi told you to find him.

"Madhavi," Roth hissed. "Never speak that wretched woman's name in my presence again, you foul bird! She's vile!"

*And **she** wants your precious Moppet...*

"No!" Roth growled, squeezing Malie's hand hard enough to make the girl cry out in pain. "Now look what you've done! Apologize this instant!"

I'm not the one who crushed her hand. Idiot.

Roth continued to growl at his *audeas* but lifted Malie up into his arms to soothe her all the same as he continued walking, now determined to find his Moppet before the dragon banshee could dig her claws into him.

***

The destruction in Sapphire City appeared more intense than what was observed earlier in Tatengel. Ash no longer fell from the clouds. The miasma had moved on, leaving a dull gray sky with very little sun. he frozen wasteland that remained belayed the once stunning city. Patches of ice crunched beneath each step that Ghost took. The cursed name stuck because Roth couldn't say *Prizrak*. That idiot never shut up. The peace was welcome, even in its profound sadness. The other one, the woman with the wings that tormented him in his dreams, wanted someone found. Ghost wanted to feel the cold against his skin, the ice radiate from his fingers, and the breath leave her lungs. As soon as he and Roth were given leave, Ghost vanished to find what was *his*. He felt it, the steady pulse beneath his feet, the agony that kept the land locked away in ice.

Ghost stood beside the fallen tower, studying the cracked Shard that lay in the ash and ice. It was as large as he was; larger. Spider-web lines ricocheted throughout the large gem, allowing its Power to escape into the ether. Ghost studied it, placing his hand on its cracked surface as he shut his eyes.

The Shard, while broken, still pulsed weakly with Power. It recognized him, remembered who he used to be before he became a monster. The city was once proud and full of life. Gothic structures reached up to the sky above, each housing knowledge, divinity, strength, even Power. The Kormandi were a proud people; emphasis on the word *were*. Knowing that, *feeling* that, made rage roil inside Ghost's gut. Like the olve, the Kormandi were reduced to ashes and broken buildings. Nothing remained but smoke. The nation's crown jewel lay shattered at his feet. They'd failed.

When Ghost stepped back, he glanced at the Shard as if saying goodbye to an old friend. He did not speak, but mourned its loss all the same. He was meant to sit on the Kormandi throne once. Something changed, however, taking the throne from him. It was not something that angered him, but he could not recall *why* it was taken. All he knew was that it had to do with family, a sister or brother or...

It wouldn't surface. Perhaps it wasn't important. The things done to make him a monster robbed him of his memories and sanity. He slept fitfully, plagued with nightmares created by the she-devil, and could not find his voice. Anytime he did, it never surfaced as more than a grating rasp. Roth was the same; worse. The idiot recalled very little of his past and had more insanity racing through him than an asylum. Then there was the other one, the blind boy that Roth protected. He was like Ghost, too - a monster, twisted into something vile that spilled over to the Node he spoke for. Thinking of the Node brought the bulse at his feet into sharp focus. Ana. That was her name.

"Help," someone said from behind Ghost, disturbing his thoughts. The voice was weak, desperate, pleading. Ghost did not move. Every muscle tensed, every instinct telling him to rip the fool person apart and end their misery. He wanted to taste their flesh on his tongue. It was then he realized his fists were clenched tight, claws digging painfully into his palm. "Please, my lord. Please..."

Ghost inclined his head over a shoulder to see the person who spoke. It was a woman. Blood and soot stained her clothes, her blonde hair disheveled and dingy. The dirt on her face was marred only by tracks of tears that ran beneath her chin. When she saw him, she recoiled with a gasp, scrambling away from the monster he knew she saw. She favored her left arm, holding it close to her torso, but still tried to escape. Ghost turned slowly, listening as the woman pleaded for her life rather than for help. Her pleas didn't last long.

Bowan swooped down from above, landing hard enough on the woman to snap her spine. The Corrupted snow gryphon tore into her like a rabid animal. Ghost merely watched. Roth called his *audeas* Phier. Perhaps there was a reason for it. Like Ghost, Bowan was no longer what he once was. Ghost would have to come up with a suitable new name for his *audeas* like he'd done for himself. Something to match the ferocity shown within the once-gentle creature.

"Havok," Ghost rasped, letting the new name roll around on his tongue. It was fitting. "Leave her."

Havok let out a soul-shattering screech before launching himself into the air, curling himself into the clouds where the tower *should* have been. What remained of the Sapphire Tower spiraled up from the base. The levels switch backed on each other until it reached the point where it had cracked and fallen over onto the rest of the keep. Ghost walked toward it, drawn to the odd structure like a moth to a flame. He ignored the bodies and rubble, stepping over them as if they were bugs on the ground not worth his notice.

Despite the destruction and lingering chaos outside, the inside of the tower remained relatively unscathed. Tapestries still hung on the stone walls. Sconces stood out against the light gray stone in stark black, waiting to hold the torches that provided light in the darkness. Windows, all broken, let in what meager light filtered through the gray clouds above, washing everything out in a surreal haze. Ghost committed every detail to memory, forcing himself to recall the past that was robbed from him and match it to what he saw now.

This place was his. What remained of the people was his to command. What remained of the lands was his to rebuild in his ghastly image. He looked down at his clawed, pale hands, then back up to the surrounding walls. He laid one hand against the stone and sent his Power outward. Ice raced across the stone, became one with it until the spiral tower rebuilt itself one brick at a time, reaching to the grayed out sky above.

We'll slaughter them, Havok, Ghost said, eyes closed as he reached out to his *audeas*. *We will tear apart the ones that did this to us.*

***

It seemed as if it would have been a great effort to reach Joricho City from Tierra Vida, yet it was something Xandrix managed with ease. He remembered a time when the manor house in Joricho City had lush gardens filled with wildflowers and trimmed hedges to divide it from the rest of the manor houses. The one Daemodan now inhabited once belonged to the Esbethi consulate. Their time was split between Esbeth and the Empire. Both died in the Fall, leaving the manor to the ravages of a bloody, messy war.

Xandrix had to admit one thing about Daemodan - for all he may or may not do, he put in the effort to make things habitable. The manor no longer held the glamor it once did, but the grounds were clean. In fact, all of Joricho was clean. Of all the Spawn, Daemodan was the one with the most decorum. He didn't slaughter the people that got left behind, nor did he allow them to be slaughtered. There were rules to follow for olve and demon alike. The ones that failed to do so were severely punished no matter what or who they were. In that sense, Xandrix had great respect for the man over any of the other Spawn, or even the Red himself. The others thrived on chaos. Daemodan existed in a world of order.

Still, it brought Xandrix no joy to return to the manor house in Joricho City. People stared at him as he shuffled through the gates, whispered about the condition he was in. Their lives continued mostly unerringly after the Fall. Daemodan allowed them to cling to whatever visage of happiness they felt suited them best. Xandrix hid a snarl, glowering at all of them as he passed.

The gardens were no longer vibrant and lush, but the yard was well manicured and free of any stray leaf or root. Four hideous beasts loitered in the yard, all four loosely chained to a stake in the ground. Xandrix knew better. A mere chain would not stop those beasts. They were dogs, once; the kind used for work with the large ebony sea horses the Kormandi bred. The dogs were easily the height of a man and the width of two. What Daemodan had done to them made them ferocious monsters. It was a trend, but, in this instance, it made the dogs difficult to get by and loyal *only* to Daemodan. Their low growls slowed Xandrix's steps. Habit made him put his hands up even if he knew that would not help him should the dogs choose to attack.

"I'm just coming back," Xandrix tells the hounds. "You know me."

"They don't care."

Xandrix jumped despite himself. He wasn't expecting to be seen or stopped. Attacked, maybe, but not spoken to. No one gave him the time of day. Xandrix looked up to meet Daemodan's eye. His voice was unmistakable. Generally soft-spoken and calm unless irritated beyond his considerable tolerance for stupidity.

"Dare I ask why you're alone?" Daemodan

asked from the corner of the house. He wore a sun hat, of all things, and looked as if he'd been gardening. Daemodan. Gardening. The image was laughable, yet oddly disturbing.

"There was a Hex Storm over most of Kormaine. It made them ill. And... there were complications. The Phoenix prince isn't as dead as we believed. He has Jaysen. I don't know what happened to Roth," Xandrix reported. "I was taken captive."

"Not quite the mighty hunter you thought you were, are you?" Daemodan purred. Xandrix tried not to snarl. "Not only were you captured, but you return empty-handed. Explain to me what use you still have - if you have any at all."

Xandrix's nostrils flared. He did not come so far to be eliminated. However, he was acutely aware of how the dogs growled at him, all of them smelling his anger and fear.

"They're in Tierra Vida," Xandrix said. "The Phoenix prince, his son, and his nephew. They sent the Kormandi King to Itahl."

Daemodan sneered. No one liked that nation, not even the Spawn or the demons. Even *they* had laws and standards. The Itahli did not seem to have any at all.

"And Ghost?" Daemodan asked. Xandrix shook his head.

"I don't know. With Madhavi, last I knew," he said.

"My wayward sister has gone silent," Daemodan said, moving toward the front of the house again. The dogs watched him, parting when Daemodan came close to them, before knitting themselves back together in a tense line. "No doubt looking for Jaysen. Her obsession with my ward is rather disturbing. I may yet find use of you."

Xandrix watched the dragon-born man walk up the steps to the manor house, barely containing the desire he felt to lash out at Daemodan for the clear dismissal. "I could return you to Ba'el if you'd rather."

Xandrix shook with a mix of fury and fear at the mention of that name. He felt his claws dig into the flesh of his palm, blowing out those emotions through clenched teeth. "No."

"Good," Daemodan said, calling the dogs to heel. "Hose yourself off before coming inside. You smell. And try not to be all day about it either."

Chapter Seven

Darkness enveloped him. A sweet, heady scent filled his nostrils. It pulled him from the darkness to a place of comfort and familiarity. As soon as Jaysen opened his eyes, the darkness receded to a field of bright red poppies. They swayed in an unseen breeze that tousled his hair. Pieces of it flew in front of his eyes, making him blink. It was blue - a soft pale color that seemed bright to his eyes. He felt his jaw drop slightly at the realization that he had never seen the color of his hair before now.

"Didn't we agree to stay out of the Sea of Stars?" Kaleo asked from behind him. Jaysen jumped despite the comfort he felt around his friend, then immediately replaced the fear with annoyance, frowning as he turned to face the young avian. They met nightly for 'lessons' that Jaysen insisted Kaleo needed for his own protection. Really, he was just lonely and didn't want to admit it. Sitting next to a grumpy chimera was not as fun as it might seem. It was boring and depressing half the time, annoying and infuriating the other half. His wound was healing too slowly, leaving him nearly helpless in an unfamiliar place.

"We're not in the Sea," Jaysen replied, hearing the slight lisp on his rasping voice, frowning at that too. It was as if nearly dying suddenly put everything about him into stark focus.

"What's wrong?" Kaleo asked, noticing his reaction. Jaysen shook his head. He was about to growl that Kaleo should mind his business, should stay out of Yira's realm entirely, then softened. He needed to trust someone. Kaleo was the only friend Jaysen had.

"What color is my hair?" Jaysen finally asked.

"What?" Kaleo chuckled. Jaysen bit back the rising frustration that naturally came to him.

"My hair. What color is it?" he repeated instead, trying not to growl out each syllable. Kaleo shrugged, looking at Jaysen in a more scrutinizing fashion.

"Sort of powder blue. Why? It's normal coloring for a tywyll. Most of you is, just... ashy, I suppose. Not as gray as you could be. Except your hands. Those are black to the elbows."

And just like that, as if suddenly colored, Jaysen felt himself shift and change within Yira's Realm to the exact description Kaleo gave. Kaleo's response might have been comical if Jaysen had not been so shocked by what occurred. No one had affected him within Yira's Realm in years. Their lessons were working.

"Did... I just color you in?" Kaleo asked. Jaysen looked down at himself, noting that his clothing had not changed. They remained the same drab, washed-out color that reminded Jaysen of what oatmeal might look like just based on its taste. It was horribly bland and, thus, had to have an equally bland color. The rest of him, however, from clawed hands to hair now matched Kaleo's description perfectly.

"How did you do that?" Jaysen asked, then quickly added. "I didn't teach you that."

"*Why* did I do that? You have better control than I do," Kaleo said. "Haven't you ever asked what you look like before?"

"Don't be stupid. Why the hells would I ask what I look like? I can't see it anyway!" Jaysen barked. "Roth always tells me that my eyes are there, but that's all he says. Crazy idiot." Jaysen paused. "Do… they have a color?"

"Your eyes?" Kaleo asked softly, then shook his head. "No, not really. I see where the iris should be, but it's so pale it may as well be white."

Jaysen nodded quietly. He wasn't sure that he expected anything different, but the knowledge that his lack of sight could not be changed seemed to hurt a little.

"Your clothes didn't change," Kaleo pointed out. Now that they were the focus, they seemed to shimmer as if waiting for instruction. Both young men frowned at the oddness of it. "Are they always so drab?"

"How should I know!"

"Because you're the one that puts them on!" Kaleo laughed. "No one helps you? You just… what? Grab tunic and trousers and hope for the best?"

"Isn't that what everyone does?" Jaysen snapped.

"No," Kaleo chortled. "You're not a bad looker. It wouldn't kill you to put in some effort into looking less like a paper bag."

"I'm a what?" Jaysen replied, having never heard that term 'looker' before. It seemed rather odd to say to someone that could not see.

"You're cute," Kaleo chuckled. "That's what it means. You're not bad to look at. A 'looker', as it were."

Jaysen frowned, still not really understanding the term or what it was meant to imply. Kaleo merely sighed and smirked.

"Are you feeling any better?" Kaleo began, clearing his throat. He was still grinning. Jaysen shrugged.

"I don't know how I should feel after being skewered."

Kaleo winced. Jaysen sighed. Things had become so strained between them. Even during their lessons, there was an odd tension between them. Jaysen had once resigned himself to losing his one friend, but then that same friend became his only savior. When death crept in all around him, it was Kaleo's voice that brought him back from the brink. Jaysen felt he owed the young avian for that, yet had no real way of repaying him. The lessons were the best he could do.

"Guess we should try something new today," Jaysen said. "Since we're already here."

"Sure," Kaleo shrugged, the shit-eating grin finally fading from his cheeks. "Lara's been teaching me to pick pockets. We can try doing something like that here instead."

Jaysen snorted. Kaleo spoke highly of the girl named Lara. He was clearly smitten with her, even to the blind. Jaysen could hear it in Kaleo's voice, each inflection carrying hints of adulation in it anytime he spoke of the girl. It was disgusting.

"Why would you need to pick pockets in a dream?" Jaysen said in a deadpan voice. Kaleo glanced at him, but shrugged again.

"I don't know. Was just an idea."

"Form better ideas," Jaysen retorted.

Kaleo laughed. The sound of it was melodious, carrying off into the spectral breeze that filled the Poppy Fields. It made Jaysen's lips almost curl into a smile. Almost.

"Fine. Focusing Power then, since I'm still not good at that," Kaleo said. He wasn't. Power worked differently in Yira's Realm. Things did not always have the same effect they did in the waking world. Kaleo wasn't wrong either - he was terrible at it.

"Ok. We'll start here in the Fields where it's..." Jaysen's words trailed off as the Poppy Fields grew dark again, the sky above them angry and roiling with black clouds and forks of lightning. "What are you doing?"

"Nothing. This isn't me," Kaleo said with the same look of fear on *his* face that Jaysen felt on his own. Something was terribly wrong.

"Wake Up!" Jaysen barked at Kaleo, feeling his stomach knot when Kaleo remained. "Kaleo, Wake Up!"

"I can't!" Kaleo argued. "What the hells is this?"

Neither had the chance to answer, both boys jumping to the side as a fat bolt of lightning struck the ground between them. They flew through a whirlwind of light, each of them landing hard on their sides feet from where they'd just been standing. Jaysen blinked the bright spots from his vision, unaccustomed to such things.

"Kaleo!"

There was no answer.

"*Kaleo!*" he repeated, forcing himself to his feet. What he saw made him freeze to his marrow.

Kaleo hung suspended in the air, head back between his shoulder blades. Rivulets of blood ran down his arms, dripping from splayed fingers. His wings looked broken, even if Jaysen *knew* they weren't. Jaysen froze for half a heartbeat, then just charged right at his friend, tackling him back down to the poppies whip-lashing beneath them. As soon as he did, both of them vanished from the Poppy Fields as if a bubble of terror had popped over their heads...

...and ripped them into the waking world. Jaysen's eyes opened to complete darkness even as he gasped, chest heaving. He heard the rustling of animals nearby, smelled their fur and feather. A raptor on the hunt. The squeal of the prey confirmed his guess. His face was on the pillow given to him, claws curled deep into the soil beneath him. He heard Fionn's steady breathing nearby and took comfort in that, heart aching for Tanis.

The footsteps that followed made Jaysen's back stiffen and every hair stand on edge. He didn't know whether to fight or flee. Not that he was capable of doing either in his current conditions.

"Jaysen," Kaleo said, his voice pitched low and breathless. All the air rushed out of Jaysen's lungs in a single growl.

"What just happened?" he snarled, still shaking with fear and confusion.

"I dunno. I don't... Are you ok?" Kaleo said, voice shaking. He sat beside Jaysen. Normally Jaysen would huff or scoot away, but he needed that closeness now, needed to smell his friend, to feel him and *know* he was ok. Other than the fear and a light scent of copper, Kaleo smelled fine.

"Fine," Jaysen clipped. He let the breath he'd been holding go, then inclined his head toward Kaleo. "You?"

"Yeah. I'm ok," Kaleo said. He moved in a way that suggested he might be touching his face. Given the scent of copper, he was probably scrubbing his nose clean of the blood that ran from it. Jaysen was familiar enough with what that was like to know the motions and scent of a nosebleed. Daemodan got them fairly often, blaming them on allergies.

"We're supposed to be safe in the Fields, Jays. That's the second time something's happened to us there. Why?"

Jaysen merely shrugged, shaking his head. He didn't know why, had no explanations or theories, only fear and worry. "Madhavi, maybe. She's hunting you. That's why I told you it wasn't safe in Yira's Realm."

"Did she do this to you?" Kaleo asked after another moment of silence. "Madhavi? Did she…"

The question faded even as Kaleo touched Jaysen's hand to indicate what he meant. Jaysen merely shook his head, throat closing up.

"Worse," he croaked, forcing that fear back down into the pit of his stomach where it belonged. Silence followed again. It did not bother Jaysen. They'd spent so many hours in silence that it felt natural to him to do so; natural to Kaleo too, for the avian did not complain. Both were just glad to be *awake* instead of in the Fields.

Kaleo shifted after a while beside Jaysen, wrapping a wing around the Corrupted tywyll's shoulders. The close contact was something uncomfortable and unfamiliar to Jaysen in the waking world. Kaleo had done the same in the dream world many times, though it had taken a very long time to trust the avian to come that close or even touch him. It had never happened in the waking world.

Jaysen felt his muscles tense. The instinct to fight back grew stronger until Kaleo started singing a soothing song in low tones meant for Jaysen's ears only. It still woke Fionn, for Jaysen could hear the giant creature shift in the grass nearby, smelled his breath as it blew in their direction. Kaleo used to sing for him in Yira's Realm, too. The boy would 'perform' for Jaysen as practice and even tried teaching Jaysen how a violin worked once. It was a fabulous failure that Jaysen remembered fondly - one of the few fond memories he had.

The song continued, flowing seamlessly into another in a language Jaysen was not familiar with. He finally gave in, his body giving a little shudder at the intimate touch before he relaxed, leaning heavily into the loose embrace.

***

A cool breeze blew in from the sea later that afternoon, bringing the sweet, salty scent of the ocean right along with it. Kaleo sat alone with his feet in the frothy waves. His mind wandered to the horrible nightmare he and Jaysen shared. It made him shiver, and made focusing on anything else a monumental task. The bard's dreams still bothered him, too. While Jaysen and Kaleo were having their own nightmare, the bard had had another about the duende. Luckily, he hadn't set anything ablaze this time, but it was bothersome all the same. There was something in them that spoke of things to come, that worried Kaleo.

"Do you want to stay alone or can I sit?" Lara asked as she came to stand behind him. He smiled at the sea, but then turned his smile to her. She was beautiful, still wearing her stupid cap to hide the horns of her race. He didn't mind it anymore like he did when they first met.

"You can sit," he answered, gesturing at a spot beside him. She rolled up her trews and sat, feet already bare.

"You've been quiet today. Are you ok?" she asked, golden-amber eyes staring out to the sea while he stared at her. He was so glad she was there with him and had no words to tell her. He felt stupid for it. He sang ballads, *wrote* them, but couldn't string together a proper sentence around one silly girl to save his life. Jaysen said he was stupid. Kaleo was inclined to agree. Lara, blessedly, didn't seem to mind.

When she looked at him for his answer, he flushed and looked away, down at the sand beneath his knees. "Just thinking."

"About?" she pressed, the wind catching some of the long locks of hair that naturally gathered themselves into loose tubes.

He shrugged. "A lot of things. Dreams mostly. Mine; Reven's. They're unsettling."

Lara offered comfort by placing her hand on Kaleo's arm. He looked at it and felt his face grow hot again.

"You can talk to me if you want to. I don't mind."

He grinned and nodded, looking at her again with so much tension in his stomach he thought he might be sick. Instead, he leaned in and kissed her. She let him, kissing him back. It was something sweet, innocent, but urgent at the same time. Kaleo felt it at his core and fought it down.

He brought his hand up to her face, holding her to him, only to tear away sharply when whistles echoed at them from the ocean, along with shouts and cries for aid.

"What the bloody hells?" Kaleo said as they both stood so fast they wavered and had to catch each other for balance or risk falling over. Two ships came toward them, large ones, not like the small rafts that were moored to the shore. They were large fishing ships; or perhaps something more akin to pirate ships. That was one spot where Kaleo's knowledge was rather limited - ships.

"Make way!" someone shouted. "We come with injured!"

Kaleo's heart sank, eyes closing as the nightmares slammed back into the forefront of his memory.

"Please no..." he whispered, squeezing Lara's hand tight before releasing it. "Go find help. Go!"

She nodded, running back to the Grove about a mile down from where Kaleo walked out to. He liked the peace, the silence. He ran out into the shallows to join one of the men that jumped off a flat ship that washed itself up right onto the sandy beach while the other anchored itself just offshore and began dropping a dingy that would bring others.

"What happened?" Kaleo asked. The man that came to him with ropes almost as thick as his arms was half-olven, a fisherman by the looks of his hands and markings on his arms.

"Survivors," the man barked in a thick accent that was difficult for Kaleo to understand. "Asphondel."

"Kaleo!"

He looked up at the sound of his name being called and felt his stomach grow cold. Ettrian looked at him. He was family, Syrus Oenel's son by his partner, Eloiny.

"Oh no..." Kaleo breathed out as a flap splashed down into the water. People flowed out, sad or sobbing, worried. "No... no..."

So many of them were injured. The ones with demon wounds cried out, desperately trying to fight the curse such a thing brought on their heads. But it was not to them he looked. He looked at Ettrian, at his little brother, Gael - at the man that they carried out in a sling.

"Ferren, where's Hayden and Ali?" Kaleo immediately asked as he helped carry his grandfather to the shore. The man was a mess, ripped apart from head to toe and turning faster than Kaleo thought possible. "Ferren!"

The duende man - also injured if not as badly as Kaleo's grandfather - merely looked at Kaleo sadly but said nothing.

"Serai!" Kaleo hollered even as he began healing some of his grandfather's wounds so that the man would stop bleeding so much. He knew his voice would not carry that far, but the instinct to holler for the red-haired woman kicked in anyway. "Gael, are you hurt? Gael!"

The boy shook his head. He was only eleven years old. Tear tracks ran down his face, carving a path through the dirt and grime that covered him.

"Uncle E?"

"M'fine," Ettrian said. Kaleo nodded, helping Ferren next as he looked back toward the Grove with worry knotting his stomach more and more. Syrus wouldn't make the trip there. Half these people wouldn't.

So, Kaleo did the next best thing he could think of, the thing a *bard* taught him just before their flight from Mahala - how to soothe others with his voice. He'd done it for Jaysen and now intended to do the same for the duende stumbling onto the surrounding shore. He sang. He sang despite the odd looks others gave him, sang while holding on to Syrus Oenel, while others stood around helplessly. He sang and let his voice be heard, let the ocean carry it out to the ship anchored out at sea.

"Kaleo," someone said. The tone was gentle, concerned, but enough to cut the song off sharply. As soon as it ended, all the life rushed right out of him. He hadn't been singing for long, but he felt raw and his throat hurt. He immediately felt himself falling, but then felt hands holding him up.

"It's all right. Relax," the same soothing voice said. "Relax."

"Sy…" Kaleo tried, but it hurt to speak, so he stopped.

"Shh… Serai has him. It's ok. We'll help them. Just relax. I've got you."

Somehow, that made it better. To hear those words spoken to him made the rest of his muscles liquify and his head loll to his chest.

Chapter Eight

The number of people near Yira's Grove far outweighed the straggling, meager handful of lingering 'embers' left behind at the Temple to Sulis. The Baron liked the name he'd used for them, seeing the stragglers that followed as tiny embers desperately clinging to life after a smoldering flame was snuffed out. They aimed to hit the fabled Grove where their supposed savior was. Except, everything the Baron saw was in total chaos.

People ran over the sanded grass around time-worn stones and pillars, or along the nearby shore carrying armloads of bandages, torn sheets, and rough-hewn bowls filled with green paste. Others shouted for aid, while more carried makeshift litters that held the wounded. Watching them made the Baron look away briefly. Many of the wounded were turning, fighting a battle they could not win as their souls were twisted and made evil. It wasn't a pleasant thing to watch, nor was it something that he wanted to relive. He felt that evil inside himself, slowly twisting him in ways he knew he would not be able to fight off forever. For now, the Baron ignored the burning acid moving through his veins and let Halora help him limp along toward the one individual that looked like they were in charge.

The man looked rough, to be honest. He, like many of the others the Baron saw, was dirty, with dark circles beneath his eyes. The scar over the right eye was the most prominent feature about the man's face outside of his hazel-blue eyes. They tickled some part of the Baron's memory that would not surface. It wasn't important. Exhausted or not, the man with the scar seemed to be the one delegating tasks, supplies, and people.

"You are in charge?" the Baron asked as he walked up with Halora beneath his shoulder. The Baron heard her soft gasp when she saw the man in charge.

"I don't know that I'd call it that," the man replied as he looked at the Baron, taking a moment to gauge how badly injured he was and what he was going to do with the new human in town. The look he gave to the Embers was the same, taking stock of who the Baron brought with him. It was quick, precise, and exactly what the Baron needed.

"P-prince Gannon," Halora stammered, twitching beneath the Baron as if debating whether she should curtsey or remain where she was. The tired-looking man simply shook his head.

"No. He's dead," the tirsai man said. "You can call me Reven. How many do you bring with you?"

"Forty, maybe," the Baron answered, wincing slightly as Halora shifted beneath him. Reven took up the slack.

"Let's get you settled," Reven said, helping the Baron to a spot where he could sit. "Girl, I don't know your name. Take the others over to Navid. Centaur, grumpy disposition, tall, can't miss him. He doesn't blend well."

"Y-yes, your highness," Halora said, bobbing a quick curtsey as she directed the others to follow her.

"Reven," he corrected as he settled the Baron on a smooth stone with runes so old and worn they had become part of the stone, an imprint of a forgotten age. "I need a bloody sign so I don't have to keep repeating myself."

The Baron snorted a dry chuckle, then winced again. Reven frowned, looking him over carefully until finding the wound that would eventually spell the Baron's demise. He could see it on Reven's face - resignation.

"Stay here. I'll bring someone that might be able to help," Reven said. The Baron caught his arm and shook his head. It wasn't worth the effort. From what the Baron could see, there were already too many people that needed help, with too few that could do so.

"Nadya," the Baron said. "And Aeron. They are here?"

Reven nodded. "Yes. I can take you to them if you'd like."

The Baron nodded in response. Reven studied him again and sighed.

"On second thought, why don't I just bring them to you," Reven said. "Stay put. You've already put too much strain on yourself."

This time, the Baron didn't argue. He sat on the smooth stone and let his eyes drift closed for a few blessed seconds. The sound of the ocean overpowered the chaos he'd walked in on, creating a soothing song for the weary and downtrodden. He pondered over what Halora had said, recognizing the tired-looking olve as the Phoenix prince. He was rumored to be dead, though he had heard Aeron's story a few times over. The man was injured, lost his mind, and fled. Aeron gave chase but lost the trail and ended up in Kormaine with Demyan and Nadya - and stayed. It wasn't the Baron's place to ask why given what he saw around him. Had the young man known? Would it have made a difference if he had? He had the arrogance of a leader but the experience of a toddler. Perhaps it was best that he remained where he was.

"Gabriel!"

The Baron's eyes snapped open at the sound of Nadya's voice. She ran to him, throwing her arms around him in a hug so tight he groaned.

"That hurts," he said to her in Kormandi. She did not loosen her grip.

"I thought you were dead. You idiot. I thought you were dead."

The Baron held her as tightly as he could manage after that, letting himself sink into the soft blonde curls around her shoulder. When he looked up, Aeron stood to the side with a surprise standing behind him. Adrian Verit and Nastya Golubev, both trusted friends of Nadya *and* the Baron. He smiled at them while still holding on to Nadya, letting a seed of hope spark inside him for the first time since fleeing his home.

***

Kaleo slept deep and long. The dreams came to him one right after the other. He saw people running like Reven had explained, saw them laughing and dancing. He saw people he knew, yet they were still just out of touch in the dream, like he could not quite speak their names on his tongue. He saw the darkened Poppy Fields, the sky above black as pitch and angry. He heard the cackling sound of laughter carried on the wind, only to find himself falling. It seemed like such an odd sensation. He had wings! He could fly! Yet he fell endlessly, desperately reaching out for anything to hold fast to until something finally gripped him back.

You overtaxed yourself, little one.

"Fionn?" Kaleo asked, looking up at the giant chimera from the comfort and cradling grace of a sea full of lavender and fresh sage. The smell soothed his aches, his fears, his heart.

Try not to do that again, shall we? It worries me.

"I don't understand. What did I do?"

The bard will explain. Wake up now. You've slept long enough, and it is not safe in Yira's Realm any longer.

"But-"

Wake up!

Kaleo gasped, eyes popping open. He slept inside a humid tent rather than a bed of lavender and sage. The sounds of the shore drifted to his ears, as well as the sound of people talking or calling out to each other outside. It was dark and disgusting in temperature. His entire body felt sore, and his throat burned as if he'd swallowed a thousand fiery coals. Beside him was a clay cup filled with a dark liquid that smelled awful and far too sweet, with a tiny piece of parchment nestled against it.

:: Drink the tea. It will help, little bard. - R::

Kaleo snorted as he picked up the cup and sniffed the tea. His nose wrinkled of its own volition, but he looked at the note again and did as he was told - he drank it all down in one long gulp and then gagged.

"Oh, that is awful..." he breathed out. A few of the dark leaves still sat at the bottom of the cup, taunting him. "Yes, *you* are awful."

The tea leaves did not respond. He sighed, setting the cup back down so he could redress himself and go outside. Part of him wished he had not done that, half tempted to dart back into the tent to get away from the surrounding chaos.

People moved quickly around the grove, carrying bloodied rags or fresh bandaging that, to Kaleo's knowledge, appeared out of nowhere. Others carried water or more tiny clay pots like the one Kaleo had in his tent. He smelled food cooking over the scent of the sea and blood, of herbs being used to heal and soothe the wounded. There were more people in the grove than before, too. Not just the new arrivals, but other tirsai, the ones who had been with his aunt. That was easily the most confounding part of it all.

"Good morning," Lara said, sitting beside the tent flap. She startled him, making him jump in the air slightly and clutch at his chest. She giggled. "Sorry."

"How long have you been sitting there?" Kaleo asked. Lara shrugged.

"An hour, maybe. Not long. The bard asked for me to sit with you."

"You could've come inside, you know," Kaleo said. She smirked without looking up at him, making him turn bright red. It was not the first time they slept in each other's company, but his absurd emotional range still betrayed him. Rather than dwell on his uncooperative thought processes, he cleared his throat and looked around again. "What happened? Where did all these people come from? I remember the boats coming and then-"

"You sang," Lara explained simply. "Most are from Asphondel. The last that could leave. They were safe, but the demons found them. Now they are here - what is left of them. There aren't many. More have died from the demon wounds. Serai is doing what she can. The rest came with a human man who talks like he is chewing rocks. He says that the woman who came looking for you in Mahala was here. He told her to leave."

Kaleo frowned at Lara's explanation. He didn't know a human that spoke like he chewed rocks. The only fool with a boorish brogue that Kaleo knew was Liam. That idiot's drawl was unmistakable. He kept his eyes focused on the movement all around him, feeling hot yet oddly drained at the same time. Lara stood, dusting sand from her trews, and took his hand. She looked at everyone with him, seemed to have the same thoughts and confusions he did, but remained at his side so they could be confused *together*.

"Thanks for staying with me," Kaleo croaked. It still hurt a little to speak despite the wondrous effects of that gods-awful tea. He almost yearned for another cup if it meant his throat would stop burning. Lara smiled at him, then pointed at the crowd when she saw the human she spoke of earlier.

"Him. That is the man who brought the others from the ruins," Lara said.

The man was, in fact, human, with dark hair and vibrant blue eyes. Nadya and Aeron followed in his wake, each on either side of the limping man. He used a staff to keep himself upright with one hand and gestured at things around them with the other. Kaleo smirked, recognizing the man immediately.

"Baron Karov," he said. "A noble from Kormaine. He goes by the Baron. My father knew him. He's a good man. Loyal to the Kormandi crown. I didn't think he'd made it out. The man must have a roach's luck."

Lara snorted a dry chuckle but took steps toward where Reven sat. Kaleo let her tug him along, still feeling too sore and drained to argue much. The bard sat near a fire with Ettrian and Gael. There were a few others that Kaleo didn't recognize around the fire as well, each blot of orange and red hosting far too many people around its warmth. Not that people congregated because of the cold. This was different; this was a need to feel safe and secure. Navid lounged nearby, the centaur making Kaleo feel better by presence alone as he did to the others that loitered with the bard.

Reven played idle songs on his violin. It seemed to help keep people calm and put a note of ease in the surrounding chaos. When Kaleo walked over with Lara, the bard looked up with his eyes and grinned.

"Good morning," the bard said to him while he continued to play. "You're just in time to watch the sunrise."

"Is it? Morning?" Kaleo countered. The bard nodded. "You didn't have to let me sleep so long."

Reven finished his song, then looked at Kaleo with a gentle grin.

"And you didn't have to sing everyone's wounds away, but you did. Sleep well-earned. But we'll need to work on that. You can't be exhausting yourself every time you use your resonance abilities," the bard winked. Kaleo flushed, looking around.

"Syrus-"

"Is fine. He needs rest," Reven explained. "Navid's been filling me in. It's a lot to take in, but Serai purged him of the poison in his blood. She's done the same for the Baron despite loud protests. They'll both be ok."

"The girl you saw in your dreams, Alivae - she's not here, Reven she-"

"I know," Reven cut in sadly. "She didn't make it on to the ship."

Kaleo just stared at the bard for a moment, at his grandfather resting near the fire, his features gaunt and pale, scarred where the wounds were left untreated for too long. Serai worked miracles, but Kaleo knew that some miracles just didn't cut it. He looked at the bard again, noting the strain in the man's tired eyes.

He'd been overtaxing himself too, it seemed. It probably did not help to have *everything* dumped on him all at once without a net to support him.

Kaleo's family tree was a complicated one. He'd tried to get away with explaining as little as possible when Reven first asked him, only mentioning himself, L'nae and Noelani. He'd heard the bard asking Azure about Idris a few times since being at the Grove, and now this. Despite what the tirsai nobility said, Gannon Oenel was *not* the son of the long dead emperor of the Phoenix Empire. Instead, he was the unfortunate accident of a coupling between the emperor's brother, Syrus, and the emperor's wife - also long dead now.

Shame and absurdities being what they were, Syrus was banished from the Empire. He made his way to the duende tribes instead, building a life with them. The man had too many children to count, participating in fertility rites as regularly as any duende would. The four children Kaleo knew the best were the four his grandfather had with his partner, Eloiny: Alivae, Hayden, Ettrian, and Gael. Gannon would take him to visit his extended family often.

Just *thinking* about all that made Kaleo's brain hurt. He could not imagine what Reven must be feeling. The bard remembered nothing before the Fall; anything before being found by Ajana. Saying that the new information was 'a lot' was the understatement of the cycle.

Kaleo felt Lara's fingers flex in his hand before he realized he was nearly crushing them with his tumultuous thoughts. He released her immediately, bringing his hand up to scratch his chest, to scratch at the spot where the phoenix tattoo would have gone had the Empire survived, and frowned.

"Sorry I wasn't awake to field any of this for you," Kaleo said quietly. The statement must have been unexpected, for the bard looked up and shrugged. The shrug was followed by a glance to the sky where Azure cartwheeled above them.

"I had help," Reven said. "You put too much on yourself, urchin. It isn't good for your health."

"Speaking from experience, master bard?" Kaleo smirked as he sat next to Ettrian. The young duende held his younger brother in his lap, both silent and observant of their surroundings. Neither seemed phased by the change in their brother.

"The only experience I have, urchin. Laziness is the key to happiness," Reven said, bringing the violin back to his shoulder, settling in to play until the sun crested above the horizon.

***

By evening the following day, the Asphondeli survivors had settled nicely with the tirsai refugees. At one point in time, the tirsai and duende would have been hard pressed to give each other the time of day. Now they relied on each other for survival, treating each other as brothers, neighbors, and allies. The appearance of the Baron eased a great deal of Reven's doubts and concerns. His first order of business had been checking on Aeron and Nadya. The Baron's second order of business had been to question Reven on Demyan's whereabouts. Reven told him what he knew: the Kormandi king and his queen requested to go to Itahl, so Reven helped them get there. The rest was left to the Baron to sort out.

The man was frightfully efficient. Within the first few hours of his arrival, he'd sent runners to the nearest town that had a courier, and another to the nearest town with supplies. Aeron and Nadya followed the man's example. He took charge while deferring to Aeron. It was astonishing and rather brilliant when Reven sat to examine it for longer than five minutes. It clearly established a chain of command without undermining what Aeron was trying to build, yet also worked to teach the boy what he needed to know for him to actually *lead* these people. They were so desperate for guidance, they took it from anyone willing to give even the smallest shred of it. Maeve had squandered it, but Reven wondered if Aeron would be able to do better.

However, with the Baron's arrival, even suddenly felt superfluous. Serai assured him that he was not, that he was still the people's hope, still needed. Part of Reven wanted to believe it, the other part simply wanted to take this gift and run before something else happened.

Is that really what you want? his mind chimed in. Reven sighed, throwing a glare out to the open ocean as if it had sent him the offending thought.

"There you are," Serai said as she came to sit beside him. "I have been looking for you."

Reven smiled at her, kissing her cheek when she sat down. She laced her fingers with his and leaned her head on his shoulder. She'd been doing so much of late, healing everyone she could, offering miracles no one else could provide.

"Did I miss a date?" he teased. He felt her smile against him, felt her radiate like a small sun with delight. She looked up at him instead of answering, kissing him soundly. It was entirely unexpected. "Well, that's nice. What did I do to deserve that?"

Serai smiled at him. So much had gone wrong since their arrival: losing Xandrix, nightmares that terrified people, loss of control, fleeing refugees. The list was as endless as it was exhausting.

"You have found your family," she said with the most adorable wrinkle of her freckled nose. Reven couldn't help but grin back.

"Technically, they found me," he corrected. "And two are missing. Well, three if you count the little one, but I'm not ready for that yet."

"Which are missing?" Serai asked curiously.

"I have another son and another daughter," Reven sighed. "Idris and Marie. They're older than Kaleo. Apparently, I was far less virtuous in my previous life. Seems ironic. I steal things or swindle people of their money for a living now, but my former self was the less virtuous. I suppose it doesn't matter. It's just all so complicated, Serai."

"Children are complicated," she said. He snorted. "You do not remember them?"

"Not at all. I want to though. I'm tired of *not* knowing anything - or anyone. Azure told me about them. Not even Kaleo was aware they were mine. And then the little one. And new siblings and an actual father. My cursed family is humongous, but I know *one* person."

"Seven," Serai corrected. "You know Aeron and the girls. Liam and Ajana are your family, too. I am your family. The rest will get to know you when you get to know them, just like we did. And we shall find the others too," Serai said, as if it were that easy. Perhaps it was, and Reven was overthinking it. Or perhaps there was a measure of guilt that raced through him for wanting to seek his other children when he barely knew the first one. When he thought about it logically, it sounded stupid, yet Reven's mind often ran around in confounding circles.

"Do you think Kaleo will be upset?" Reven finally asked, needing to know he wasn't crazy or overthinking.

"That you have other children?" Serai repeated. Reven nodded. "No. Have you told him?"

Reven shook his head. Serai watched him,

studying him in her quirky way. They listened to the sound of the sea, or the gulls overhead. Serai gave his hand a squeeze, smiling at him. They remained quiet for a time, staring at the sea. When Reven looked back at Serai, she was watching him with a wistful grin on her face. He leaned in and captured her lips in a kiss, taking full advantage of the time they had until they were both spent and exhausted along the shore.

***

"Did you know about his wife? How he loved her? Will you keep him for yourself?"

Serai sat in the dark that evening. The people struggled, but were happy to be starting a new. The symbolism of the tirsai was not lost on Serai. They were a true phoenix rising from the ashes. She admired them.

Yet, it was not the tirsai that had her mind turning in ways she was not expecting. A glance to her left set some worries at ease. Reven slept peacefully on the warm sand. Serai reached across to brush a strand of hair from his face. He complained it was too long, but she convinced him to leave it alone. She liked it longer. He rolled onto his front so she could see his back. Several scars tore apart an otherwise beautiful tree of life tattooed on his lightly tanned skin. How many hours had she spent since meeting him tracing that tattoo? She loved it as much as she loved every other part of him.

Serai's mind wandered so much. She thought of the invisible wife, the one he could not remember. She thought of Xandrix and where he had gone or why. She thought of Jaysen and the pain he was in, or about Kaleo and the other spectral children existing out there somewhere in the ether. Mostly, she thought of *Reven*; of how much that man filled her heart.

"Come back to bed," Reven muttered. He felt

her fingers tracing the tattoo. Serai did not realize she'd reached for him until he spoke. She did as he requested, pressing herself close to him, skin to skin, feeling the warmth that radiated off him. He shivered but remained silent. He always told her she was cold, but never pushed her away. She let her arm drape over his side, kissing spots on the tattoo instead of tracing it.

"I love you," Serai said in a soft, breathy whisper. Her heart became his so quickly, her head still spun. She was positive he would not hear her muted words until she felt his muscles tense. A moment later, he turned to face her. His tired eyes searched her face, looking for truth or lies. He didn't trust anyone, still raw from Liam's betrayal. Other things tested his trust as well - Kaleo, who was his son; the people that knew him as Gannon; the things he saw; his own *audeas*. All told him different, sometimes conflicting things, which kept the trust he gave closely guarded.

When he looked at her, however, she saw doubt in his eyes. Serai smiled at him instead, tucking hair away from his face and repeated, "I love you." She'd spent thirteen months of her life with Reven Si'ahl. He saved her, showed her patience when others showed disdain, taught her as much as she taught him. He was everything to her. When she touched him, however, she not only felt his doubt, but *saw* why.

"I love you," he said, holding Zuri in his arms. She lifted her head off his chest to fix him with a sharp look.

"Do not say that. You cannot."

"Why?" he asked.

"You know why," she said, rising from the bed. "I'm thinkin' our time together is over, highness."

"Zuri," he pleaded, sitting up. "What will it take for you to accept me? I already gave you what you wanted."

She looked down at the small swell of her belly, then over her shoulder at him, but said nothing.

Serai felt her breath catch in her chest, realizing too late that Reven saw the same thing she did. He groaned, gripping the sides of his head tightly. She immediately regretted the words spoken to him, not because she did not feel them, but because they caused him pain.

"I am sorry," she said, pulling him to her. "Shh… breathe. Let it go. The past cannot hurt you anymore. I will not allow it."

Reven let out a haunting whimper, slowly relaxing beneath her touch, until he was breathing steady against her chest again. She held him that way in the silence of the late night hour, her mind whirling even as the memories continued to crash through. He'd had his heart broken by this woman who asked for a child. The invisible wife was no better, caring for him, but never loving him. She saw moments of passion mixed with moments of rage between Gannon and these two women. There was only one who simply let him exist with no expectations, the one who gave him his daughter, Marie. Yet the love they had was different; mutual need for companionship.

"Say something else," he said against her breast, arms tight around her waist. She looked down at his head.

"What do you mean?" she asked. She was no longer afraid to ask for clarifications from him. His world was so vastly different from the one she knew that even the language had changed.

"Don't say 'I love you'. Say something else. Something different," he whispered. His muscles tensed again, as if waiting for the fallout of words he did not want to hear. So, Serai thought about it, stroked his hair, and bit her lip, then finally smiled.

"You are my home," she said instead of the standard 'I love you'. When she felt him smile, she knew he understood. He squeezed her tightly and whispered so softly she almost lost it, "You're my home, too."

Chapter Nine

Marie kept her head down as she moved through the brick-paved streets of Rudia like a shadow. She, Idris, and Jax had made their way to Amadour, the small city on the border of Damaskha and Itahl earlier that morning. A room was secured, and a plan was plotted out. The first step was reconnaissance. While Jax could provide a great deal of detail about what he'd seen with the king and queen, seeing those details was important to what they were going to have to do. Starting a war with Itahl was not in Damaskha's best interest. Marie followed Jax across the border under the cover of night, working her way through the alleys and streets near the palace with the duende man. The Itahli looked at the duende with as much derision and hate as they did to casters. Much to his great frustration, Idris stayed behind in Amadour. His skills for infiltration were phenomenal, but his Power was bound to light up like a candle in a dark room. And, despite having enough Power to *destroy* a city, Marie didn't want to take that risk. She moved from one corner to the next, carefully listening to conversations and complaints. She spoke at length to one of the working girls in the low quarter, learning the Kormandi king's precise location. The Itahli queen was hosting him and his wife in the west wing of her palace.

The news made Marie snarl under her breath after she left the busty woman with a good tip and a full tankard of ale for her information. From time to time, she watched a group of masked figures walk by as if they owned the street they walked on. Hunters of Itahl tracked down the unfortunate born with Power and ended them. It was nasty business that Marie did not like thinking about. They were the reason Idris stayed behind. Too many rumors spread about the Hunters, too many people vanishing in the night, or families torn apart, all for the 'greater good of the people'. It was horse shit.

Marie finished her circuit around the palace, talked with a few more lovely working men and women, then met up with Jax again.

"What'd you find?" she murmured to him as they walked together along the perfectly paved streets. She would say this: Itahl had some of the most stunning architecture and technological advances of any nation she'd ever been to. Granted, that was a terribly short list, but what the Itahli did was impressive nonetheless.

"She's moved 'em," Jax grumbled. "I managed t'get in. They're not where they was when I left. No one would let me see 'em. They're plannin' somethin'."

The news made Marie growl. She remained quiet after that, guiding Jax out of the city limits, promptly making their way back across the border to the inn in Amadour where Idris waited.

"Tell me you've got good news," Idris said once

they'd returned. Marie shook her head as she took the cloak off and threw it on the back of the nearby chair.

"That's not a reassurin' look, Marie."

"The king's somewhere in the palace. Jax knew where, but when he went to check, they told him the king and queen got moved, and wouldn't let him near them," Marie said, throwing herself into the chair. Jax took up a spot on the wall, jaw working like he was chewing stones for all of his agitation.

"So, then, what are we workin' with?" Idris persisted.

"The palace," Marie said with a lazy flop of her hand. "Hunters that know what the king is, and a ruthless woman sittin' on the Itahli throne. That 'alliance' was done for a reason. I wouldn't be surprised if the Itahli were responsible for how quickly Kormaine fell. Five years and suddenly everything goes south? It doesn't add up, Idris. You know it doesn't."

Idris sighed, throwing himself on the bed in frustration, growling into the pillows. The room only had one tiny bed barely suitable for one person, let alone three. They hadn't expected to stay long, if at all. The room had a desk, a washstand, and a trunk. It was basic, bare-bones, but it was sufficient for what they needed - until now. Now they needed a plan, tools, supplies, perhaps even reinforcements. Above all, they were going to need to find a way to get *Idris* into Itahl. Marie was good, but she wasn't *that* good. She knew her limits and, by the looks of the duende man holding up the wall, Jax knew his limits, too. Idris had none.

"How we gonna pull that off?" Jax grumbled. "We're only three. No one is that good, *comrade*. Not even the Baron."

Idris snorted. "Preston is."

Preston Casce ran the Maison du Hombre. He taught Idris everything he knew, allowing Idris to train

Marie. Preston could walk in and out in full view of the entire nation and never be questioned. Idris was good, but he wasn't that good. Yet. This was not going to be easy.

"Preston isn't here, *comrade*," Jax pointed out. "Why do you get th'bed?"

"Seniority," Idris grumbled. Marie could tell his mind was already sorting out the problem, working through the puzzle one little piece at a time. "Do we have paper?"

Marie glanced lazily at the desk, stretching just enough to reach a scrap of paper. She flung it at Idris, then did the same for the ink pen. They were wonderful devices that put quills to shame. Being this close to Itahl had its benefits. Amadour was well-equipped with fun little trinkets and toys stolen from the Itahli.

Idris rolled over, stretching his wings one at a time. He penned a quick letter as he stretched his wings, waiting until the ink was dry before folding it up and stamping it with the wax provided on the desk.

"Get this delivered. The king only. I think I have an idea."

Marie looked at Jax, watching the duende man take the letter before looking at Idris with a smirk. This was going to be a story for the ages.

***

Kendal Ovet paced back and forth in the large apartments she and Demyan shared in the royal palace of Itahl. It was an odd arrangement for them. They did not share quarters in Kormaine. Demyan had been too busy to do much of anything but nod at her in the wake of their very fast, very awkward wedding. Kendal still barely knew him, and now he raised such wild accusations about her people and nation she wanted to scream. She felt her heart race and blood boil as she listened to the man she married *lie* to her, pleading for her to *believe* his lies. She frowned at the rugs beneath her feet, pacing a line into the plush patterns before finally rounding on her husband.

"Demyan, stop!" Kendal screeched. The man silenced immediately with a minor flinch, averting his eyes to the stone floor instead of her. Some of the fight left Kendal's shoulders when she saw him flinch, but she held her ground. "Why are you saying these things? Are you mad at me? Are you unhappy here? Is that why?"

Demyan shook his head, but remained silent. The frustration Kendal felt came back tenfold. He was so infuriatingly silent!

"You can't tell me these lies and then not tell me why, Demyan."

"They are not lies!" he insisted. "You do not feel what I do! We are not safe here! *I am* not safe here!"

"*Why* aren't you safe here!" Kendal threw back, voice raised enough to make Demyan frown and look down at the stone floors again. He behaved like a scolded servant more than a king. It was confounding. Kendal took in a deep breath and calmed her rage, placing a hand on her belly as if to still that anger into something less volatile by touch alone.

She did not feel what Demyan did. He told Kendal he felt something screaming beneath the palace, a Power that was in pain, begging for help. He claimed the Source, what gave the Itahli everything they had, had sentience; that it could feel, and suffered so the Itahli could have their technologies. It was the most absurd thing Kendal had ever heard. She knew her husband had Power. He was the only one in the *nation* currently. Every other Sinner was taken into custody by the Hunters and cleansed of their sin. Demyan was spared out of respect for his backwards beliefs - for now. Kendal already asked the queen if anything could be done for him. She cared about what happened to him. His Power helped get them through Kormaine but at what cost? Clearly it was driving him mad or worse.

"I am not crazy," Demyan said, a frown on his face and low growl in his hoarse voice. She frowned in return and threw the nearest object at him.

"Stay out of my head!" she screeched as he flinched from the hairbrush she grabbed. It careened into the armoire, shattering the ivory to a million little pieces.

"Then listen to what I am saying! I would not lie to you, *ai*! Never," he pleaded. The word he used was unfamiliar to her, yet struck her through everything he had said.

"What did you call me?" Kendal dared, nostrils flaring as she waited for the answer. Demyan's mouth worked silently until he swallowed hard and looked down again.

"*Ai*," he repeated. "It means 'love'."

Kendal's rage tempered to a small flicker. She sighed, studying her husband closely before moving to stand in front of him. He was tall and thin, all limbs, but handsome after a fashion. The tight coils of blonde on his head fell in an unruly disarray no matter what he tried to do with them as they grew out in this tumultuous time. His eyes were the most striking feature - a stunning sapphire blue. It was a trait the Kormandi were quite proud of, comparing it to the Shard that had existed at the top of the Sapphire Tower.

Demyan would not look at her even when she came close to him. She raised her hand to lift his chin, and he flinched, turning away with eyes closed, expecting a blow. It broke her heart to see. She immediately regretted throwing the ivory brush.

"*Gomen*," she said, gently caressing his face.

It was one of the very few words she knew because Demyan used it so much, constantly apologizing to her for his actions or fumbling words. When he looked at her, there was fear in his eyes and helplessness. She wished she could make it go away. Instead, she reached up and kissed him.

They had not shared anything remotely resembling intimate. The farthest they'd gotten was a hand-in-hand walk that was quickly interrupted by impending doom that turned into *actual* doom. She was surprised he didn't pull away from her. Quite the opposite. He put his hand over hers and deepened the kiss, letting his other arm slide around her waist to pull her closer.

Kendal steeled herself for what she was about to do, brows bunching.

'*Show me. Show me what you saw,*' she thought, knowing he would hear it like a gong in a church. His slight flinch told her she was correct, but he deepened the kiss even more, squeezing her tight as he flooded her mind with images of torment and horror, all stemming from the Source. Kendal heard what he had, *felt* the pain it was in and listened to it cry out for help before she became overwhelmed with what he shared and pulled away with a cry, falling to her knees, hand on her head.

"*Gomen,*" Demyan said, moving to help her but stopping as if afraid of hurting her.

"Why?" Kendal sobbed. "Why would they do this? It's in so much *pain.*"

Demyan didn't say anything, moving silently to the floor beside her so he could take her into his arms and hold her while she sobbed over the terrible truth she'd just learned.

Her people were murderers.

Chapter Ten

Floorboards creaked with every step Daemodan took. The air inside Madhavi's cottage tasted stale inside his nose and mouth. A fine layer of dust covered the usually immaculate furnishings, the odd trinkets kept on the windowsills, and mismatched teacups his sister collected as treasures. He glanced up to the ceiling, painted with white and yellow stars to resemble the night sky. In another part of the cottage, a mural of the moons and their phases created a pattern of intersecting circles. So much dedication to a goddess she barely understood and rarely worshipped. The potential Madhavi wasted disgusted Daemodan.

"She's not here."

Daemodan glanced over his shoulder to face the woman that spoke; one of his sister's pets. Lines of wisdom carved her face into great canyons on rough leather skin; a duende woman. He could tell her hair had once been a dark, lovely auburn, now lightened to a desiccated red. Her eyes held the same desiccation and numb compliance.

"I can see that," Daemodan said. "Where has she gone?"

The woman remained silent. Daemodan sighed, rolling his eyes as he flicked a wrist. The action snapped the woman's neck. He had no time for games. He continued through the cottage, walking slowly up the steps with his wings tucked in to fit into the narrow staircase. Those creaked as much as the floorboards, if not more. Despite the outward appearance of the cottage, it was in gross disrepair. Everything the woman had was an illusion.

The second floor was not much better than the first. Dust covered the furnishings or lingered in the air. The rooms she kept were small and cramped, usually full of her playthings. Glass hung from the ceiling all across the second level, each one turning idly on their invisible strings. In the corner room, four beds filled the space, all in disarray, but only one held an occupant.

"She left you behind, highness," Daemodan mused. "Interesting. Not like her to leave you so unattended."

The prince of the fae was Madhavi's greatest treasure. She coveted the man like one might covet a prized horse. She kept him in a slumber so deep not even Death could make a body so still. Daemodan was certain that death-like sleep was the only reason no one had come for him yet; specifically, the man's sire. It would not do well to have the god of the fae intervene in what they were planning. Madhavi played a very dangerous game.

Daemodan looked down at the sleeping man. To say that he slept seemed incorrect. What Madhavi did to her victims was more than simple sleep. She kept them suspended in a different realm, their minds locked in a world of her design. Daemodan could only imagine what that must be like - the woman *had* no imagination.

"Don't suppose you know where my sister has gone?" Daemodan sighed, idly conversing with the sleeping prince.

"Probably hunting the same thing you are," said a new voice that startled the half-dragon, regardless of what he might say to himself. "You should keep better watch of your creations."

"Says the one who's been on holiday the last four years," Daemodan sneered, glaring over his shoulder in a way that turned him to face his younger brother. Cavian could be as ruthless as Madhavi. Blessedly, he was not as stupid.

"I went to your house, but your lap dog said you'd come here. Can't sleep?" Cavian smirked, taking slow steps toward Daemodan. They had similar features, the most prominent from their father, while the rest came from the woman that bore them as it was with Daemodan.

"As if I would come to her for sleeping draughts. I'd never wake," Daemodan sniffed. "She's taken Jaysen. I'm tired of her toying with him. I think I fancy taking something of hers in retaliation."

Cavian looked at the man on the bed, then at Daemodan with an arched brow.

"Oh, she won't like that," Cavian purred, but grinned wickedly. "I'll do you one better: I'll wake him for you so you're not carrying a sack of bones around with you."

"If?" Daemodan sighed with a roll of his eyes. He knew better. Cavian's smile broadened.

"Don't trust me, Dae?"

"Cavian, what do you want?" Daemodan sighed. He rubbed his brow, feeling the vein at his temple throbbing. Everything seemed to be falling apart at the seams. Daemodan knew that wasn't true, but his sire's armies were as coordinated as a creature with four left feet. Losing Jaysen, Roth *and* Ghost at the same time Madhavi slithered away while Cavian reappeared was not coincidental. Daemodan did not believe in coincidences. They got lucky with the tirsai, had to work hard to get the duende in Asphondel just like they'd had to work to get the northern part of Kormaine. Yet neither push yielded what his sire wanted, which put unwanted pressure on Daemodan. Cavian's presence made that pressure worse.

"Thought I might borrow some of your brain power. I'm looking for something. It's been elusive until recently."

"But?" Daemodan sighed; again. Cavian was more than capable of finding things *without* Daemodan's hunters.

"It's in the Necropolis. Guarded."

Daemodan groaned. "What could you possibly seek that would be *there*, Cavian? The Necropolis is not really a place *anyone* should traverse into if it can be avoided."

If rumor was to be believed, several of the fleeing olve still hid in the Necropolis even after the most recent clean-out of the Asphondeli forests. But refugees were not the only things in the Necropolis - neither were the dead.

"The Sword of Fate," Cavian smirked. Daemodan's jaw dropped.

"Are you mad?" Daemodan asked. The Sword of Fate was one of the Tools of Creation. Rumor was only a god could wield it - something Cavian was not.

"You don't have to help. It'll be amusing watching you carry a fae sack around with you."

"Fine," Daemodan growled. "Fine. It belongs

to Tantris, god of Death. They gave it to Alma for safe keeping. Wake him up."

"I thought Azrus was the god of death," Cavian intoned. Daemodan forced himself to breathe slowly so he didn't rip out his brother's throat.

"So does everyone else. Azrus is the *Harbinger*. They ferry the souls *after* Tantris has cut their threads. The prince, Cavian."

Daemodan stepped aside with a gesture at the man in the bed. Cavian merely smirked, moving up to the bed while tilting his head curiously.

"He'd be cute if he wasn't emaciated. She needs to get better at that," Cavian commented.

"Brings a whole new meaning to the term 'sleeping with the fae' doesn't it?" Daemodan snorted.

"I'm proud of you, Dae. I didn't think you had a sense of humor," Cavian said as he studied the fae prince closely. He placed a single finger on the man's brow, turning his head again as if listening for something. "Oh, she's got this one in deep. Make us some tea, would you?"

"I'm not making you tea, Cavian."

"Spoil sport," Cavian replied, already shutting his eyes. Daemodan did not pretend to know what it was his siblings did. The two manipulated Yira's realm like children manipulated dolls. Daemodan had intellect and resources; patience. None of which the twins had. "Damn. She really-"

Both Daemodan and Cavian cried out in surprise when the prince's eyes opened suddenly and his body convulsed upward. His back arched, head hanging between his shoulders until, like a broken doll repairing itself, he shifted and twitched forward to a slumped position with his wings draped heavily across the bed.

"What in all of bloody hells," Daemodan

breathed, shoving himself away from Cavian. The idiot stood behind him, using one of Daemodan's wings as a shield.

"Is this your doing, Daemodan? Some new way to Corrupt them?" Cavian spat. Daemodan glowered at him.

"You assume she's let me near her little pet since she got him," Daemodan snarled back, shoving Cavian in front of him again. "Find out what's wrong."

The prince's head tilted to the side with a crack of his neck. Cavian froze. The fae prince had wings that might have been beautiful once, the feathers iridescent and tipped in gold now dulled to a mottled violet hue. Black veins wrapped themselves around his arms and chest like tattoos, curling all the way up his neck and into the base of his skull. His eyes lacked a pupil - an oddity of the fae - and were as red as blood wine. If it wasn't Corruption, Daemodan was looking at, then it was fairly close to it.

"You find out. This is your study of expertise," Cavian growled again, this time nearly tripping to shove Daemodan forward. Coward. However, he wasn't wrong. It *was* Daemodan's field of expertise.

"Welcome back to the land of the living, highness," Daemodan began. "Can you hear me?"

The man growled, lip curling to reveal fangs. It was Corruption for certain, though one done through Yira's realm. Daemodan had seen the fae prince *once* when he was captured and never went near him again. No one else would have been allowed to go near him either, except maybe Jaysen. Madhavi did so love to torment the poor, blind child. Daemodan would need to have words with his bitch of a sister for playing with things she didn't understand.

"Clearly you can," Daemodan said in a tone that held more curiosity than actual concern, meant for his own thoughts than for the man to actually respond to.

"Where is she?" the man growled in a voice that was like Death speaking across rough gravel.

"Not here, I'm afraid," Daemodan grinned. "I'm happy to help you find her. She has something of mine. I'd like it back. I don't think I ever got your name, highness."

"Daemodan, what are you doing?" Cavian hissed. The fae prince focused on him instead.

"Oh, don't mind, Cavian," Daemodan said. "He's not worth your time or thought. He's not worth anything, actually."

"Prat," Cavian growled. Daemodan smirked.

Again, the fae prince glanced at Cavian and growled, as if sensing what Cavian could do. Daemodan didn't want to waste more time, so stepped in front of the man's view, blocking Cavian entirely.

"I can give you a name if you'd rather," Daemodan persisted.

"Taelon," he finally snarled. Other than anger issues, he was well in his right mind. It was something the other Corrupted did not always have. Certainly not Roth or the Kormandi King. Both went mad in different ways, but mad nonetheless. Perhaps there was something to Madhavi's tampering, after all. Daemodan would have to research it further.

"A true pleasure, highness," Daemodan grinned. "I don't suppose you saw a tywyll boy while you … rested? Clawed hands. Blind."

"Faded," Taelon said. It was not a question, but a statement of fact that arched Daemodan's brow. "She had him there sometimes."

"Interesting," Daemodan grunted. Madhavi was going to pay dearly for harming Jaysen; again. "Not always?"

"He was called. A voice. No one called for me."

"Hrm, probably because no one knew to. But that brings up a new question - who knew to call for Jaysen?" Daemodan asked with another glance at Cavian. The idiot only shrugged. "Well, that gives us a place to start, at least. Thank you, Taelon. I'd imagine you'd rather not stay here. Shall we?"

Daemodan gestured to the doorway. Taelon snarled, lip curling again in suspicion this time before Daemodan finally shoved Cavian ahead of him, leaving the room. Taelon followed.

***

The divine power imbued within the old temple still held enough sway over the land to make Madhavi step cautiously through the ruins. Being there made her skin crawl uncomfortably. There were a handful of sad, pathetic stragglers that made the old temple grounds their home. They practiced with swords that would have been fine if not for the layer of tarnish and rust covering them. They all seemed to have been excavated directly from the dirt beneath them. A handful of bedrolls and a mid-sized tent dotted the exterior of the temple, with one large tent off to the side. Madhavi wound her way through the dense jungle foliage to that tent.

"... stand for this. There has to be recourse for this insubordination, highness."

It was a man who spoke. His crisp, proper words made Madhavi smirk. Even now the tirsai held tightly to things like insubordination and propriety. It was absurd. The tirsai were a joke. One of the easiest things her father had ever done was toppling the 'mighty' Empire of the Phoenix. There was nothing left of the olve that boasted the largest, strongest, mightiest empire since the Destruction.

"Horse shit," Madhavi murmured under her breath. The sound of her own voice brought her out of her own head. She waited until the voices in the tent died down before moving closer, parting the worn canvas. There wasn't an element in nature that the tent would protect the inhabitants from.

The interior of the tent was as bare as the exterior. A single table stood in the center with a map rolled out across its length. How quaint.

Madhavi slunk to the table, letting her clawed hand graze over the thick parchment the map was drawn on. It showed the island of Tierra Vida. The major cities were all marked down, smaller fishing towns, areas held by the savage races, and areas that have yet to be explored. One area in particular was marked 'traitors'.

"Interesting..." Madhavi purred. "Can't maintain control of your people highness?"

The tent flap snapped open then, curling Madhavi's lips. She heard the sound of steel on leather as she turned around slowly. The tirsai princess paled in comparison to her elder sister, but she was attractive in her own right. Handsome rather than beautiful, strong even in her weakened condition, a fighter. She was perfect.

"I expected more of your subjects, your grace," Madhavi smiled. "Have you misplaced them?"

"Shut up, witch! What are you doing here!"

"Looking for you, actually," Madhavi smiled. "We have some things to discuss."

"I have nothing to discuss with the likes of you, demon!" Maeve Oenel spat. Madhavi pouted.

"That hurts, pet. You don't even know why I've come yet."

"I am *no one's* pet!" Maeve snarled. She was like a feral alley cat hissing at shadows. It was adorable.

The woman had spirit, an ember inside of her that needed to be rekindled before the smoke choked her.

"Care to prove that, highness?" Madhavi teased. "You've had your people stolen from you - twice. That can't be good for the ego. But they're here, within reach, aren't they? What's stopping you from becoming the *queen* you were meant to be?"

The debate on Maeve Oenels face was displayed as clearly as a statue in a courtyard. The woman knew Madhavi was dangerous, but that temptation was too great to ignore.

"Speak quickly," Maeve barked. Madhavi's smile turned predatory.

"There's something I want. Someone. Two of them, actually."

"Retrieve them yourself," Maeve snarled through clenched teeth. Madhavi grinned, tapping her lips as she looked the princess up and down.

"Impossible," Madhavi admitted finally. "One would know I'm coming and warn the other. I have my eye on them both, but I need boots on the ground, so to speak. Someone like you."

"And who might this person be?" Maeve sneered as Madhavi circled her.

"You're nephew. The pretty one with the wings." Maeve growled. "I'll happily take him off your hands. You'll never have to deal with him again. I promise."

"You said there were two things."

Madhavi chuckled. "So smart. So worthy. My lamb will fall in with the flock as soon as I have the lovely boy with wings. Whats his name? No one will tell me."

"Kaleo," Maeve hissed through gritted teeth.

"The voice... Beautiful," Madhavi mused, feeling herself shiver in anticipation of this new game.

"What do you say, highness?"

"What do I get in return, demon? I know how your kind operate," Maeve continued. Progress was progress even if her assumption was incorrect. Madhavi was no demon.

"I can give you whatever you want, pet. Power, money, beauty, revenge. Name it."

Maeve stood quiet for a time, contemplating her choices as Madhavi circled her. There was something the woman wanted, even if she was not ready to voice it yet. All mortals were the same.

"Come now, pet, don't make me guess," Madhavi purred, trailing gentle fingers on Maeve's neck. The woman turned sharply to slap Madhavi, but Madhavi was faster. She caught the tirsai woman's wrist and pulled her close. "Careful, pet. I might get the wrong impression."

"Let go!"

"Or what? Show me that fire. Let me taste it."

Maeve wrenched her arm away from Madhavi and raised her sword again.

"My bastard of a brother. I want his Power or no deal."

"So demanding, pet. But I like it," Madhavi smiled, daring to move closer to Maeve once more. The woman swallowed her fear, frown deepening. She kept her sword level with Madhavi's throat but made no motion to use it even as her nostrils flared. She was bristling. It was fabulous and intoxicating to watch. Madhavi wanted more of this woman's rage. She wanted to feel it, taste it, use it.

"My patience is waning, witch," Maeve continued. Madhavi chuckled.

"All things take time, pet. Patience. Give me two days. If you don't have what you want by then, you're free to remove my head. I won't fight you.

Fair?"

Madhavi held her hand out to Maeve. The woman looked at it as if it were poisoned, the debate clear on her face. Eventually, she took it, giving it a firm shake with a curt nod. This was going to be a game worth playing.

***

The Temple to Sulis was quiet and dark compared to the brightness of the beach near the Grove. Only a handful of Esbethi soldiers loitered near the temple ruins. Reven had been careful to avoid them when coming to seek solace within the temple walls. His mind still turned itself over and over with guilt and indecision. Reven admired the Baron, even if he wasn't entirely certain he trusted the man. Reven supposed the same was true for himself. Gods knew he had several questionable methods. Aeron and Nadya trusted the man, though, which counted for something. Reven's survival perpetuated itself by *not* trusting people. It was a trait Serai was trying to break him of.

The bard wanted a place to think, to sort out the things he'd learned recently about his absurdly complicated family and make sense of the wild array of emotions he was feeling *away* from everyone, somewhere private. The temple fit that description.

The most difficult thing so far was his stupidly large family. Half of the new refugees knew him by his old name, all of them related to or friends of his biological father. It was *absurd*. That man continued to recover at a glacial pace. It seemed so odd to know his father lived. But he also knew that *he* had children from different women - three at the very least, more if Liam's garble of complaints and hisses were to be believed. The different women didn't surprise Reven much, but the children did. He never really felt he was much of a family man. Kaleo tried to tell him otherwise, tried to tell him how things *used* to be, but that was not how things were *now*. He was barely fit to be upright and functional for himself, let alone for anyone else.

Hiding again, Beloved?

Thinking, the bard answered, this time mentally as it should be between *audaen* and *audeas*.

He learned so much in recent days. So much turned entirely upside down in his life, too. Yes, answers to his past were something he'd craved, but not like this. What he received was a hammer blow to his heart and head over and over until he wanted to scream. He could have been happy as a bard with a spotty memory. He could *still* be happy as a bard with a spotty memory. Kaleo changed all of it, changed what he wanted and how he lived his life. Serai did too if in different ways. Part of him wanted to take what he had and vanish into the wind to start over somewhere new. It didn't have to be Mahala - though his house made him rethink it once or twice. He *really* liked that house. But now there were Idris and Marie and his extended family and father and cursed *hope*...

Perhaps we can convince them to go somewhere less hot, Azure offered, making Reven snicker. *Start a commune in the snow.*

You're a bird of fire, Reven mentally chuckled.

"You've a lot of nerve coming here."

Reven sighed. *Maeve* was another issue entirely. Yet another relative, one that hated him for breathing for as long as memory existed, according to anyone he asked. This tart in armor behind him had struck his son and squandered away six years of time, complaining about the hand they'd been dealt. Despite being out of sorts, Reven knew starving people when he saw them and knew that nearly six years was plenty of time to rebuild a life.

"Planning on having me arrested?" Reven said,

without turning around. He liked the statue at the head of the temple. It was simple but powerful in its appearance and embodied everything he believed the forgotten goddess represented. Everything Maeve Oenel was not. "Or sending the Esbethi for *my* son?"

Maeve snorted, her steps moving closer until he could feel her breath on his neck - as well as the steel of her dagger.

"Tell me why I shouldn't kill you right here and now?" she said. "Or send my lieutenant to do the same to that winged shit following you around?"

"In the habit of killing family, Captain?"

"We aren't family," she hissed. The blade cut into the skin with a sharp sting, blood welling as it slid down into the collar of his shirt.

Now it was Reven's turn to snort. "Glad we've cleared that up. That doesn't mean you can threaten me whenever you want. I don't take kindly to such things, *Captain*."

He felt his veins burn with Power as he filled himself with it. Reven heard the woman scream as he sent a pulse out from his core to push her away from him. It rocked the loose marble from the surrounding walls. They crashed to the floor, cracking it further as he turned to face his so-called sister with blanched, angry eyes.

"Don't threaten me," he said in surprisingly even tones. "And don't you *ever* threaten *my son*."

"*Bastard* son!" Maeve scoffed, getting to her feet again. "Just like you are."

Reven smirked. "Peas in a pod, m'lady. You know he doesn't like you much. I can see why. You're a bitch. Do you actually care about anyone but yourself?"

Maeve growled at him, nostrils flaring as she unsheathed her sword. Reven just watched her, looking up to his shoulder when Azure landed on it.

"That little shit will be the first one to di-"

Reven cut her off, slamming her against the wall again without laying a single finger on her. The woman could not speak, kicking while trying to pull something invisible off her neck.

"That makes twice, m'lady. You won't get a third chance. Oh, and don't come near the Grove. You won't walk out of there alive."

He did not let her drop to the floor until he left the temple. Azure fluffed his feathers up as Reven walked out in full of the remaining handful, eyes still searing white with rage.

~

The crack of bone on flesh echoed across the beach. Reven grunted, shaking out his hand as Liam fell to the sanded grass with an audible thump. The news of what transpired between Reven and Maeve spread like wildfire through the Grove as soon as he set foot among the worn down stones. Reven blamed Azure for that one, the orange-blue phoenix gossiping away to Runya and the other magical beasts loitering around. The magical beasts, Reven discovered, that Aeron *and* Ettrian could talk to. By the time the news reached Liam, the thief-taker was in a fit state that was quelled with a fist to the face.

"Jack ass!" Liam barked.

"Sod off?" Reven retorted, still shaking his hand out.

"Ya don't know nothin' 'bout what's what 'round 'ere! Ya can't even remember yer-"

"Ass from my head," Reven finished, having heard the statement countless times in the five years he'd been with Liam. "I know. And no one - *no one*, Liam - is going to just threaten me or my urchin. So either piss or get off the pot, Master Roe."

Kaleo beamed at him. Lara stood beside Kaleo, fingers entwined with the young avian's, Reven noticed. That made him grin internally, happy that his urchin found a bit of romance in all this madness.

"This is yer fault, ya schite! Yer th'one what took on stupid crap! Now look!" Liam hollered. "Shoulda been drown th'second you was born!"

Reven kicked Liam in the face, sending a spray of blood across the sand and the duende man sprawling.

"That is the *second* time someone has said something about drowning my urchin at birth today! I'm over it! What sort of barbaric assholes do that, anyway! Gods alive…" Reven breathed, turning to face those that were nearby - and the rest of the refugees that watched the drama unfold. Reven's demeanor changed immediately as he raised his hand and grinned at those watching. "It's fine! He's drunk! Threatened Kaleo; again."

Everyone nodded as they returned to their lives with no further explanation needed. Kaleo merely smirked, giving Reven the reason he needed to *stay* with his *son* no matter what - - or where.

Chapter Eleven

Sapphire City looked different from above. Clouds that once carried ash and snow to the broken cobbles hid the sunlight between gentle curves, allowing rays to break through occasionally. Icicles dripped onto the ground, turning the ash-filled, bloodied ground into a thick paste of pink-tinged muck. The light glinted off the new tower, sending a cascade of rainbows across the city. It was an oddly festive, if gloomy, wonderland. Roth loved it immediately.

He's here. His beast is at the top of the tower.

Roth narrowed his eyes, glancing up to the highest point of the tower before being forced to bring a hand up to shield his vision eyes. Malie leaned against his shoulder, bundled in so many layers, it was difficult to discern that anything living nestled inside of it.

It's shrieking at me.

"Yes, I hear it," Roth murmured aloud as the echoing shriek of Ghost's confused creature reached his sensitive ears. "You may kill it."

Roth did not wait to see if Phier killed the confused beast. He continued on into the tower. It was part stone, part ice - confused, just like Ghost's beast. It had taken some time to find where Ghost had gone. While Roth wanted to find his Moppet, he had questions he knew Ghost would know. Despite not speaking, Ghost paid more attention to detail than Roth did.

The only visible part of Malie were her large, sapphire-blue eyes. They stared out at the icy-cold surroundings with wonder and a touch of fear that Roth could smell even through all the pilings keeping her warm. He liked that too. He could see living here with Ghost, but he would miss his Evie. Perhaps after he found his Moppet, he would find Evie again.

"Do you like it here? It's rather... bland. Not enough color," Roth asked Malie as he ascended the wide, winding staircase to the top of the ice tower. "So much white inside. It's absurd. Don't you think so?"

Malie nodded her head, the movement making her coverings shift slightly to cover one eye. Tiny fingers, peeked out to push the coverings up before darting back into the warmth.

"What color would you paint it?"

Malie thought about the question but did not answer immediately. When she did, it was in a muted, croaked whisper and only to say, "Green."

"I do like that color, yes. Perhaps we shall paint it green then," Roth said. He put his hand on the icy wall and let it trail behind him as they continued to ascend, leaving a streak of green in its wake. Malie giggled.

Which was when Ghost decided to show himself, snarling in Roth's face when they reached the third floor. Malie squeaked and hid in her pile of coverings, trembling with tiny sobs. It was delicious.

"Now look," Roth scolded all the same. "You've frightened her. Are you happy with yourself? She's fragile! It's alright, Malie, I won't let him eat you. You're mine now, remember? He's just confused. Like his beast and this tower. Aren't you?"

"What are you doing here?" Ghost snarled. It was then, Roth realized, that he understood Ghost - and Malie too, for that matter. Both spoke in a rumbling language that sounded like rocks rolling down a mountainside. Roth spoke the same language, though he could not fathom how or why he knew such a horrible-sounding form of communication. Perhaps Ghost would know. "Get out!"

"You don't even know why I'm here yet," Roth countered.

"I don't care!" Ghost snarled, coming close to Roth. The idiot was shorter than Roth by a good hand or more. His intimidation tactic seemed flawed to Roth, but points were given for good effort.

"Please," Roth clucked, brushing past Ghost to explore this floor that the man so viciously guarded. "What are you hiding here anyway? Women? Men? Babies! It's babies, isn't it! Tell me it's babies - no! No, don't tell me it's babies, it'll be too tempting. Is it babies?"

"Get. Out."

"You're no fun at all, are you? No wonder you're so grumpy. All alone in this cold ice tower lacking in color and life. Here," Roth said, handing Malie over. "This is Malie. She's mine. She's fragile. But you may hold her. She's like a floof, she makes everything more tolerable."

Ghost growled at Malie. The girl merely batted her long, pale lashes as she'd done with Roth. Ghost stopped growling.

"See? Isn't that better?" Roth said. "I have questions. You listen better. Where has my Moppet gone? I can't recall."

"Madhavi wants him."

"I'm aware," Roth snarled, all joviality dissipating in seconds. "He's. Fragile. He needs to be protected. That bitch only wants to cause more harm."

Ghost snorted. Roth snapped. His clawed hand shot out, fingers encircling Ghost's throat, claws pressing into the soft, black-veined flesh. The act made Ghost drop Malie. The girl squeaked, scrambling away while the two Corrupted men fought.

So many believed Roth to be an imbecile. He forgot things quite often, but he was no fool. He was more observant than most gave him credit for and listened to everything. He remembered when the manor only held himself and his Evie, when Daemodan had slipped away while his Moppet recovered from a terrible malaise. It was right after Ghost had been created. His creation, like Roth's, had gone poorly. Something was not right. The man would not speak. It bothered Daemodan. Roth had bothered Daemodan too. He remembered the beautiful angel that came to him in his sleep - - the same angel that tormented him until he became more compliant. He remembered Madhavi. They both did.

Ghost snarled back at him, making croaking noises, filling himself with Power, but he could not focus long enough to use it. Roth squeezed tighter.

"You're pathetic," Roth hissed. "Your tower of ice won't save you. She'll come for you, eventually. She always does. She doesn't like it when her pets wander. That's what we are to her - pets, dogs for her to torment. Is that what you want, your grace?"

Roth's own words washed the rage away. He *knew* Ghost. Roth let the creature go, listening to Ghost cough and growl. Ghost was important once, to the people of Kormaine. Roth was important too, but he could not recall why. Thinking about it made his hade hurt, made him growl and turn in circles as if seeking some invisible tormentor.

Phier... he said. No, whimpered. It was a pathetic noise wrenched from the dark recesses of his mind that *remembered* what as done to him. It was not *just* Madhavi that hurt him. Daemodan tortured his body, made him a monster. Madhavi tortured his mind, making him her toy.

He heard the roar of rage, the heat of blackened fire, then heard only whimpering sobs. His eyes scanned the melted ice for the source of the noise. Slowly, Ghost unfolded himself revealing Malie's tear-soaked face. A small bubble formed in her left nostril. Ghost protected her.

"I need to find my Moppet. They made him so fragile. I need... My Evie. Do you know where they've gone?" Roth asked as he lifted Malie into his arms so he could gently wipe her tears. Ghost hesitated, then finally nodded.

"I will show you," the other Corrupted said.

Phier, Roth said. *We're leaving.*

***

Dead leaves and twigs crunched beneath Cavian's feet. There was literally no way to be silent with so much dead verdure around him. It was a shame his sire was so hellbent on turning the world around him into the actual Hells. As if that realm didn't have enough space to spew its vileness, now it needed space on the Prime realm. It was not for Cavian to question much. He didn't have time for it. He sought something else entirely. As soon as he found it, he intended on leaving Doranelle all together. He was done with his sire's schemes and his siblings' idiocies. Perhaps he'd visit Terra or Evanlin. They were nice Orbs.

A crunch to his left made him freeze in position, wings tucking in tight against his back as he tilted his head to listen for what tried to hide in such absurdly loud surroundings. Whatever it was didn't move, but Cavian could hear the rapid heartbeat and shallow breaths. It made him smile for several reasons. First, noise meant survivors. Second, it meant he was not the only one trying to be silent and failing. That was, perhaps, more important than the first.

"I hear you," Cavian purred. "You can't hide. No one can. This cursed forest makes too much noise with all this dead and burned crap laying around. It'd be better for you to just come out and show yourself rather than play a game you can't win."

Cavian waited as the person debated. They always did. Eventually logic beat bravado, however. It always did. What emerged was rather pleasant to look at. A duende female. No, not duende, at least, not entirely. Her skin was too pale to be full duende. She held her bow like the forest-dwelling olve did. It was well crafted, wrapped in runes and worn leather. She aimed it at him, eye fixed on his heart. He smiled.

"That seems a bit forward. We only just met," Cavian smiled. He moved a few steps forward to lean against a nearby tree. At least, he thought it was a tree. It was difficult to tell at this point in the game. The woman moved her bow with him.

"Honestly, I expected more of you to come out. You must be pretty good with that if you've survived this long on your own."

"Who said she's alone?" A new voice said right as Cavian felt the cold steel of a blade at his throat. Typical.

Cavian put his hands up. There was nothing he'd be able to do before that blade cut him open or, worse, the arrow pierced his heart. While he might be able to take out his new friends, it would come at the cost of his own life. He rather liked living. Daemodan's 'help' only lasted long enough to be a distraction for something bigger upon reaching the last strike point. It did nothing for a meager group of survivors.

A third person moved in to bind Cavian's hands behind his back. As soon as the cold ivory snapped shut over his wrists, he knew he'd grossly underestimated his chances with the local folk. He'd guessed there might be one or two stragglers, but the last push through the forest sent most of them running. They killed or captured any left - or, so Cavian had been told. He would have to remember to repay Rodmilla's information with something vile.

"Move," the woman said, jerking her bow in the direction she wanted him to go. He didn't argue. The man with the blade stayed close, iron at Cavian's back instead. It burned even through the cloth. He looked like the woman; related perhaps. The third took him by the elbow, a tirsai woman. The second remained out of sight.

They marched him through the crunching leaves, right to the edge of the very place he'd been aiming for. How convenient.

The Necropolis was, quite possibly, one of the most stunning examples of ancient architecture Cavian had ever seen. Many scholars shared his sentiment. The entire city had been grown from the marble and granite that naturally existed in Asphondel. It was easily older than the Destruction, perhaps even older than the Calamity that occurred over seven thousand years gone. The marble gave away no secrets. Its sole purpose was to house the dead. It had done so for time eternal. Nothing living remained long within the cradle of the Necropolis.

Cavian observed what he could, glancing

around for something that might give away the location of the sword. The Necropolis did not just hold the dead. It also had treasures of pure imagination, all buried with their final owners. The only reason any of it remained intact was the very duende that marched him through the narrow byways around him. The duende took responsibility of the dead, one of their tribes dedicating their lives to its protection for literal millennia. It was a fascinating study.

A root tripped him up as they walked, sending him tumbling to his knees. The olve pushing him along didn't seem to care for his comfort or lack thereof. They merely hauled him back up to his feet and continued on. Cavian let out a sneer but remained silent, taking careful note of every turn, every tomb, every structure they passed. When it was all said and done, they shoved him into a gated tomb beneath a larger structure, locking it up tight. Cavian looked around, placing his hands on the iron bars. The halfie woman thwacked his fingers, making him hiss and tuck his hands back in.

"That was rather rude," he said. She was the only one to linger, keeping watch over him as if he had the wherewithal to go anywhere but where he was. "I never did get your name?"

"Nor will ya," she said. She carried the accent of the Asphondeli. The tirsai of the Phoenix had a more refined accent. Cavian didn't care for it much. He heard it in his own words from time to time, but tried to hide it. It sounded too pompous for his liking.

"Afraid I'll use it for mischief?" Cavian teased, bringing his hands around the iron bars again. She glowered at him for it. Cavian merely grinned. "Does this bother you, sweet?"

She thwacked him again. The woman had a decidedly accurate aim. If she kept going, his knuckles would be bleeding by the next thwack.

"Well, if I can't call you sweet, what can I call you? 'Love' seems too forward. We're not at that point in our relationship, I don't think."

"I've a name," she hissed. Cavian's grin turned into a devilish smile.

"One you won't tell me," he reminded her. It only served to redden her cheeks and deepen the scowl on her face. At least he wouldn't be bored in his captivity. "I have to call you something."

"Ya can just shut yer trap instead," she snarled, stepping close to the bars as if to strike him through them. He stepped back. He was quiet for a full count of twenty before continuing.

"Tell you what, *naru*," he began, noting her look of surprise at the use of the olven tongue. "What? Surprised I speak the olven trade cant? I promise it isn't the only language I speak so if you're thinking of 'hiding' things from me by speaking in tongues, just don't bother. What was I saying.... Oh, I was going to ask if you'd indulge me some information. That's all I came for, you know. Your little band of thieves and brigands wasn't even supposed to be here. I was told you were all dead."

"Ya was told wrong," she spit back.

"Clearly," Cavian intoned flatly. "I'm looking for something. Maybe you're familiar with it, maybe you're not. You can just nod if you are. Ever heard of the Sword of Fate?"

She blinked in annoyance at him.

"I'll take that as a 'no'. What tribe are you?"

She peered at him, scowling again. He stepped back to his original spot, placing his shackled hands around the bars again.

"I told you, I'm looking for some*thing*, not some*one*. Telling me your name isn't going to give me some absurd power over you. All I'd do with it anyway is make you smile once. It would suit you better than all that scowling you're doing. Here, how about an easier question: are you one of the Dead Speakers?"

"No," she grumbled.

"Was that so hard?" Cavian continued. "Don't answer that. Could you find me someone who is?"

"No," she repeated. "Stop talkin'."

"You've taken my Power, my freedom, and my ability to call you by name and now you're going to take my ability to speak?"

"I can take yer life if ya'd rather," she countered. Cavian smiled. This was going to be so much fun.

***

A curious breeze rolled over the Grove. It held something ominous on it, something that made the bard shiver even as he stared out at the sea. His vision unfocused, thoughts wandering to what that breeze was trying to tell him. He could feel it in his skin, the way it tightened across his bones and muscles with what was to come.

"Reven?" Serai said, giving his hand a little squeeze. "You are ok?"

"Fine," he murmured, offering her a soft grin that didn't touch his eyes. His vision remained unfocused, but he nodded and repeated, "Fine."

"The boy asked a question," she said. Reven blinked at that point, refocusing his eyes to glance over at the poor young man he'd been ignoring. A tirsai boy of roughly fifteen or sixteen summers stood in front of him. He wore a kerchief around his neck despite the heat, something that hide scars that just barely peeked out from beneath the fabric.

"Apologies," Reven offered. "You asked something."

"Will you play, highness?" the boy said, gesturing at the violin Reven had in his lap. He'd been tuning it when he felt the odd breeze. "Like you used to."

Reven paused a moment, looking around for Kaleo. The young avian was not immediately present. Neither was Lara, so the bard didn't think too much about why his urchin was absent. He saw a small handful of children loitering a few feet away, all of them varying in age from seven to seventeen. Navid was not far, and Rielle sat just across the Grove beside Ettrian and his little brother, Gael. Shouting across the Grove at either of them didn't seem very becoming. Liam sat beside Reven opposite of where Serai did and just snorted, shaking his head. It was that noise and gesture that decided Reven.

"My memory is not as good as it was before. Perhaps you'd be kind enough to remind me how I used to play?"

"With the children, highness. You'd come to the low quarter and let them come sing and play with you."

"Azrus take me, were they any good?" Reven said with a minor wrinkle of his nose. The boy snorted out a dry laugh. His smile brightened his face even as he shook his head.

"No. It was awful, but they loved it."

Reven glanced behind the boy at the small group of children and smirked. "I imagine these are the children who would like to play with a great bard?"

The boy looked at the group behind him and gestured for them to join him. They shuffled over in a tight little group of wide eyes and barely contained giggles. It made Serai giggle and Liam groan under his breath. Reven ignored Liam.

"Can we play too?" one of the duende children asked. Ettrian, Reven noticed, watched closely. The tirsai children stared at him, as did the young man who'd come to speak to Reven.

"What's your name?" Reven asked the one brave enough to come ask.

"Emile," he answered. "Of House Delphus, highness."

"House? Can I ask where you see any houses that are not made of canvas, Emile?" Reven continued. Emile's face colored. "Emile, all we've got left is what you see around you. There's no Empire anymore. There's no throne."

"Hey," Aeron grumbled. Reven sighed. He'd not wanted to do this in public, but it was a conversation that was building. Perhaps that was what the ominous breeze meant.

"You don't, Aeron. You're not an Emperor - you're a child. You don't have a nation, you have a Grove on a small continent somewhere south of the only empire left in the entirety of Doranelle. These people need someone *with experience* to lead them out of the cesspool your aunt dropped them into. That isn't your fault, it's hers, but don't make the same mistake she did by pretending you're something you're not."

"Alright then, master bard, if there's no throne and I'm too inexperienced to take what's rightfully mine, then who's going to bloody rule? You?" Aeron threw back.

"Gods no!" Reven scoffed. "I don't want that responsibility."

"That is why you should be the one to have it," Nadya chimed in. The Kormandi princess sat beside Aeron, earning her the worst scowl Reven had ever seen on a woman.

"What's Aeron scowling for?" Kaleo asked as he and Lara rejoined the crowd.

You're not subtle at all, urchin, Reven teased,

making the avian blush.

"Nadya thinks uncle should rule!" Aeron blurted finally.

"No thank you," Reven said.

"You'd be good at it," Kaleo shrugged. Aeron socked him. "OW!"

"Alright, children, we will not start another war. We haven't even won the first one. One problem at a time. Come here, small one," Reven gestured at the small duende child who asked to play as well. The child moved forward.

"I've a drum. I brung it wif us when we ran!" the girl said, producing a tiny, worn, leather dulcimer.

"I see that. Do you know something? This wonderful gem of freckles beside me plays the drum as well," Reven said with a smile at Serai. She beamed in return. "Well, come on then, give us a beat."

The girl positively radiated happiness. She played while other children gathered. Reven lifted his violin to his chin and followed the odd beat as best he could. The girl could not have been more than six summers. Aeron stood and stomped off to wallow in his displeasure. Kaleo collected his guitar from nearby and put a tambourine in Liam's hands.

"Wha's this then? I don't play," Liam said.

"Learn, Roe," Reven said.

The children sang or played what few instruments they had. Some just clapped along or giggled. It was the most hideous thing Reven had heard in his short memory - - and it was glorious.

Chapter Twelve

Demyan maintained a gentle, unassuming grin as he moved through the halls of the castle-palace several hours after his 'argument' with Kendal. He allowed himself two days after his plea for aid was sent to learn the identical halls and where they went, where guards were stationed, and why. Sometimes it was simply for the sQueen's protection, other times it was to hide something. He learned that quickly too, so that by the time he walked the halls on the fifth day since seeing the Speakers in the Shards, he knew which places to avoid and which ones he could easily slip into unseen. A building so large not only had beautifully wrought halls and balconies but also a multitude of hidden passages for the servants. It was those that Demyan made the most use of. The servants were kind, treating him like the idiot foreign king they believed him to be, always guiding him back out of the passages into a different part of the castle-palace.

The 'argument' with his wife was spurned by a letter that had arrived in the early hours of the morning. It was not signed, but promised assistance in getting him *away* from Itahl. It brought a sigh of relief to him when he read it, for it meant the Baron's contact read the missive Demyan had sent. He did not want to abandon his bride, but they did not want to raise suspicion either. They would not hurt *her*; they would torture and murder *him* like they were doing to the others. Kendal had gone to the temple to pray, to think - to find help. Demyan wanted to find proof of what the Itahli were doing.

He nodded at passing gentry, priests and acolytes, walking with purpose as if he knew exactly where he was going. Aeron taught him to always walk with his head up and eyes focused forward. It was difficult for him. His conditioning as a slave taught him to do the exact opposite. In this instance, he managed to play the part of a king, hands placed lightly inside of wide sleeves and pressed against his belly to calm his nerves. The guards that were at the doors that lead down to the Source were not present like they were the day Kendal brought him, which made him frown. They'd been present every day since. He expressed his concerns to her that first evening too, listening to her laugh and dismiss them as vapors of paranoia. She knew differently now, as desperate as he was to get out of the country. First, they needed out of the castle-keep.

One problem at a time, Koji, he told himself.

Talking to ourselves, Love. Are you well? You've not used that name since I met you, Aisling asked. The name was given to a small, terrified boy who was made a slave in a world that was lifetimes away, it seemed. Only two other people called him by that name. One was dead, and one was as far from him as Aisling was. How he wanted to be with her. He could do it; he could leave, but then nothing would change.

Yes.

For the time being, he put his *audeas* out of his mind, took in a deep breath, and walked through the double doors in front of him with head held high and back as straight as he could make it.

The smell hit him first. It made him gag, his features twisting up into a grimace. He was all too familiar with the stench of rotting meat, which was what his nose caught on to first, followed by the burning tickle of acid. He moved quietly down the stone halls with their blue tubes lining the ceiling, illuminating everything in a pale wash of light. The pulsing vertigo he'd felt the first night Kendal brought him had diminished, something that worried him.

Where are you, lovey? I don't sense you.

Aisling, again. She remained outside the city walls, where it was safer for her to be. Her voice spoke all languages and none, making it very easy for Demyan to understand her.

Hunting, he told her. *I am fine, Aisling.*

Oh? And since when does my shy creature hunt? Do you even eat meat, lovey?

He didn't, but that was not the point. Now he made a face that was directed at his *audeas* even if she could not see it. Then something occurred to him.

Aisling, can you find Aeron?

His only friend would know what to do in situations like this and might even have a safe haven for him to flee to should the need arise before his requested help did.

It may take some time, but I can probably manage. Runya speaks very highly of him.

The new name made Demyan pause forward momentum and frown.

Runya?

*His **audeas**, lovey. You didn't know?*

That must have been a new development.

Aeron was still recovering last Demyan knew. Good. He'd worried for his friend.

Find him, please.

Aisling assured him she would, asked for him to be careful, and said nothing more, leaving him in silence again. In hindsight, he wished he'd waited a little longer to send his *audeas* on an Aeron-hunting errand. Her mental voice was comforting. With her 'gone', he continued moving forward until rounding the corner that brought him face to face with the *two* giant shards; the third was missing. Demyan's stomach dropped out to the floor when he saw why - the body of one of the Speakers lay on a table, the chest cavity open and the insides exposed. He gagged again and turned away.

HELP US!

Demyan cried out, dropping to his knees as his hands flew to his ears. The voice was not heard in the normal sense, but it was heard all the same, ripping across his mind in a desperate plea. The confidence he felt earlier vanished, replaced by rising panic.

"You are not one of them."

The new voice *did* reach his ears, making him spin and land hard on his rear. A young man of roughly equal age to himself spoke from a grate embedded in the stone floor, looking up at Demyan with stunning cerulean blue eyes. His hair was fiery red and too long, the curls matted into clumps that needed to be cut. Demyan crawled to him, examining the bars and the hole in which he squatted. It was not very big and the young man wore ivory manacles on his wrists that dug into the flesh. Demyan did not know what they were and suddenly felt a new wave of panic when he tried to form words to communicate.

"Demyan," he offered, gesturing at himself. It was a start.

"Seren," the young man said. Progress. That…

was as far as Demyan could get. He understood more than he could speak. Demyan offered Seren a reassuring grin, then studied the grate. For all talk of science and alchemy, their mechanisms were frightfully simple. The *youkai* of the Imperium made more complex things in their sleep. It took very little effort to find the spring that held the heavy iron bars down onto the floor. The trick was placing such things just out of reach of the prisoner - not that Seren would have been able to reach through the bars with the manacles on his wrist. He looked at them, then at Demyan, who studied those as well, but could not find a way to remove them. They appeared to be one solid piece of ivory and made him feel dizzy any time he touched them.

"*They steal my Power,*" Seren said in a language that brought Demyan's attention up to his face sharply. Seren was taller but more frail and spoke in the same 'everything' language that Aisling used. Demyan nodded, unable to use the same language back, but at least able to acknowledge that he understood.

"*We need to free them,*" Demyan said in the language of the *youkai* while pointing at the two still trapped in the giant Shards. Seren shook his head.

"*It will kill them. I watched them do it to her.*"

Seren looked at the body on the table, so Demyan looked too, then quickly looked away again. The screaming in his head increased for a moment, then tempered itself. He looked at the Shards, head turning sharply, when he heard the doors at the other end of the hall opening. Someone was coming.

Without thinking, he grabbed hold of Seren and ran in the opposite direction, ignoring the queasiness that came from touching the manacles on the young man's wrists. They hid in the dark, Demyan gesturing for Seren to remain silent while he gave the manacles another look, feeling all around them despite the discomfort until finding the tiniest of notches on each one. As soon as he did, he pressed them, both snapping open with a clatter.

"Did you hear that?"

"Shit," Demyan hissed, the word learned from Aeron. He didn't know where to go or how to get out of the subterranean death lab, so did the next best thing: he Traveled.

It was not his best ability by far, but it was useful at times. He Traveled back to the apartments he'd been sharing with Kendal, catching Seren when the young man landed hard on top of him with a wince.

"Gommen..."

Seren only nodded. It was then that Demyan realized the poor thing was not wearing a single stitch of clothing and flushed bright crimson to the roots of his blonde curls.

"We need to leave," he said instead, sticking to the language he knew best as he extracted himself to find Seren something to wear. *"It isn't safe here for us anymore."*

Seren nodded, rubbing his wrists. He dressed as quickly as Demyan could throw clothing at him, all of it fine and well-made, but simple. The rest Demyan threw into two satchels and handed them to Seren.

"Carry them, keep your head down, and follow me," he instructed, hoping to pass Seren off as a servant. Again Seren nodded, mutely following Demyan out of the room to the expanse of halls in the castle-palace. Demyan felt queasy with how tight his stomach wound inside of him. He walked with head up as he'd been taught, perfectly neutral, unassuming grin in place. Now and then he nodded at someone who passed or glanced behind him to Seren who, so far, was doing as instructed. They would never make it out of the castle-palace, however, and Demyan knew it. He

saw it in how people ran past them or whispered. He even made a good show of it, stopping to ask a servant what was happening.

"Someone's broke into the palace, my lord," she answered. "Are they sending you to the Temple?"

Demyan nodded. "It is safer."

The servant nodded back, accepting of the answer, and helped them out a servant's corridor to the fresh air beyond. She gave direction to Seren, showing him how to get to the Temple faster so the king would be safe. As soon as she was gone, Demyan grabbed Seren's wrist again, dragging him to an unseen corner and Traveled a second time, this time to a dirt field as far as his ability would take him and blacked out.

***

The rapping echo of wood on wood reverberated through the wide hall of the *Amaterasu*. Each member of the Seat of Heaven sat in a gilded chair carved of *koa* wood. It was unique to their nation and highly sought after, fetching high prices across the globe. Incense burned from a ceramic ball that hung from the center of the room, bringing peace to the gathering of the Amaterasu. Each member paid respect and reverence to the *Amatta* and *Amat*, their stations above all others, as they listened to the grievances posed before them.

"We are most disturbed to think that a member of this court would attack another, not just once, but several times," Lady Kahananui said. She sat with back straight and nose high in the air. Her pale lavender wings set her apart from others in the room that had pale blue or gray against the Amat and Amatta's silver. She married well, earned her place, and had even discussed arrangements to have her daughter wed to the missing *amati* - the very one accused of turning against the Amaterasu. It was a good match; *was* being the operative word.

"The incident is under investigation. We have been unable to locate Kaleo-"

"He's in Tierra Vida," Tondra Caelestis interrupted as she entered the room. The Tempest certainly earned her namesake, with a reputation as brutal as the summer storms that swept through the island nation. Even members of the Amaterasu tread cautiously around her - everyone but the *amatessa*. Noelani, scoffed and rolled her eyes.

"He's always 'in Tierra Vida', Tondra. He never stays long. What proof do you even have that he's-"

"Maeve Oenel," Tondra cut in again, this time looking at the Amat and Amatta. "He has overthrown her rule at the temple ruins where the refugees had been with the help of that cursed bard. He has several hundred of her people in a grove near the southern shore just west of Brecken - - and has several of the Phoenix and Kormandi royalty held hostage with him."

"Hostage? Are you kidding, Tondra? Kaleo would never do something like that," Kalelako said. He spoke as their Anointed One, blessed with the wisdom of the ancients and the Power of the cosmos.

"Kal, he attacked *us*," Noelani barked.

"He put you to sleep," Kalelako corrected, glancing over at the amatessa placidly.

"And robbed you of your Power," Tondra added. Kalelako gave Tondra an even glare.

"Much like you robbed an innocent man of his. In fact, if Kaleo had given me even a quarter of what you pumped into that bard, I'd have you in chains right now, Captain. Your methods leave much to be desired."

"My methods have kept this nation safe, your grace," Tondra hissed.

"Enough," the Amatta said. "Kaleo is not a malicious child. He never has been. I agree with Kalelako - he would not hold *anyone* hostage, Tondra. Maeve Oenel's word is not worth much among this court. She has only ever been interested in her own selfish needs since she could walk. Kaleo helped bring new policies and forward thinking to a nation that once slaughtered on sight and solidified an alliance with the most powerful nation in existence at the time. *If* the phoenix prince is with Kaleo, then I am certain it is to finally rebuild rather than sit idly by as Maeve has done."

"The boy is a bastard accorded the title of amati," Tondra sneered. Her disgust was emulated on the faces of other members of the Amaterasu. "He has no place in this world!"

"Be careful how you speak of my great-grandson, *'alihikaua,*" the Amata said, using Tondra's formal title. "I want to know what he's doing in Tierra Vida and with whom. I want Kal to go with you."

"I'm going too," Noelani said.

"No," Kalelako and Tondra said in unison. Noelani frowned and put her nose in the air, silver wings bristling and puffing with annoyance.

"Noe," Kalelako continued. "Your place is here with L'nae."

"It is because of L'nae that I want to go, Kal. I am done getting second-hand information on what my son is doing! L'nae asks for him every night. I owe it to her to find the truth about why her brother's gone missing."

"Noe," Kalelako sighed just as the heavy *koa* doors opened. Every head whipped around to glower at the fool that dared barge in without invitation or announcement.

"Forgive me, your grace," Ioana, Noelani's handmaid, said, holding L'nae's hand. "The *amatess* requested that she be allowed to speak on her brother's behalf."

The tiny avian girl stuck her chin out, head held high and back as straight as any of the adults sitting in the room. Noelani's face turned red with embarrassment and rage that she shared with her handmaid for allowing such a childish act to interrupt something so serious. The Amatta, however, merely smiled, extending her age-spotted hand to her great-granddaughter.

"Come, child," the Amatta said, beckoning L'nae forward. The girl went, holding a tiny boar beneath her left arm as she walked. The others of the Amaterasu laughed or whispered, silenced only when L'nae shot them a scathing glare.

"The amatessa said you're looking for Kaleo," L'nae began when she reached the Amatta's side, climbing up into the elder woman's lap, boar and all.

"We are. Do you know where he's gone?"

"No," L'nae said. "But you should leave him alone. He's happier when he's not here. He told me he was going to find our daddy."

"L'nae," Noelani warned. The Amatta silenced her with a single look.

"Continue, child," the Amatta said. L'nae looked at her mother, lips pursed in defiance.

"I asked him if he found our daddy when he was here. He said he found someone better. I know that's not what he meant. I heard momma and Kal talking. She kept asking Kal to 'be sure' it wasn't my daddy, but that's who Kaleo found."

"This bard everyone speaks of?" the Amatta asked. L'nae nodded.

"Kaleo promised to come back for me. Just like he promised to find our daddy."

"You are absolutely not going anywhere near Kaleo!" Noelani hissed. L'nae leveled an even glare at her mother, making the Tempest narrow her almond eyes at the girl. Too much of the bastard child had rubbed off on the heir-apparent. Too much of their *father*.

"Noelani," the Amatta snipped. "L'nae, do you want to be with your brother?"

"Grandmother!" Noelani screeched. It was Kalelako that stilled her this time, reaching over to take hold of her hand in full view of the Amaterasu. Their relationship was forbidden, but that did not seem to stop them. The whole room whispered about that, too.

"I want to help him," L'nae answered. The Amatta smiled at the girl, glancing over to the Amat who also smiled.

"Then we shall see what we can do. Kalelako - take an emissary to Tierra Vida. We have sat idle for long enough."

***

Footsteps crunched along the dead leaves that littered the ground outside of Rudia. The roads were not paved beyond the city. The intricately laid brick turned to hard-packed gravel flanked by orchards and farms for as far as the eye could see. Demyan desperately wanted to stop at a barn even if it was just to sleep with the animals for a night but they did not dare. Both he and Seren radiated Power like suns and the Hunters did not waste time with their hunt. By the time he regained consciousness, rumors had spread that the Kormandi king had been taken by a servant Sinner. By the time they saw their first farm, several of the Hunters and city guards had ridden by on metal horses that growled like fierce monsters as they thundered by. Demyan kept them off the main road, darting from tree to tree in the dark and sleeping *in* the trees when they could no longer keep their eyes open for two nights straight, then pushing through once more.

Neither said much. Demyan knew Seren understood him. Even so, the young man did not say anything at all. He did not ask Seren his age, but Demyan estimated him to be within a few years of his own age, at twenty-two or twenty-three. They'd stolen a sack full of apples the first night and munched on them silently as they walked to keep their strength up, but it was getting difficult. Two days out of the city only brought them to more orchards and more farms that were stirred up by the Hunters to look for escaped Sinners.

Demyan thought about Traveling more than once but didn't have a clear destination in mind. It was too dangerous to just pop away to somewhere unseen. They might land *inside* a tree or, worse, among Hunters. So they walked, keeping as far from the road as possible while still in sight of it, moving from tree to tree or shrub to shrub.

"*Where are we going?*" Seren finally asked when the sun began to set on the third day.

"*Damaskha. We shouldn't be far from the border,*" Demyan replied. He sounded tired even to his own ears. He knew the general direction to follow based on the maps he'd studied in the castle tower. There were hundreds of them from all nations. He'd memorized Kormaine's first, then Itahl's when Kendal was brought to him. Thinking about her made his heart ache with guilt. He should not have left her behind. Any other thought after, however, ended as soon as he felt pain rip through his shoulder, throwing him backwards into a stack of crates filled with apples.

"Demyan!" Seren cried, ducking behind the crates as another bullet came careening at *him* from somewhere unseen. The pain robbed Demyan of thought, making him cry out as it burned its way through his entire body. It was not *just* a bullet. It couldn't be. There was too much agony racing through him for it to be just a bullet.

He was vaguely aware of screaming, back arching up sharply. He knew Seren was doing something, heard the Hunters shouting and thunderous noises that Demyan could not sort out as he hollered until his throat was raw.

Idris cursed when he heard the screaming, heeling the horses he and Jax rode on to a full run. They'd had a plan. It was a *good* plan. That plan just went out the window. Both men heard the gunshots and saw the bright flashes of Power in the distance. Hells, Idris *felt* the Power in the distance.

"Hunters!" Jax said as they came upon a group of them set on one red-haired young man and the one screaming.

"Keep them busy!" Idris said, taking to the sky on strong wings, filling himself with Power as he soared up into the clouds coalescing above him. Jax simply looked at him but did as he was asked, getting the attention of the Hunters away from the two pinned down in the orchard and on himself instead. Idris focused everything he had on the surrounding clouds until they were black with rage, crackling with energy that he sent down as fat bolts of lightning at the five Hunters on the road and the other *eight* slinking through the orchards. He continued his barrage until every single one of the Itahli pricks were little more than a scorch mark on the ground.

The storm continued even after the Hunters were dispatched, giving Idris and Jax cover to do what needed to be done. Rain pounded the ground, saturating it in minutes. Idris no longer heard the screaming, which made him worry even as he came to land in the orchard nearby. The red-head jumped in surprise, ready to fight, but Idris raised his hands.

"I'm here to help you, *mes amis*," Idris said. Jax knelt on the ground beside the Kormandi king. "*Merde.*"

"He will not last long if we can't get this bullet out of him," Jax said. Hunters did their jobs too well. Every weapon they used was intended to eliminate people with Power. Idris knelt beside Jax, looking the king over, too. He was so young. His face was a mask of pain, mouth twisted into a grimace that barely allowed breath to pass through.

Idris shook his head, taking a dagger from his boot. "Hold him down."

Jax winced but held the king down, turning his head as Idris used the tip of his dagger to dig the offending little orb out of the king's shoulder. Doing so ripped another scream out of the poor kid that Idris apologized for as he dug deeper until the bullet finally popped out, rolling lazily onto the grass with a hiss as the poison on it corroded the earth beneath it.

"*What the hells do they put on that?!*" Jax asked in Kormandi.

"You don't wanna know," Idris sneered. "We can't stay here."

Jax nodded, lifting the king up as the rain poured down around them. Idris looked at the red-headed man, his hair a matted mess that stuck to his neck and back.

"What's your name?" Idris asked. The man glanced around, swallowing fear that Idris could feel. "I'm not gonna hurt you. I'm here to help him. What's your name?"

"Seren," the man finally answered, looking up sharply when they all heard more thunderous roars along the road.

"*Something tells me those Hunters aren't going to*

stop until he's found, Idris," Jax said. *"And the queen is not with them."*

Idris cursed again, looking around with a mild growl. *"The king is who matters most. She's not here, she gets left behind. Let's go. I don't have enough in me to take on more of these assholes."*

Jax nodded, getting the king to the horses still loitering nearby. They could not Travel with him in those conditions. They just had to pray the horses were fast enough to outrun the Itahli's iron steeds until they reached Amadour.

Chapter Thirteen

Aeron Solvanis, former heir-apparent to what remained of the people of the Phoenix, stared up at Nadya Ovet, princess of Kormaine, from the flat of his back for the eleventh time in a row. It should not have been possible for her to best him so many times in a row. Once or twice, yes, but not *eleven*. Reven Si'ahl, the new heir-apparent and 'simple bard', chortled off to the side with the other 'men' rather than helping. Much like he had 'helped' the Embers start coming to a much more democratic decision to put *Reven* on the throne, despite claiming to not want it.

"She best you again?" Eila asked as she and her twin walked by with Ettrian Si'ahl, Reven's half-brother. The surname must have been lodged in the bard's memory for the man to adopt it as his own. Aeron thought it was stupid, though that was his general opinion of anything relating to his uncle of late.

"I thought you were stronger," Rielle teased.

"She's faster," Ettrian said, carrying sacks of grain toward the cook pots. He'd gone to Brecken with the girls.

"Not helping!" Aeron snarled after them as he rolled up to a seated position. "Fine, let me fight Kaleo."

"That's-" Kaleo began. The Baron cut him off.

"Fine. Nadya, give Kaleo your sword?" the man said.

"How is that fair? Hers is lighter than a normal sword," Aeron whined. Reven smirked as if privvy to an inside joke.

"Give *Aeron* your sword then," the Baron grumbled. Aeron smirked, accepted the weapon switch, and readied to whollop his cousin.

When he rolled around gasping for breath, he was certain he'd stepped into some strange nightmare. Kaleo had *never* beat Aeron before. He'd always been small and bratty.

"Strength is only good if you can hit them," the Baron explained. "This is the problem with your people. You are only taught strength, names, 'houses'. Who taught you, Kaleo?"

"Kalelako," Kaleo answered. He was the Esbethi Anointed One. Aeron knew him in name only. The Baron nodded, gesturing at Reven.

"You did not fight good before. Now you hit Liam all the time. Who taught you?"

"Ajana," Reven smirked while Liam grumbled. The Baron nodded again.

"You learn what is good for you. Not for me. Not for Nadya or for your cousin. For you. It is this way in politics too. Again."

Others watched, listened, waited. Aeron tempered his reaction for them. The Baron's words were as much for them as much as they were for Aeron. He needed to remember that, even if it all felt like a personal attack recently. The tirsai would need to unlearn everything they knew if they hoped to move forward with the duende and succeed. *He* needed to unlearn everything.

So, he stood up with a minor groan and growl ready to spar again.

"Yer grace!" Ettrian called. "We've a visitor!"

It's Aisling, my love, Runya said to him. Demyan's *audeas*.

Is Demyan with her?

No.

Aeron was moving in an instant. Kaleo and Nadya followed. Others filed in after them. Both of Aeron's sisters pet a large, snow-owl gryphon at the outskirts of the Grove.

"Has something happened?" Aeron asked as he came close to her.

My shy creature tasked me with finding you.

"Is he well?" Aeron persisted, knowing Ettrian was the only one to hear Aisling besides himself.

Concerned, though he will not tell me why. I'd imagine it may have to do with the gross amount of Power there.

"Power? In *Itahl*?" Ettrian blurted. The young man looked like his father. He was smart and shared Aeron's thought even if he didn't temper his tongue as well.

"Oh ye summer children," Reven chortled while Liam snorted. "How do you think they make all their atuomations and machines?"

"Science?" all the 'children' said, to include Ettrian. Reven shook his head.

"Roe, how many 'Power pools' are in Itahl?"

Liam held up three fingers. Reven gestured at them. Aeron felt his jaw drop.

"That's imposs-"

No!

"What? What's wrong?" Aeron asked. Aisling

did not answer, screeching as she took to the air and vanished in a flurry of ice crystals.

***

The Temple of Yira sat at the center of the Home district. It was a marvel of design and beauty. Twisting spires rose up to the heavens from the main building, creating a dreamscape worthy of the goddess worshipped there. For Kendal Ovet, it was her home and haven for many years. Now the stunning architecture and beautifully stained glass had become her prison.

"Please," Kendal asked of the guard tasked with her 'protection'. "Is there any news of my husband?"

"All we know, your grace, is a Sinner took him. The Hunters are tracking them down. The Hunters will find them."

Kendal nodded. That was what she feared. The Hunters knew what Demyan was. They would not be merciful.

She moved to the open window overlooking the Home quarter. There was snow on the ground, but not like in Kormaine. She missed the glittering white blankets of stars. She saw Yira's hand in everything. Prayer was her solace. So, she prayed for Demyan's safety, prayed to see him again, then jumped when a deafening crack of thunder ricocheted across the sky. Kendal's eyes snapped open. The sky was no longer a dull blue, but a furious shade of charcoal gray. Angry blue lightning forked along the hideous clouds before lancing down to the ground, illuminating a figure in the darkened sky.

"Yira protect us," Kendal breathed, backing away slowly from the window.

"Yira's not the one helping now, your grace."

Kendal yelped as someone took her arm. An

acolyte, someone she'd never seen. The young woman was older than Kendal with black hair and oddly colored hazel blue eyes rimmed in amber.

"Who are you?" Kendal dared.

"A friend. I'm taking you to the king," the woman said. Her words were heavily accented in the Damaskhan nasally smoothe drawl of words that was so similar to how the Itahli spoke.

"You're Damaskhan," Kendal said.

"*Oui*," the woman winked, clearly proud of her nationality. "Now come on, get your things. We're leaving, *cherie*."

"The guard," Kendal said, as she threw a few things into a small bag. Most of her belongings were still at the castle keep.

"Won't bother us," the woman said. "We gotta hurry, *cherie*."

"What's your name?" Kendal asked, as she secured her cloak around her shoulders. Not that it would protect her from the torrential downpour flooding the streets.

"Marie," the woman smiled in the same way she'd said '*oui*' - with pride and a touch of sass. Kendal liked her immediately.

"Thank you, Marie."

***

Exhaustion threatened to drag Idris down. He'd used too much Power calling the storm. It still gave them cover to a point. The Itahli's iron horses didn't operate well in the rain. To be fair, Idris didn't operate well in the rain either. He felt saturated to his core, holding the Kormandi king as they raced the distance back to Amadour. Jax kept the other young man with him, the added weight slowing both horses.

Marie waited for them at the inn. The plan was to go immediately to Grolly by Port Stone. Now, Idris needed to think of a new plan. The king should not travel by Port in his condition. If things got desperate, perhaps he would stick to the original plan, but it was dangerous to do so. The Hunters would look at the Port logs first.

Idris! Be careful, love!

The warning came seconds before a flurry of ice blinded Idris. A snow gryphon appeared from that ice, frightening the horse. The animal reared up, throwing Idris and the wounded king from the horse. Idris landed hard on his back with the king atop him. All air left his lungs, rain poured down around him. He heard Jaz and the other horse; heard the wild, angry cry of the snow gryphon - - then felt the searing heat of his *audeas* imposing herself between Idris and the gryphon.

"Come on," Jax said, tugging Idris up out of the mud. It weighed his wings down and tugged in places he didn't want to have tugged. Wings were beneficial most times, but not in the mud. "Get up! I have Demyan!"

Idris coughed, expelling rain water from his lungs as he finally got to his feet. Liss, his beautiful phoenix, quite literally set the air on fire to protect him.

"She is Demyan's," the red-haired man said. "The gryphon. She felt his pain."

Idris groaned and looked behind them. He couldn't see the Hunters, but he could hear the growl of their iron horses over the thundering storm.

"We outta time," Idris spat, his city accent coming through more heavily with the rise in his stress levels. "Liss!" *Stop*, he continued mentally to his beloved phoenix. *We're outta time. We need to go!*

Where? I will take you, she replied. Idris only hesitated a moment, thinking of Marie. *I will tell her. Where, love?*

Our haven, Idris said. He then grabbed hold of

Jax and Seren, shutting his eyes tight as the heat of the phoenix flame engulfed them all, taking them away from the rain and the Hunters to safety.

~~

Demyan's eyes rolled open briefly. He did not recognize his surroundings. Everything was sore - even his skin, like he'd sat out in the sun for far too long.

Rest, my shy creature. I'm here. You're safe now.

Aisling's voice relaxed every tense muscle, making Demyan melt into the soft padding beneath him.

Kendal? he managed.

They're looking for her. Rest now.

Demyan did not have the energy to argue. He let his eyes close and his body drift, sleeping in peace and safety for the first time in his life.

Chapter Fourteen

Wind chimes echoed into the open air around a small fish pond surrounded by stunted little frond trees and beautiful blossoms. The scent of them carried into the air. Soft music from a stringed instrument drifted out into the surrounding area from somewhere unseen, creating a serene atmosphere. The entire scene felt serene, but wrong at the same time. It was unfamiliar, a place Kendal had never been.

She felt the water of the pond drift around her feet, the fish nibbling lightly at her toes. She watched them, moving each little digit curiously.

"You're Kendal, aren't you?" someone said, startling her. The surrounding serenity shattered, replaced with the sharp wood scent of a bathhouse. The water turned to ice, making her tremble as she scrambled out of a shallow tub.

"It's alright, you're safe," an avian with teal wings said as he helped her out of the tub...

...to a field of bright red poppies and crystal

blue skies. It was stunning. The scent of the poppies drifted to her nose, each red and orange petal swaying in a spectral breeze.

"It's just a dream," the avian explained. She recognized him from Mahala.

"You're the bard's apprentice," Kendal said. He smiled and nodded. "You've been given Yira's gift."

Dreams were different for each person, unique to their lives and experiences, the memories they had or their greatest desires. Dreams were no more sacred than secrets - eventually, they were all laid bare for *someone* to see. Kendal had learned to accept the Lady of Dreams's gifts during her training at the Temple. She recalled that it did not sit well with the young avian before her that the Kormandi king - a *Speaker* - sought safe haven in Itahl. She knew now that the nation was notorious for slaughtering those with Power, or worse. Guilt weighed her down, darkening the surrounding sky.

"Demyan..." she began, blinking wide, brown eyes welling with tears at the avian. She didn't know his name.

"He's safe," he said. "We're looking for you. Are you safe? Are you still in Itahl?"

Kendal shook her head. "Amadour. We just arrived. I'm sorry, I don't know your name," she drawled, sniffing back the tears. The sky cleared some too, with her relief at knowing Demyan was safe.

"Kaleo," he smiled, the field brightening to its original crystal clear blue. "You said 'we'. Who are you with?"

"Marie. She's from Damaskha. We were supposed to meet her brother here in Amadour, but he never showed. Demyan sent for help. Jax brought help from Baron Karov."

"Can you get to Grolly?" Kaleo asked. "You'll

be safer there than Amadour. That's where Demyan is headed last we heard."

Kendal nodded. "I will talk to Marie. I think that's where we were headed to anyway Is Demyan with you now?"

"No, I'm in Tierra Vida with Aeron. Demyan is with my brother. I'm not sure where. I got it second-hand from the *audeases*." Kendal blinked in confusion. "Demyan's *audeas* told Aeron's who told mine. It's complicated."

"Oh," Kendal nodded. She was still learning to accept the knowledge learned when Demyan showed her what Itahl did to Sinners. She was still learning that Power was not a sin at all. Even *knowing* all of that, it still frightened her. Kaleo merely smiled patiently. "I guess I'll just tell Marie to go to Grolly. She's real worried about her brother."

"I don't think I know Marie," Kaleo said. She heard the regret in his voice and nodded.

"She's real nice," Kendal said of her savior. "Is this where I can find you if I need to get a message to you?"

Kaleo nodded. "If you pop in and find a tywyll guy with claws, just leave him alone. That's Jaysen. He was in Mahala with us."

"The one that got stabbed real bad. I remember," Kendal smiled then let it fade as the rest sank in. "Wait, you said you weren't in Mahala no more, right?"

"Right. I'm in Tierra Vida, near Brecken. Things got... weird."

Again, Kendal merely nodded. "Thank you Kaleo. Stay safe."

"You too."

***

Marie sat at the desk in the room she'd begged of her mother. The Companion Houses used curtains of beads or sheer cloth rather than doors save for one - the one the mistress or master of the house kept for themselves. In this instance, it was the room Idris's mother used. Marie took it, with little in the way of explanation for the woman's questions or demands of *Marie's* mother. She fingered the dagger at her side as she waited and contemplated the next steps.

Kendal Ovet sat on the bed, watching her. She'd said to go to Grolly after speaking to Kaleo in a dream. Marie had found a member of the Maison du Hombre to explain the situation, someone she trusted. Sungnier Rotem had returned to the Maison, reporting to Preston what had occurred and to see if anything could be done to help the Kormandi king's new bride. Even Preston waited, however, worrying over Idris.

Their haven would only last for so long.

***

Seren sat silently on a stool, freshly washed, in clean clothes with a comb in his hand that did nothing but snag the matted curls of his wild hair. They intended on going to Grolly once Demyan woke. Demyan needed a surgeon to be sure he did not have any lingering issues, but Idris only trusted a handful of people to do something so delicate. His sister was one of those people, but she had been left behind. It worried the aurum a great deal. Seren felt it, saw it in how the man twitched his golden-tipped wings or let a dagger spin slowly on the small desk in the room. Every now and then, Seren glanced at Idris curiously. He could feel Idris's Power. It differed from what a normal Speaker had, raw and kissed with divinity.

"You're staring," Idris said. Seren blinked. The

man had broken the comb. "Want help?"

"Where will we go?" Seren asked. They'd discussed it, but Seran heard the aurum's thoughts. Idris glanced at Seren, letting the thoughts roll around in his mind a little more before answering.

"Tierra Vida," Idris finally said. Seren didn't question, merely nodding in understanding.

"We are supposed to go to Grolly," Jax argued. Idris looked at the duende man with murderous intent.

Liss had brought them to a wondrous place, a haven full of life like Seren had seen only in his long-resting dreams. The trees all around them stretched to the sky, their trunks wide and strong, roots digging deep into the earth. Each tree was adorned in the colors and twinkling lights of the family inside it. Tywylls in Rellan shared generational homes, all of them tracing lineage back two, sometimes three cycles. It made Seren's heart swell. He knew some of the family names, even if he did not know the individuals. It was something familiar.

"This house has no colors," Seren commented as he continued to run the comb through his tangled curls. The lights around Idris's home were white.

"No," Idris said, watching Seren with a mild frown. "I'm not tywyll."

Seren nodded, hearing a snap. He had broken the comb.

Seren looked at Idris, eyes full of remorse. Idris merely smirked with a glance at Jax who scowled for being ignored. Seren watched Idris rise, sitting very still when the man moved behind him to pull out the broken part of the comb.

"How did you end up in Itahl" Idris asked as he ran calloused fingers through Seren's hair until it was less tangled. Seren tried not to wince when they caught on snags.

"I woke there," Seren said. He'd answered all of Idris's other questions, he saw no reason to stop. "Men in masks stood over me in a dark place. I felt pain... Califia. She passed into Azrus's hold as I woke."

"Calafia?" Idris asked. Seren felt the other man's fingers massaging his scalp, working small bunches of Seren's hair together in tight braids that kept the curls at bay.

"My princess," Seren said. "My *audeas*."

Idris's fingers slowed briefly before resuming once more. He remained quiet for a time, focused on helping Seren tame his mane. Jax watched them, making Seren nervous.

"He's not as mean as he looks," Idris said in the Damaskhan tongue. Jax snorted, staying close to the king, protecting him as fiercely as his *audeas* did.

"Yes, I am," Jax replied, stone-faced. Idris laughed, clapping Seren on the shoulder when he finished taming Seren's curls into three thick braids that fell to Seren's mid back.

"Thank you," Seren said.

"Nnnggh." The noise came from the Kormandi king. Seren watched his brows bunch together as he rolled on the bed, eyes fluttering open slowly. Jax looked at Idris with concern. They'd expected him to rest longer. To be honest, Seren had too.

Consciousness did not return quickly, especially from the things the Hunters used. Their methods were brutal and lethal. Seren had seen their cruelty first hand, suffering through it with the others who could not be saved.

Idris sighed, tossing the broken comb to the desk with a loud 'thunk' that made Seren jump.

"Sorry," Idris said as he moved to the bed where the king lay. Demyan continued to groan until his eyes finally lifted heavily off his eyes. Idris waited, watching the king work his way back to consciousness.

"Aeron..." Demyan muttered in a dry rasp.

"He is not here, *mes amis*," Idris said. "But we can get you to him *after* you rest some. You took a big hit from those Hunters."

Demyan frowned slightly but nodded and drifted back to a restless sleep that was more in line with what the Hunters' poisons did to a person. Seren remained silent, observant of the young king, of his protector and the assassin keeping them all together.

***

Marie kept a tight grip on the Kormandi queen's hand as she wove her way through the busy side streets and alleys of Grolly. The girl was instructed to keep her hood up and head down. Everyone in Grolly knew Marie, but if anyone even whispered about the queen of Kormaine, the gossip chains would spread through the streets like wildfire in a dry field. She needed supplies, a moment to think without intruding mothers, and a safer haven than the Chateau or even Grolly itself.

"Come," Marie said once they reached their destination. "We'll be safe here."

"For how long?" Kendal asked while Marie unlocked five different locks. Idris could be a little paranoid. "Where are we?"

"My brother's apartment. Maybe you'll wanna hold your nose," Marie warned. She had reason. The stench of stale wine and sex hit her nose first, followed by the natural musk of a man.

"Oof! Lady's stars, no offense to your brother, but don't he got soap or something?" the queen said, letting her accent slip into a longer, less refined drawl than normal. The woman was of humble roots. Marie's did the same from time to time, the drawl of the Damaskhans more nasally than that of the Itahli.

"Only when I remind him," Marie gigged. "I'm sorry, *cherie*, but it's the safest place for you to be right now."

"Stars above..." the woman said, fanning her nose, stepping in. "I may thank him for his help by cleaning."

Marie giggled again, glad to hear the sound echoed in the queen. The Hunters had charged through Amadour right as Marie and Kendal made it to the Port Circle. It was only a matter of time before they learned where the women had gone.

"They're still lookin' for us, aren't they?" Kendal finally asked. Marie paused, her hand on one of the many go-bags her brother kept. She sighed and nodded, turning to face Kendal.

"*Oui*. It's what Hunters do. They hunt. You didn't know, did you?" Kendal shook her head. Marie continued. "Does anyone in Itahl know?"

"It isn't what we're taught," Kendal explained. "Why would we know?" Marie nodded this time. "Where will we go?"

"Where all lost ones go, *cherie*," Marie grinned. "To Tierra Vida."

Chapter Fifteen

The cavern echoed from all directions. It was unsettling to Xandrix. Perhaps, at one time in his life it might have been comforting, but he left the undercities when he was still a child, barely fifteen summers gone. The man that helped him stood beside him once more, frowning at the pool of sapphire blue. It took up most of the space in the cavern. To call it a cavern seemed inadequate. The walls were intricately carved into buildings, homes, alcoves, shops. The pool was the centerpiece of the town square leading to a place of worship as intricately carved as the ones on the surface that had been grown from the marble beneath the ground.

Xandrix dared to take a step forward, feeling inadequate. After all he'd done to spare Taelon the pain of Corruption, it had happened anyway. The bitch had done it in the Dream Realm, letting it seep through Taelon's soul until he turned in the waking world as well.

"We're going to find her, Xan. We'll find the

bitch, too, and tear her apart," Taelon said, startling Xandrix. Had he heard his thoughts? "You think loud. Most people do."

Xandrix gave the man's back a rueful look but averted his eyes and pointedly *stopped* thinking. He was surrounded by too much Power, constantly in the presence of near gods; in this case, literally. Taelon was as highly desired by the Red as the Speakers were. The cursed dragon wanted control of Power. What better way to do so than by capturing the God of Power's son?

"Daemodan wants us to find Jaysen," Xandrix said instead. He'd been surprised to find Taelon with Daemodan in the first place, but chose to ignore it.

"I'm not interested in what Daemodan wants. He hasn't done us any favors. He kept you as a pet, a hunter, and used that boy to hunt others. It's sick. He isn't your commander."

"He's my creator," Xandrix answered. It was automatic. It had been drilled into him from the very first day. Even before the Corruption began, Daemodan made sure to tell all the captors he would be their creator, their liberator. What they were intended to be liberated from, Xandrix still did not know.

Taelon turned around, looking down at Xandrix. The Corrupted fey prince was very tall. Even twisted, his skin had an opalescent shimmer to it. The darkened veins on his hands and arms only made that shimmer stand out more. His eyes were different, more bloodshot and full of rage. Xandrix understood that rage. It came of being a monster. It was rage at what had been done, at being helpless to stop or change what had happened.

"Tormentor," Taelon corrected. "All he did was torment you like that bitch tormented me. And we're going to tear them all apart one by one until the only thing left will be stories of the Red and his spawn and what they *tried* to do. *After* we find Daynali."

Xandrix frowned witj shame. He wanted the same, wanted to rip apart every single demon, every one of the spawn, the Red, everything that had destroyed what he held so dear. Yet, anytime he tried, he felt the burn in his veins that stopped him as if what they had done insured he would never raise a hand to them. It was how he lost Taelon's wife.

"I... can't," Xandrix forced out, as if realizing it for the first time in almost six years. "I..."

"It isn't a request," Taelon scoffed, walking by Xandrix to the small building he'd claimed as his own across from the glowing blue pool at the center courtyard of the undercity. Xandrix looked over his shoulder, feeling a shiver of fear course through him. *Fear*. He'd survived threats, near death, and torment so profound he could not even repeat it with nothing but rage, and *now* he felt fear from the one person he'd worked so hard to protect.

"You failed at keeping her safe," Taelon said, his voice carrying up into the high ceiling of the cavern, bouncing off the stalagmites hanging from above. "Now you get to repay that failure. Find Gannon. He's the one that matters most to them right now."

Xandrix frowned, the shame turning to confusion. "Why?" he dared.

Taelon turned to face him. "He controls the Heart of the Phoenix. Find him. And try not to fail this time. It won't end well for you."

***

Roth looked at the remains of a manor house in the hills. It was hideous. Burning it had been a kindness. Freezing the flames seemed like a bit much, but it entertained Malie. Two monsters and a child. There was a joke in there somewhere, but Roth couldn't think of it. Instead, he refocused his attention on Ghost, idly gnawing on someone's bone.

"Found something?" Roth asked. Ghost looked at him, but did not answer. He'd found something. Roth grinned, lifting Malie up onto his shoulders. He stepped over to where Ghost stood and immediately felt it - Power. It was like the sweet, fluffy webbing that evaporated the moment it hit your tongue - elusive but delicious. "What made this, I wonder?"

Ghost studied it as curiously as Roth did, if not more so. He let his senses stretch outward, feeling, smelling, tasting. One scent in particular made him recoil and snarl at the open air. Malie held tighter to his head.

"She was here," Roth hissed.

"Not as easy to find as we thought," a new voice said. Both Roth and Ghost whirled, expecting a fight. Instead, Roth groaned.

"Oh it's just you, Nasty Pants. Where have you been?" Roth asked when he saw Xandrix. He didn't know the sparkly man with him and didn't particularly care.

"What are you wearing?" Xandrix asked. Roth looked at himself. He wore a loose gown made of linen and colorful sashes of silk.

"Why? Do you like it? You may borrow it if you pro-"

"On your head," Xandrix interrupted. All attention went to Malie, who wiggled her little toes at Roth's mostly bare chest where the scarred, black remnants of a tattoo could be seen.

"Oh, that's Malie. You can't eat her. She's mine," Roth explained. "Say hullo to Nasty Pants, Malie. Who's your sparkly friend, Nasty Pants?"

Malie waved. Xandrix palmed his face. "This is Taelon, you idiot. You *know* him."

"I think I'd remember someone that glitters so nicely, sir. Also, I don't care much for his name. May I call you Sparkles?" Taelon frowned at him. Malie giggled. "Man of few words. You'll get on nicely with Ghost. Have you seen my Moppet, Sparkles? He's fragile, you see."

"The boy without color?" Sparkles asked Xandrix.

"Yes. Jaysen," Xandrix said. "He's in Tierra Vida with the prince."

"Life dirt," Roth translated automatically, wrinkling his nose in disgust. "I don't care for that either."

"Enough, Danyel," Sparkles sighed. The name made Roth shiver. It was familiar, but hidden behind a veil of thick smoke. He felt that veil part slightly, the smoke curling along the edges of his memory.

"Why did you call me that?" Roth asked in a soft, curious tone.

"Because that's your name."

"No… I don't care for it," Roth whispered, taking a step back. "Ghost, we need to find my Moppet…"

"Danyel," Sparkles sighed again. Roth knew him. He felt that pain in his chest again, like he had before.

"No," he croaked, holding tightly to Malie's legs. "I don't care for it. I don't… I waited for you. You never came. You… left me. Why didn't you come?"

"I couldn't. They had me too. We're going to make them pay, Danyel. I promise," *Taelon* snarled. Roth nodded.

"Yes. Good. That's good, Sparkles. I'll help you. Ghost too, and his confused creature, and Phier, and my Moppet. Have you seen him? He's fragile, you see."

"Tierra Vida," Sparkles said as he took Malie off Roth's shoulders, relieving the girl of the claws around her thin legs. "Take Ghost. Go get him. Come back to Daemodan's manse. We'll be there."

Roth looked at Malie, then Sparkles. "She's not for eating."

"No, not for eating. I promise. Go."

Roth nodded, then felt around for that sweet elusive Power again until he found the smallest thread, letting that pull him and Ghost along to the place of Life's Dirt.

***

Cavian let his head bounce lightly against the cool marble wall behind him. He repeated the gesture ad nauseum while staring at the top of his makeshift prison.

"Sword of Fate, ever heard of it?" he asked as someone walked by. Boredom set in quickly. Too quickly. No one answered him anyway. "Sword of Fate ever -"

"Do you ever stop?" His guard asked. It was a duende man who spoke more like a tirsai.

"Not usually."

"Don't give him the time of day, Maddy," Cavian's new favorite creature said as she came to relieve the guard.

"You sure you're OK with him?" 'Maddy' asked. She nodded. When they were alone, Cavian smiled.

"Missed me that much, flower?"

"Oh, shut yet trap," his little snap dragon said. "Here, eat somethin'."

She shoved a bowl of milky-looking water at him, sloshing some of the contents out of the bowl. Cavian smirked.

"I can't drink my gruel if you spill all of it, flower," he purred at her. She'd stopped glowering and moved on to flat glares. He was making progress.

Much to her great dismay, he was sure, she was put in charge of his watch. The only other one to come by was the duende with odd speech patterns. They looked similar.

'Maddy' was only mildly interesting. *She* made him smile, so unwilling to indulge him. A stone holding fast against the surrounding rapids. Cavian merely needed time. Eventually, all stones wore down.

"Do I really disgust you, flower? Or do you just *think* I disgust you?"

"Yer a demon," she replied, as if that were answer enough. His smile broadened.

"Actually, I'm not," Cavian said. "Don't let appearances fool you. My father may have passed some unfortunate genetics my way, but my mother was olven. Tirsai to be exact."

The look of shock always amused Cavian. he knew what he looked like, knew the associations he carried. He used those things to his advantage. It was still entertaining to see the reactions.

"Did he rape her?!"

Cavian gave mock offense. "Don't be crass, flower. My father may be a lunatic of monstrous proportions, but he loved my mother. And she him. Willingly gave him three children before she died."

"Don't ya lie-"

"I've not lied to you once, flower. Why would I start now? For attention?" Cavian scoffed. "I'm bored, flower, not melodramatic, no matter what my brother says."

She snorted at him. He smiled then felt his hackles rise. She noticed when he shivered and shifted his shoulders. "What?"

"I don't know. I don't like it. Take these off me," he said, shoving his hands at her. It was her turn to scoff.

"I'm not doin' that. Yer real funny-"

"And I'm not playing around, woman. Something isn't right. Take. These. Off," Cavian growled, baring teeth at her. The air tingled, making the hairs on his arms stand on end. It did the same to her, for she looked at her arm, then over her shoulder when someone cried out in alarm.

"I swear on my mother's grave, flower, I will not harm you or let anything else harm you. Please!" Cavian pleaded, again shoving his hands towards her. He could see the debate on her face, the fear and worry when one cry turned to two, then three, then four...

"Move," she finally said, unlocking the iron bars and pushing them in, locking them again after she'd entered his prison.

"What are-" he began, cutting off when she put her fingers on the ivory binders, releasing them from around his wrists. A rush of Power flooded him, making him momentarily unsteady. "Come on. If ya turn on me, I'll feckin' kill ya."

As soon as she touched him, he felt a thrill race through him.

"Says the fabulously delicate creature that just locked us in."

"Shut up!" she hissed, pulling him to one of the dull little alcoves. She pressed in on a worn name plaque, opening a hidden passage that lead further into the Necropolis.

"You said you weren't one of the Dead Keepers."

"I didn't *say* nothin', and I'm not one. I just know how t'pay attention."

"I think I may just be falling in love with you, flower," Cavian teased, getting in a good look at her bottom as he crawled into the opening after her, before she kicked him in the face for his wandering gaze. It was absolutely worth the pain.

***

Madhavi moved quietly through the blanket of whirling stars around her. She rarely hunted in the waking world. Her strength lay within Yira's embrace, among the tumultuous stars that called to her. She found her prey there, whirling and flickering in fast beats.

A peek into the fallen prince's dream nearly sent Madhavi crashing into a nightmare composed of razor sharp pieces all coalescing into an amalgam of fear, confusion, and loss.

Madhavi pulled back to the safety of her starting point with a click of her tongue. A sleek black cat rubbed against her leg. Mr. Pads always greeted her. He was a staple of the cozy room that smelled of tea leaves and cookies.

"Well, that's going to cause problems," Madhavi said aloud. No one answered, but she was used to that. It would be far more difficult to eliminate the fallen prince in the waking world.

Rather than linger where nothing could be accomplished, Madhavi woke, eyes opening to a dense forest. She did not need full sleep to manipulate Yira's Realm, like others did.

"Certainly explains a few things," Madhavi said to herself as she stood to her full height and stretched. Her wings fluffed out and her back arched; it was a glorious feeling.

"Napping, demon spawn?"

Madhavi sighed, letting the stretch go with a heavy sigh. Maeve stood behind her. They'd planned to meet later, in the evening when it was easier to hide from prying eyes.

"You've not made progress on your side of our bargain," Maeve intoned. She was not happy - - or patient.

"And you, pet, have an absurd demand if you expect it done in two short days," Madhavi purred. "What's changed?"

Maeve nearly snarled, "The Esbethi are here."

Chapter Sixteen

A coterie of avian soldiers stood with three people that made Reven arch a brow. Two were women, the third a man with black wings. Reven had never seen such coloring on an avian before. The two women appeared to be related. One had silver wings and hair, the other a wing color akin to storm clouds in the sky with silver flecks. Kaleo looked as if he might vomit or bring down holy fire upon their heads. To his credit, Aeron had the same face - a cross between rage and nausea that confused the bard a great deal. But it was no longer to Aeron that the people looked. Nadya had made quick work of landing Reven on the throne, much to Aeron's gross upset. So, Reven did what any bard would do - he pretended and looked at their visitors with a smile that slowly faded.

"Hey," Gannon said softly. "You coming?"

"No," Noelani sighed dramatically, fanning herself, *silver wings catching the festival lights just so.* "I think I'll just go back home."

"Home… to Joricho?" Gannon asked, glancing at

the others that were moving further and further away without noticing their absence. Noelani glared at him and turned away, heading back towards the palace instead of toward the festival.

"Why would I go home to Joricho, Gannon? There's no one there. I'm here because mother and father are still away. Just... go have fun."

"Reven?" Serai asked, squeezing his hand. He sucked in a breath, blinking the memory away while trying not to gasp. He knew her, the woman with silver wings.

"I'm fine," he whispered, without any conviction in his words whatsoever. Serai noticed. "I'm fine, Serai."

"It's good to see you safe, highness," the man with black wings stated as he stepped in front of the two women. Kaleo stepped forward, lining up with Reven and Serai. Aeron tried to shoulder in too, but Nadya held him one step behind Reven, making the boy pout like an insolent child.

"Which one?" Aeron dared. Everyone looked at the brat he made himself out to be; Reven hid a smirk and gave him a quick glance.

Aeron muttered something about *his* throne and looked at his feet after that, however. Until, of course, the woman with the storm-gray wings shouldered her way forward.

"Where is he?" the woman demanded.

"Good to see you too, Captain Caelestis?" Kaleo retorted in a lazy tone that made Reven smirk more. His 'children' were full of some kind of sass all of a sudden. As interesting as the interchange was, the man with black wings caught Reven's attention the most. He radiated Power like a sun, blinding and strong.

He is a Speaker, Beloved, Azure said. *Like you. The Esbethi call him their Anointed One.*

Kaleo is the same. Did they call him anointed too? Reven asked, eyes narrowing some.

I don't think they knew, Beloved. He had not been Claimed when the Empire fell. Not even you knew.

"The bard, you little bastard!" the woman with the storm-gray wings growled. "Hand over the bard!"

Her hand rested on the pommel of her weapon, ready to draw. The other soldiers copied her motions. It brought fear and wariness from the others gathered. Reven felt it as keenly as he felt his own anxiety.

"Stop," the black-winged man said. "That isn't why we're here, Tondra."

"Then why are you here-" Reven started with a minor pause and glance at Kaleo.

"Anao. Kalelako Anao," Kaleo whispered.

"Lord Anao," Reven finished. Kalelako grinned. The woman with the silver wings frowned, however, taking Kalelako's hand as she watched Reven closely.

"Emissary from the Amatta," Kalelako explained. Not that it offered much of an explanation, but Reven kept that to himself. He focused on the woman with silver wings, the one that still ran through his memory at various points.

"Is there a problem, Kal?" Kaleo asked.

"No. Well... potentially," he replied, then focused on Reven. "You don't know us, do you?"

"I don't know," Reven answered honestly. "I feel like I should, but... Sorry, I have manners somewhere. Reven Si'ahl, master bard, junior thief-taker, and heir apparent, it seems. And you are, m'lady?"

"Si'ahl?" the woman with the silver wings said, stepping forward now. Reven regarded her, eyes narrowing.

"Yes," he said, with a quick glance at Kaleo, who moved closer to the bard's side. "I... *do* know you, don't I?"

"Noelani," Kaleo said quietly. Reven inclined his head toward the boy and nodded. His wife. Or, *ex*-wife. Or something. Kaleo's *step*-mother, as he was always so quick to correct. She was stunning.

"Of course you know me, Gannon. I don't know what Kaleo's been filling your head with, but he went through great effort to retrieve you from our holding cells," Noelani stated. Reven snapped his fingers at Kalelako in sudden recognition.

"That's where I know you - you were in there with me," Reven exclaimed happily. "See, I'm not a total loss."

Kaleo merely shook his head and sighed. Reven took the small wins where he could get them.

"This isn't a joke, Gannon," Noelani continued. Reven nodded while glancing at his feet before looking at this radiant creature with the personality of a field of nettles.

"I'm not trying to turn it into one, your gr-"

"Where were you born?" Noelani cut in, drawing Reven's full, undivided attention back to her. She was going to be a handful.

"I don't know. I know who you *think* I am. Unfortunately, I have to inform you I am not *that* man. That man is gone. The pieces that made him have all shattered, much to the dismay of many, I'm sure. I hope you haven't come all this way just for me. That didn't go so well for you last time."

Noelani's eyes widened, her wings bristling. The woman with the storm-gray wings tightened her hold on the handle of her sword.

"Rumor travels quickly, your grace. And, since my *last* home was so rudely destroyed by whoever this witch of a woman with the sword is, I've claimed a tent in this Grove, instead. Please, don't destroy this one too. It wouldn't be fair to the innocent people watching right now to ruin *their* home just to get to me. There are other ways to get my attention."

The look he gave her flushed her cheeks a bright crimson and made him smirk. Serai squeezed his hand so tight he grunted and looked down at her, noting the mild frown on her face. Kaleo and Aeron, however, smirked as much as Reven did. Even the Baron and Navid hid mild amusement.

"Kal," Noelani whispered. The Anointed One nodded and stepped forward toward Reven. Kaleo and Aeron stepped in front of the bard.

"I'm just checking, 'Leo," Kalelako said. "I was doing the same thing when you ... attacked us in the holding cells. That's part of why I'm here."

"I put her to sleep and drugged you, Kal. It was hardly an attack," Kaleo countered.

"Yes, but 'attack' is easier to say than all of that," Kalelako sighed, wilting so that his wings sagged to the damp sand where everyone congregated. Reven had to bite his lip to keep from laughing. "I promise, no tricks. The Amatta wants assurances, not rumors. It matters, Kaleo. You know that."

Kaleo sighed, shifting his feet in the sand. He glanced at Reven first, then Navid, who nodded. Only then did Kaleo step aside with a look of apology directed at Reven. The bard met it with one of understanding.

"I will apologize in advance for any discomfort, highness," Kalelako said. "Is that your preferred title still?"

"Was it ever?" Reven retorted. Kal grinned. "The mean one too - what's her name?"

The man smiled. "Tondra. She's mean to everyone. And you're free to call me Kal, Master Si'ahl."

*"Kal taught me. He's not so bad. He's a better parent than she is. Not nearly as crabby **or** paranoid."*

"So she wears the pants, and he's the comforting mother?" Reven teased. *The boy laughed and nodded, taking a drink of the spiced wine the bard offered. The performance had gone well, bringing women and money to their door well until morning. The boy was adapting quickly to the life of a vagabond. It suited him.*

Reven gasped at the *new* memory and looked at Kalelako, taking a step back.

"You... helped him," Reven said. "He speaks of you like... like a father."

It *hurt* for Reven to say that, to know that the man that stood before him had taken a position that should belong to Reven. Kaleo looked at him as did Serai, both flanking either side of him again. Kalelako looked at Kaleo too, then down at the sand.

"I never meant to replace you. Only to be a friend to your children when they needed it."

Reven felt tears welling in his eyes, chest tightening with grief. It was a painful mourning of things he could not get back, years lost to ... what? Madness? Mental instability?

Power.

The answer did not come from Azure but from an equally familiar voice. Argento. He'd said it was too much Power that shattered his mind, that robbed him of a life lived for so long, that forced him to rebuild a new one.

"I'm sorry," Kalelako said, stepping back without touching Reven at all. "It's him."

"You didn't even-" Noelani began.

"I didn't need to. It's him."

Tondra moved forward at that point as if to arrest Reven; again. Kaleo and Serai blocked her path. The woman sneered at them, nostrils flaring and wings rising up in a posture of power.

"I believe Kal," Reven began, absently rubbing

his brow while he forced himself to remain steady. "Said you were here as an emissary, not brute force. Unless you have charges to levy against me, I suggest you stand down, *Tondra*," Reven said with enough of a threat in his voice to drop the woman's wings a few inches.

"I *do* have charges against Kaleo," Tondra sneered.

"I will singe you on the spot," Kaleo growled. He filled himself with Power. Reven felt it and sighed, putting a hand on Kaleo's shoulder.

"You have no authority-" Tondra began only to be cut off.

"No," Reven said, stepping forward again. "But I do. Now, if you don't have anything *useful* to add to whatever this is, then go stand over there or you'll have a new reason for chasing him down when I *encourage* him call a storm down on your head and anyone that happens to be unlucky enough to stand beside you. Kindly shut your trap."

Tondra growled, making as if to attack or fly or something, when Kalelako stopped her.

"The Amaterasu apologizes for any insult and for its inaction in the past. We've come to rectify that. Please. Our nations aren't enemies and we have a lot to catch up on."

***

Kaleo lay within the field of vibrant poppies beside Jaysen. They stared at the endless blue sky above them. It still seemed to hold stars within Yira's Realm as if she were constantly reminding them of her presence. Kaleo told Jaysen what was happening at the Grove, about the duende and the Esbethi - his step-mother and her annoyances. It altered Jaysen's attitude oddly to hear what Kaleo had to say, made him more sullen, so Kaleo simply stopped talking and let his friend sulk.

"How are you feeling?" Kaleo finally asked when he could no longer stand the silence. Jaysen shrugged.

"Tired," he croaked out. The boy never spoke in much more than a whisper as it was, his voice naturally gritty and rough like sandpaper. "Lost. Empty."

Kaleo's heart broke for his friend. He felt partially to blame for what happened to Tanis. He should not have been in Kormaine, should not have run off like he had to play hero without a plan. It was not just Jaysen who'd lost or been injured. Reven had too and then lost his house. Aeron had *died.* Demyan was somewhere in Itahl now. All for what? A child's promise?

"I'm sorry," Kaleo finally said.

"Why?" Jaysen asked, still staring at the sky above them. "You didn't kill her. You didn't stab me."

"It wouldn't have happened if you hadn't... if you hadn't tried to help me. Thanks for that, by the way."

Jaysen fell silent again. Kaleo knew they did not need to talk, but the silence between them was uncomfortable. They used to be content in silence, sitting in each other's company without a single word spoken through their entire meeting. But, this time, there seemed to be something else in that silence that Kaleo could not place, helping him stamp down that rush of embarrassment before Jaysen caught on to it.

"How long will you stay here?" Jaysen sighed.

"I don't know. The Baron's scouts have found a haunted castle on the north shore that we might be able to use. People keep asking when we're going home."

"You don't have a home," Jaysen pointed out. Kaleo frowned, turning to look at Jaysen now rather than the sky. "You don't. We took it."

"Did you?" Kaleo finally asked. "I mean, did

you, personally, have anything to do with what happened in my home? Did you even know?" Jaysen remained quiet.

"You knew?" Kaleo dared, his voice cracking with a sudden rise in emotion. "How... why? Why would you do that?"

"I didn't know that's where you lived, Kaleo."

"Yes, you did! I told you! A lot! Because any time I ever asked you where *you* lived, all you'd tell me is 'somewhere hot'!"

Kaleo's palms sweat with the sudden fury he felt, his face growing hot and throat tightening with every word he barked. The sky above roiled with that anger, changed by it. The blue shifted to a dark, ugly gray that rumbled and roared above them. Kaleo knew how much Jaysen suffered and guessed at what the other boy was forced to do, but that did not reduce the sudden ire and hate for what happened.

"It *was* hot," Jaysen frowned as he sat up, looking up at the sky with a mild glare of annoyance on his face. *Annoyance.*

"You could have warned me, said something, asked for help - anything!"

"So you could do what? Tell your father? He was one of things we were after. You wouldn't have been able to stop them, anyway. You can't save the world, Kaleo. Stop trying."

"If I stopped trying, you'd be dead in a city of ice and ashes by now!" Kaleo barked, rising to his feet. "Did you send them to Kormaine too? Is that why you were there? To ... you were looking for Demyan, weren't you?!"

Jaysen remained passive, glancing at Kaleo with not a hint of remorse on his face. Lightning lanced across the sky, striking down hard near Jaysen.

"Don't!" Jaysen growled. His own Power surfaced, ready to let loose. Kaleo felt it as pointedly as he felt his own. It only enraged the young avian further.

"Or what! You'll kill me too, like you killed everyone else!"

"*I* didn't kill anyone!" Jaysen argued.

"But you sent them there! You may as well have been the one to cut them down!"

Another bolt struck the fields, searing the poppies to ash. It created a heady tonic on the air that made Kaleo's rage grow even more. "You're supposed to be my friend! What if they'd gotten to me too! Or worse! Would it have even bothered you!"

"I made sure you were safe!"

"Would it have mattered?!" Kaleo demanded, losing his balance when the entire Poppy Fields lurched. A fissure raced across the earth, making Kaleo bring his hands to his ears as it tore the fields apart, waking him in a fit of wild rage.

Chapter Seventeen

The temperature in Tierra Vida was vastly different from the temperature in Kormaine. Kormaine was always cold and a little overcast. Tierra Vida was warmer, more tropical even with all the mismatched pieces of land overlapping each other. Mahala had also been a very sharp change from Kormaine but they'd not been there long. Things had happened so fast with so many dips and turns that Nadya struggled to keep her head about her. Having Gabriel back with her put her mind at ease. Even the bard put her mind at ease despite his lack of memory for anything else.

Then there was Aeron. The young tirsai sat beside Gabriel discussing options for a better settlement. Gabriel sent scouts out the second he'd arrived, most of them coming back with more information about Tierra Vida than even the inhabitants knew. It was what Gabriel was good at. Those scouts brought word of a "haunted" castle. Gabriel didn't believe in ghosts. There had been a point in time when Gabriel had made Nadya's heart flutter, too. Now it was Aeron who did that to her even when he was being a sullen prat.

The sullen Phoenix prince was a miracle she still could not explain. He'd died. She'd felt it, known it in her heart, and heard his sisters sobbing even as she had quietly done the same. They'd begged for a miracle. It was an impossible miracle. But it happened. Nadya *watched* it happen. Every day since he woke, he looked at her in ways that made her face heat up even if *she* had been the one to kiss *him* in Kormaine. Nothing had happened since. Perhaps it was for the best, yet she yearned for it all the same. As it was, there was no reason to remain in his orbit outside of her own yearning heart anymore, anyway; *Aeron* was no longer a contender for the throne.

"If this castle your scouts found isn't inhabited, it would be the best place to take everyone. Easily defensible, I would think. Unless it's crawling with oddities you haven't mentioned," Aeron said to Gabriel. Reven still had Aeron discussing things with Gabriel, especially when it was clear the bard needed a break from the overwhelming activities of the Grove; or just to help Aeron learn. While the bard agreed to Nadya's push to have *him* sit on the phoenix throne, Reven made it clear it was only until *Aeron* gained the experience needed to do so himself.

Gabriel was about to answer Aeron's question when Kaleo walked by in a fit state that slapped Nadya in the face. By the frown on Aeron's face, it struck him too. The young avian was radiating rage like fire. "Hey, what's got your knickers in a twist?"

"Fuck off, Aeron," Kaleo growled, walked a few steps more, then rounded on the tirsai prince. "Did you know Jaysen was *sent* to find Mikhael and my father and all the others they've caught! He *knew*!"

Nadya blinked, feeling her stomach tighten as she sorted that out slowly. Jaysen was the boy Kaleo saved. Corrupted but not evil. Or so Kaleo had said. He didn't *seem* evil, just unfortunate.

Aeron sighed, looking up at his cousin as if Kaleo were the biggest doofus in the world. "I'm not sure why you expected someone that looks like *that* to be an innocent in all of this. He was in the catacombs, Kaleo. I saw him. With the other one and Xan."

Nadya didn't want to think about what had happened in the catacombs. Jaysen *had* been there. The other one, the one that said she was soft, sent that monstrous bird after them, too.

"It changes them," the Baron said, not at all bothered by Kaleo's mood or the interruption in the planning. "It brings out the monster deep inside. Some monsters are worse than others."

Nadya watched the rage slowly seep out of Kaleo. It was early. Most people still slept and now that the rage wasn't fueling him, Nadya could see the exhaustion in Kaleo's face. Exhaustion and defeat.

"I thought he was my friend," Kaleo said as he flopped to the sandy grass across from Nadya. "I've known him forever. Why couldn't he just… warn me or something?"

"The outcome would not have changed. You are the bastard of a lunatic. No one believed your father. They would not have believed you either," the Baron said. Nadya flushed on Kaleo's behalf, embarrassed by the words Gabriel used. Gabriel did not seem to notice and always spoke plainly, even if the words were harsh and difficult to hear.

Gannon Oenel *knew* the demons were coming. He'd Seen it many times, tried to warn his people. When they didn't listen, he warned the duende and the Kormandi instead. Both peoples lasted much longer than the tirsai. Knowing that the tirsai were arrogant enough to call the former prince a lunatic or worse, seeing what it brought them to, set a pit of rage in *her* gut but shame as well. She did not know Gannon Oenel *well*, but he did not seem the type to conjure wild fancies or tell tall tales for attention. She wondered what might have changed if they'd just listened.

"You want to put your rage into something, nebit, put it into helping us figure out where to take everyone," Aeron said. Kaleo frowned at him for the nickname. Nadya hid her smirk. "Or what to do with your cursed step-mother. Those are the options our glorious *king* gave me."

"What is Noe doing now?" Kaleo asked, pulling up blades of grass so his rage had somewhere to go.

"Making camp to the east of us," Rielle said as she and her twin sister, Eila, joined them, each flanking Kaleo. "I vote the castle."

"The plains, easier to grow things," Eila said. Rielle rolled her eyes.

"The centaurs have the plains, Eila."

"Shut up, Rielle."

"Both of you shut up," Aeron grumbled. His sisters annoyed him, as all siblings did. Nadya knew she annoyed Mikhael. It made her miss her brother a great deal.

"You asked," the girls said in unison. It was odd the way they spoke in unison, but it made Nadya smile. They were nearly equal in age to her and not afraid to face any challenge head on. She admired them.

"A broken castle is better than tents. There may be more resources there, a port to start bringing in supplies from Damaskha or Esbeth - especially if they really are willing to help," Nadya offered in agreement with Rielle and Gabriel. "Maybe, Kaleo, you could speak to your mother-"

"*Step*-mother," Kaleo corrected. Nadya merely

nodded. Rielle and Eila shoved him in each shoulder. "Ow! What was that for?"

"Being a prat," Aeron said. "That woman has been part of your life since you were born, idiot. She may have questionable personality traits, but she is the closest thing you have to an actual mother."

"Well, *she* doesn't listen to me either," Kaleo grumbled as he stood up again and stomped off. Nadya watched him for a while, looked at the coloring of his hair and wings against the olive of his skin. Before Demyan appeared, Mikhael had discussed arrangements to marry her to the Empire. Kaleo had been one of the options. Instead, Nadya was given to the Empire's High Lord Speaker, a man with a cruel streak darker than pitch. She thanked all the gods that she did not have to see that union come to light, even if she also prayed that his soul had found peace. Now she glanced at Aeron, her heart swelling for *him* instead, and watched the Phoenix prince glower at Kaleo's retreating back.

"What's got him all tizzied?" Rielle asked.

"He fighting with Lara? I like her," Eila added.

"Fighting with his boyfriend," Aeron grumbled.

"Oh," both girls said, neither one interested in that drama. Nadya frowned at Aeron for his comment. He simply looked at her and shrugged.

"I know a lot of things about my cousin. He's not as innocent as he looks. He's just dumb and emotional," Aeron said. The twins giggled. "Anyway, the castle it is then." He paused, then looked at Nadya with a smirk. "Care for a stroll, princess?"

"I will find Navid," the Baron said with a grunt as he got to his feet and left the children to their own devices.

***

Spray off the sea drifted to a small cove hidden away from Yira's Grove. It was near enough to hear the voices and clamor of people trying to eke out a survival, but not so close as to allow anyone to happen upon it by accident. Jaysen lifted himself off the pallette of blankets upon which he rested, feeling an odd rage that was overpowered with an even stranger sense of grief. Fionn remained behind him, which made that grief even worse. It gnawed at him like hunger, twisting his intestines until he thought he might be sick. He simply laid a hand on his already sore stomach and shut his eyes, brows furrowing as a few stray tears fell down his cheeks.

"Are you alright?"

Jaysen gasped, sitting up sharply only to groan, mouth hanging open as the pain he felt raced through his body. The wound Xandrix gave him continued to heal too slowly for his own good. He should be dead and now *wanted* to be if only to stop the pain he felt.

"I didn't mean to startle you. I'd have thought you'd hear me. Kaleo says you're usually pretty good about that."

The person who spoke stepped closer, their footfalls reaching Jaysen's other senses. Small tremors in the sand, the crunch of each grain beneath crinkling leather soles. He could smell lilac and honey, and something else that had his mouth watering - meat.

"Who are you?" he snarled, hand still resting lightly on his sore belly as he forced himself to relax slightly.

"Eila," she said. The name was familiar. Kaleo mentioned her and another. The twins, he called them. They looked the same from what Kaleo said, making it difficult to tell them apart.

"Where's the other one?" Jaysen said, feeling his eyes move as if to search for the one he knew must be nearby.

"The other what?" Eila asked. Jaysen sneered at her. "Do you mean Rielle? She's not here, she's back in the Grove helping our uncle. We caught a boar. Thought you might like some. I'm not really sure what Kaleo is bringing you - if he's bringing anything at all."

Jaysen didn't answer, smelling the meat while trying not to salivate like an animal. It was raw. Eila came closer, sitting across from him.

"Put out your hand," she instructed. She sounded young, yet oddly wise too. Jaysen held out his hand while he puzzled out this new nuisance to his cove. She placed the hunk of meat in his hand. It weighed him down, forcing him to use two hands. "He says you don't really like it cooked, so I didn't bother with it."

Jaysen didn't answer, bringing the raw meat to his lips, ripping off a large chunk of it without any preamble. Eila remained.

"Why aren't you like the others?" Eila asked. Jaysen didn't answer, chewing slowly in hopes that she might leave him alone. She didn't. "What makes you different? Why aren't you crazy or murderous like the others who turn?"

"Who says I'm not?" Jaysen grumbled as he tore the warm, bloody flesh in his hands apart. The smell of it created a heady tonic for him.

"Well, because Kaleo risked his life for you, for one. And he's rather upset over whatever you two fought over just now."

Jaysen didn't say anything, chewing slower as he mulled that over.

"Is it true that you sent them to us?" Eila asked, clearly overhearing whatever Kaleo was complaining about. Jaysen growled.

"Do you ever stop talking?"

"Not really," Eila said. "Does it bother you?"

"*You* bother me," Jaysen growled. She giggled. He sneered again, shoving the last of the meat into his mouth.

"You've got the manners of a pig. Hasn't anyone taught you to eat without getting it all over yourself?" she asked as he swiped the back of his hand across his mouth. "Here, stay still."

He frowned, jerking away when he felt her soft touch against his face.

"You've got blood all over you. Just stay still a minute so I can wipe it off. It's not like I can give you a mirror for you to do it on your own, now can I?"

"Why do you care?" Jaysen said. He refused to let her touch him.

"Why don't you? You're not a bad looker, but I would hazard to say that blood-soaked isn't really adding anything to your appeal."

Jaysen blinked, recalling the word that Kaleo had used when he'd changed Jaysen's appearance.

"What does that mean?" Jaysen dared.

"What does what mean?" Eila countered, taking his hand instead to put a soft rag in it before he could pull it away. "So you can wipe your *own* face."

Jaysen did so, trying to sort Eila out. "Looker. What does it mean?"

"Oh. It means you're nice to look at." Jaysen frowned at her. She giggled again. "No one's ever said that to you?"

"Kaleo did."

"That's it? No one else has ever said you look nice?" Eila asked. "Well, that hardly counts. Kaleo would go with a pig if it had a proper hole."

Jaysen arched a brow. Eila clarified. "It means he's got very low standards when it comes to partners and doesn't seem to have a preference either - though he seems attached to Lara. I like her. She's good for him."

"She's annoying too."

"Is everyone annoying or is it just that you like to pretend you hate life?"

Jaysen frowned, rolling away from her.

"You were crying earlier. You don't hate life that much or this fight wouldn't bother you so much."

"Go away," Jaysen snarled.

"I could. But I'm not really interested in sorting through the junk uncle got in the new trunk he procured. It's old and everything smells inside it. I don't want to help cook either. And you don't really *want* to be alone, do you? You just want me to think you do."

Jaysen buried himself deeper into Fionn's side.

"What did you fight over? Just that you sent the demons to us?"

"I didn't know he was there," Jaysen barked. Eila remained silent. "I didn't know…"

The hurt in Jaysen's chest made his face pinch up. The girl said nothing, but he knew she was still there. He could smell her, feel the heat of her body sitting too close to him. Then she did the most absurd thing anyone had ever done: she put her hand over his and gave it a small squeeze. It was the only time someone had touched him and not immediately made him recoil.

"I didn't know," Jaysen repeated quietly, feeling that misery well up inside him that made him want to walk into the sea and never return.

Chapter Eighteen

Reven pulled at the high collar on the tunic Ajana had found for him to wear. When he questioned why he needed it, she claimed it was so he would look less like a vagabond when he went to speak to his ex. Or wife. Or... Reven wasn't too sure on the formalities of his relationships anymore. Everything was a mottled mess in his mind anyhow.

Not more than an hour after the emissary's arrival, the *amatessa* sent an invitation to join her for tea - alone. If it had been any other woman, Reven would have ignored the invitation - or else charged a handsome price for his time. Kaleo said he could not do that this time and encouraged the bard to speak with his ex-wife. Serai was not as encouraging, frowning at the suggestion before storming off. Jealousy did not look good on his mysterious cave woman.

"Stop fidgeting," Kaleo said. "You're having tea, not going for your execution."

"I was married to her," Reven said.

"Yes," Kaleo answered from the overturned

crate he sat on. The furnishings around the Grove were meager but growing. Pallets of blankets had become mattresses, a mishmash of chairs gathered around a table missing one leg - discarded things from the local communities that the people of the Grove now guarded as treasures. The things the bard had collected were commodities he put a high value on - one being a trunk of new belongings, the other being an actual bed for him and Serai to sleep on even if it was beneath a canvas tent.

"I have a daughter with her," Reven continued.

"Yes," Kaleo repeated. He stood, moving to Reven's trunk. He pulled a different tunic out, one that had no collar, and sat open to a point just past the chest. "Here. Put that on. You'll be more comfortable and less likely to fidget while you talk to her."

After almost a year with the little avian trouble maker, Reven noticed how tall he was. They were nearly equal in height with Kaleo gaining advantage from wingspan alone.

"She just wants to talk, Reven."

"That's what worries me," Reven admitted. His stomach tightened into a million knots. Kaleo smirked.

"Since when does talking to women bother you?" the boy chortled. Everything smelled of stone and the spray of the sea.

"Since *someone* likes to remind me how awful she is," Reven threw back, snatching the new tunic from Kaleo's hands with a snap. Kaleo sighed.

"She is," Kaleo stated. "She's always been more concerned with status than anything else. She kept me as a kindness. It made her look good - and I helped her take care of L'nae. She paraded around with us like we were prized dogs, not husband and son. You still married her and, from what I could tell, seemed to genuinely love her. Not sure why, but you did."

"You're not helping," Reven grumbled as he tugged the uncomfortable thing Ajana made him wear over his head and replaced it with the one Kaleo found.

"And you're over-thinking it. You don't *have* to remember her. None of it matters anyway. You didn't remember me - you still kept me around because you liked how I played, not because you felt any responsibility for me. You don't have any responsibility to her either."

"We have a child, Kaleo," Reven repeated.

"Who's never met you and you knew nothing about even *before* you 'died'."

Reven huffed, letting the laces of the new tunic hang loose. Already he felt better, less likely to choke on his own spit.

"It's just a conversation, not a commitment. Serai might cut it off if you tried to get back with Noe, anyway."

"Still not helping, urchin," Reven said, snatching up a thin leather thong to tie back his growing, unruly hair as he left the tent. Blessedly, Kaleo remained behind. Reven didn't want to think of his son - *either* of them - *or* his daughters. He didn't want to think about Serai either. Of course, thinking about his ex-wife didn't help settle his churning stomach any more than the other potential subjects of focus, so he opted to empty his mind, steps slowing when he reached the small tea setting on the shore where he was to meet the amatessa.

The woman was a breathtaking sight to behold. Sun-kissed skin sat against a sea of shining silver feathers and long tresses of the same color. Her eyes were a vibrant silver-gray. She sat in a chair that sank slightly into the sand, back straight, with a setting of tea on a barrel beside her. The other 'chair' was another crate like the one Kaleo had been sitting on in Reven's tent.

"Hullo," Reven croaked as he moved within her periphery. She turned to face him, giving him another look up and down like she had on the shore upon the Esbethi emissary's arrival. He felt just as small and inadequate as he did then.

"Hello," she finally said, gesturing at the crate across from her. "Please."

Reven moved slowly, sitting gingerly on the crate. He was glad of it when he felt the cursed wood wobble beneath him, threatening to dump him over into the damp sand.

"This must seem strange to you," the amatessa continued.

"What?" Reven asked, feeling like a fool the second the word left his mouth.

"Seeing people you don't remember," she explained. Reven frowned, making the amatessa smirk slightly. "I spoke to Kaleo earlier. He ... filled me in."

That little... Reven thought, but merely vocalized, "Ah," before taking a sip of tea. It was weak and too sweet, but he schooled his facial expressions so as not to be rude to his host.

"Has he told you about L'nae?" she asked. She certainly did not beat around the bush.

Reven nodded, "He has. He said you hadn't known you were pregnant yet when-"

"I didn't, no," the amatessa cut in. "She asks about you sometimes. Kaleo was always filling her head with nonsense."

"She's a child," Reven shrugged. "Isn't that what her head *should* be full of?"

The amatessa arched an eyebrow at him. Clearly, she did not agree.

"My daughter-"

"Our," Reven cut in, feeling emboldened by the dismissive nature of the amatessa.

"What?"

"Our daughter," Reven repeated. The amatessa's lips pursed together.

"She's going to be Amata someday. That's what her head should be filled with," the amatessa sniffed. Reven frowned at her, setting his cup of sweetened leaf-water down.

"Is that what this is about, your grace? Making sure I don't do anything to alter your views of what *our* child should or should not be doing?"

"She has a purpose, Gannon."

"Reven," he corrected. "Gannon is dead."

"You're sitting right in front of me."

"You're right, *I* am," Reven sighed. "But *I* am not your husband, your grace. And, clearly, I'm not the father of your child either."

"No, that's not what I-"

"If it makes you feel any better, I can happily maintain my distance from *your* daughter if *you* maintain your distance from *my* urchin," Reven said as he stood from the crate, letting it tip over from his movements. "Kaleo doesn't have any parents. They're both dead. All he has left is a bard with a spotty memory. Thank you for the tea, your grace."

***

Kaleo moved through his katas at increasing speed. He needed to get the rage out of him so he didn't direct it at someone who didn't deserve it. Which, of course, was when Liam came by.

"Oi, Rev's been lookin' fer ya. Yer runeli girl said ya was out here."

Kaleo took in a deep breath and focused on the lavender waters lapping up onto the warm-sanded shores. He focused on the call of the gulls overhead and the gentle breeze that always seemed prevalent in Tierra Vida. The ocean brought him serenity; the sound of it, the smell of it, the way it moved.

"Oi."

"I heard you, Liam," Kaleo said without stopping. The duende thief-taker snorted. He stood with arms crossed, waiting as if his time were precious in some way. Kaleo merely sighed and brought his routine to an end right as the tiniest boar anyone had ever seen came running right at Kaleo and around his legs in circles.

"The bloody hewls is'at?" Liam grumbled, unfolding his arms as he looked at the boar.

"Little?" Kaleo frowned. He bent to scoop the tiny thing into his arms. He examined the boar just to be sure, feeling his heart sink into his bowels. "Oh, gods…"

"Wha'? Ya know wha' it is?" Liam droned.

"He's my sister's pet," Kaleo breathed, feeling the color drain from his face and the air leave his lungs.

"Little! You found him!"

Kaleo's jaw dropped. His six-year-old sister ran to him, hopping up to catch Little when the tiny creature leapt out of Kaleo's arms to her.

"Please tewl me tha's not who I think it is," Liam said, color draining from *his* face.

"L'nae?!"

"Hi, 'Leo! I found you! Is papa with you?"

The next thing anyone heard was both Kaleo and Liam screaming.

***

Noelani ran an ivory comb through her silver locks. She longed for a mirror and proper walls but refused to acknowledge it lest she be accused of being spoiled. The thick canvas tents set up on the shore kept the chill off the sea at bay and offered as much privacy as a tent could offer. The amatessa pondered her meeting with the bard. She needed to speak with Kalelako and Tondra - both individually and together. Both remained indisposed, however. As much as she may have demanded to go along, Noelani was not enjoying any part of traveling outside of the palace walls.

"Permission to enter, your grace?"

"Granted, Kai," Noelani said to her personal guard. The man had large, blue wings with hair and eyes just a shade lighter, denoting his lower station.

"This came for you just now, your grace," Kai said, handing her a folded parchment. She took it, unfolding it carefully with no rush - - until she read the words. Then a scream of horror ripped its way across the Esbethi encampment.

***

Reven smiled at the small girl talking his pointed ear off. She poured weak tea from a cracked pot he used to make his own tea as she spoke. She told him about the tiny boar beneath her arm and the gown she got to wear during the festival of the ancestors. She included Kaleo and Lara in her rapid fire conversations even if neither of them said much. L'nae was an absolute gem; a tiny firecracker on wings.

"Here!" Serai announced, stepping into Reven's tent. "I have found biscuits!"

"Hooray!" L'nae cheered. Serai adored her. Reven did too, if he was being honest with himself. Once the initial shock of learning she had stowed away passed, the bard found his young daughter to be a joy to have around. Kaleo did not share Reven's sentiment, coming close to passing out twice since finding her.

"'Leo, want a biscuit?" L'nae asked, holding a dessert out to him. He groaned, letting his head fall into his hands. Lara rubbed his back. "Papa?" L'nae offered instead.

"Thank you, darling," Reven accepted. Serai beamed at him. "Don't forget to ask Miss Lara and

Miss Serai."

"Seriously?" Kaleo asked, voice cracking. He raked a hand through his hair and huffed out a long, shaky sigh.

"It's only polite," Reven said, taking a nibble from his biscuit. It was awful, but he wasn't going to ruin the moment by letting on. Serai was not as subtle, wrinkling her nose and looking at the circular dessert before glancing at Reven.

"L'nae!"

"Your grace, please, let me - - nevermind."

"Hi, mommy! We're having tea! Want some?" L'nae said in the bright, jubilant innocence only a child could have. The amatessa was less than impressed with her daughter's enthusiasm.

Reven stood as his ex barged into the tent in which they all had tea. Kaleo did too. The blue-winged man with the amatessa nodded at them both, familiar with them. Reven was no longer surprised by the recognition, taking it all in stride. He caught sight of Navid standing just outside the tent, hand on the sword of his hilt, and hid a small smirk.

Standing guard, Navid? Reven asked. The centaur gave the most imperceptible nod, amusing Reven more. The amusement ended immediately, however, when the amatessa ripped L'nae off the child's seat and clutched her close like she'd been held hostage.

"How dare you!" the woman screeched.

"I beg your pardon?" Reven dared. He saw the frown on Serai and Lara's faces but ignored them for now, watching Kaleo step forward instead.

"Noe, Reven didn't do-"

Kaleo's words were cut short by a loud crack across his face that made L'nae whimper. Now Reven's ire grew.

"This is your faualt! Always filling her head

with nonsense and false hope! I was wrong to let him keep you! No!" the amatessa screeched as Reven plucked L'nae from her arms. The blue winged man made to interpose himself between Noelani and Reven but changed his mind with one fierce look from the bard - and a not so subtle entrance of the centaur with the scimitar.

"Sit down, your grace," Reven frowned. "I didn't send for you so you could assault my urchin and ruin a perfectly good tea party."

"That is MY daughter mas-"

"*Our* daughter, your grace. I agreed to keep my distance when I believed she was in Esbeth. Clearly, that is no longer the case. Also, what under the sun and moons makes you believe *you* have any say in what I did with any of my children? Then *or* now?"

"You would have drowned him in the sea if I'd said so," Noelani snipped. Reven scowled.

"I doubt it. I did no such thing to Idris or Marie and they were planned from what I understand." Kaleo shook his head even as Noelani's eyes grew wide with shock and fury. Reven smirked. "So he never told you. Can't possibly imagine why. Now, we're going to have tea and biscuits in a calm fashion so we can discuss how *we* shall deal with *our* daughter moving forward. You too, Blue. I don't know your name. Sit. Navid, you're welcome to join us as well even if I know it's a bit tight for you in here. Say hullo to Navid, love."

"Hi," L'nae waved, leaning her head on Reven's. "I like your sword."

"Thank you, highness," Navid rumbled, settling himself in the doorway as if to both join the tea party and block any other intrusion to the event. Reven was coming to like him a great deal.

"Blue, sit please," Reven repeated, gesturing for him and the amatessa to sit where there was space.

Kaleo even did the *right* thing and offered Noelani his crate.

"That's Kai. He's mommy's guard," L'nae explained. "Hi, Kai."

"Hello, amatess," the man said in return with a small grin on his face that spoke volumes of what L'nae and her tiny boar got into at home. He smiled more when Serai handed him a biscuit.

"That's Serai. She's going to be my new mommy."

"What?!" Noelani yelped. Even Kaleo flushed while holding his bruising cheek.

"Let's not get ahead of ourselves, lovey. We only just got your mum to sit down. We don't need her - or your brother - fainting. Now-"

"Uncle! Eila called. He could tell their voices apart, at least, even if the sound of one was a nuisance now. They were just getting started!

"Uncle! We've got more visitors. They're asking for you - oh, tea party."

"I'm dead," Reven deadpanned. "Would you like to join us?"

"Another time, maybe, but no," Eila said. "They're not looking for the prince. They're looking for the *bard*."

***

Kendal stood beside Marie, eyes wide as she watched movement in the tirsai camp at the Grove in Tierra Vida. It was a stunning shrine to Yira. Stars were etched into every stone. Even worn, she could see the symbol of the goddess everywhere she looked. It brought her some comfort compared to everything else she saw.

The people looked defeated yet oddly hopeful in a hodge-podge encampment of what most would consider a handful of people. There was barely enough to make a village, let alone a nation. Marie stood beside Kendal, arms linked together. They'd remained inseperable since their escape from Yira's church in Itahl. She was tired, hungry, and perpetually terrified - like the people of the Grove.

Marie said it was important to remain hidden, so they had remained hidden. Even in the heat, they both kept their hoods up and cloaks closed. As soon as Kendal saw the bard, relief flooded her. The hope she had that Demyan was here swelled in her heart. The bard held a small avian girl with storm gray wings. An entourage of unique people followed him.

Kaleo, she recognized immediately. The runeli girl with him was not someone she knew, but the woman with wild red hair Kendal recognized as well. Navid was a welcomed sight to see but the two avians that followed beside him were unfamiliar to her.

"Is there somewhere private we can speak?" Marie asked once the bard came close. Her accent stood out among the tirsai. Those nearby looked at Marie with derision, despite their current status. Kendal had no doubt her own accent would stand out just as much.

"Clearly your attention is needed elsewhere, Master Si'ahl," the avian woman clipped. "I'll have my daughter back now."

"*Our* daughter, your grace. And I think you'll want to be here for this. Eila, go find your brother. Um... I'm sorry, it takes me a while - Blue," Reven said.

"Kai." The man's name was echoed by four different people.

"Sure," the bard dismissed. "Can we borrow one of your tents? Ours are a bit small and... holey."

The one named Kai looked at those gathered - especially the woman with silver wings - before finally deciding to find the requested tent.

Chapter Nineteen

Marie stared at her father. She knew he'd made it out of the Empire; she'd helped her mother heal him and the *Madame* hide him. When he vanished, she so desperately wanted to go with her cousin to find him, but it was not allowed. When Aeron reported he'd lost her father's trail, she accepted the inevitable. Idris's and Marie's mothers had done the same, as had the twins and Navid who took the failure to heart. Now, however…

Navid sat within arm's reach of the bard as if no time had passed, no changes made to the man that stood before Marie. But the changes were insurmountable and time *had* passed. Almost six years, in fact.

"Is everything alright?" Reven asked, looking directly at Marie. She nodded with a faint grin on her face to hide what she was thinking. Not that it would help with him, but she put the effort in all the same.

"*Oui*," she lied. Things were not 'alright' but she would process things a little at a time the way Idris taught her. "Any word of the king?"

Introductions were made, along with a summary of events up to their arrival that caught everyone up on what Marie and Kendal had been through and their concerns regarding the king. Small additions were made to explain *who* Marie was to the memory-stricken bard. He took the news better than she was accepting the change.

The Amatessa continued to bristle, refusing to be far from L'nae - Marie's little sister. The girl remained by the bard's side, easily adapting to whatever situation she had before her. The Amatessa had been furious to learn about Marie, as if any of it mattered now. They were not the same people from six years ago.

Kaleo had expressed hurt at being kept in the dark about Marie - and Idris, who he'd puzzled out on his own - but otherwise accepted the growing family and moved on. Marie did too, learning of her uncles and grandfather - and just how prolific her family was. The tree was gigantic.

"None since Kaleo spoke to you last, unless I'm forgetting something," Reven said as Marie thought on her growing family. The bard looked at Kaleo to confirm his statement.

"No, I haven't heard. I'm sure they're fine."

Both Marie and Kendal nodded.

"Well, clearly we don't have much and we're in the midst of some diplomatic fun, but you're welcome to stay," Reven added.

"L'nae, let's go!" the Amatessa hissed.

"No thanks, I wanna stay with papa and 'Leo. Little does too. It's ok, mommy, I'm still learning. I learned I have a big sister and another brother and we're gonna help save a king! So, I'm gonna stay."

The Amatessa actually *growled*, shooting a seething glare at Reven before storming out of the tent calling 'Kal!' at full volume. The Annointed One followed with a heavy sigh and nod at everyone in the tent. Kai followed on their heels.

"L'nae," Kaleo began.

"Be an angel and help Serai make us some tea? Aeron and Nadya can take Kendal somewhere to rest," the bard said, cleverly dismissing everyone he no longer wanted in the tent. L'nae, Marie noticed, let her lips curl into a small grin as she noticed the trick.

One by one, the people who gathered to meet Marie and Kendal filed out of the larger, if hastily erected and patchy, tent Kai found for them until only a small handful remained, L'nae included. She helped make tea, but listened and watched everything she could.

"You're not alright, are you?" Reven asked Marie once everyone had gone. She looked at him, but shook her head, fighting back tears. Reven noticed. "I'm sorry."

"I know. Mostly I'm worried for Idris."

"Trust me, he can't be any worse off than we are," Kaleo snorted.

"Feel free to mourn your loss. The urchin did, and then he turned into a petulant schite," Reven said.

"Hey!"

Marie giggled. She liked this man very much. It was not her father, but he seemed to genuinely care and did not fear admitting his flaws - - one of which was keeping his children at arm's length.

I do mean to change that, if you'll let me, Reven said to her.

*I think I could manage that. It might be nice to be a princess, **majesty**,* Marie teased.

"Ugh, not you too," Reven groaned. Both Marie and L'nae giggled. "You heard her?"

"Yep. It's statistics."

Marie laughed. "Big word for so small a girl, *cherie*."

"Not really. I'm six. Besides, 'Leo taught me and he's not wrong. Papa is Powerful and so is 'Leo and I am sort of even if I'm small, and so are you. Statistics."

"That's good to know. Good that Kaleo taught you. And now I can teach you too. would you like that, *cherie?*" Marie asked. L'nae nodded vigorously. "And you?"

She directed her question at Reven - heir apparent, bard; her father. He looked at her with doubt in his eyes until Serai took his hand, then some of that doubt simply melted away.

"What do you think, love? Think she could teach me a thing or two?"

"I think that you could teach each other," Serai said.

"Good, because I know bollocks about leading. you can start there, Marie."

She shared a look with Kaleo and giggled again, giving Reven a deep curtsey.

"*Of course. As his majesty wishes,*" she said in Damaskhan, smiling when Reven groaned.

***

Idris felt his head falling to his chest and jerked awake. It was his turn to take watch but exhaustion had not let him recover from calling the storm. Theoretically, they were safe, but Idris was just paranoid enough to not risk it, especially when Itahli Hunters were concerned. The shuffle of feet brought Idris to immediate attention, dagger in each hand at the ready. He only stopped his continued motions because he recognized Seren.

"Sorry," the other man muttered, hands raised.

"I am thirsty."

Idris held his stance for a moment longer before storing the blades and letting out a breath. "Sorry, *mes amis.*"

Seren merely nodded and continued shuffling to the kitchen. Idris followed. His ability to trust people needed a lot of work. It wasn't easy to ignore a lifetime of training.

"You're not tired, *mes amis?*" Idris asked as he set himself to making tea rather than suffer awkward silence with Seren. The mysterious man did not seem to mind the silence, nor the company.

"I would like tea as well," Seren said while sipping water. Idris nodded, preparing a second cup while trying to ignore the fact that Seren had not answered his question. "Do I bother you?"

The question was unexpected, slowing Idris's movements before he could school the reaction. But, he gave the question serious thought.

"I don't know you," Idris shrugged. "You're very Powerful. You were held in Itahl, but you can't say why or how long. You have a sister somewhere, you think. That's it. That's what I know."

"Serai."

"*What's that?*" Idris asked in Damaskhan. Seren grinned.

"Who," he corrected. "She is my sister." Idris nodded again. "Marie is yours. You spoke of her."

"She is. I'm worried for her, and upset that we left her behind."

"Liss cannot find her?"

It bothered Idris that this stranger could hear and speak to his *audeas*. He knew some had that talent, but it had never been used on *Liss.*

"She says you are protective," Seren smiled. Idris frowned.

Is my beloved dark angel jealous? Liss teased. Idris's frown deepened.

No. I don't like strangers knowing my business.

He is no stranger, Idris, Liss said gently. *He is one of the N'charra.*

Idris's eyebrow came up curiously. Before he could ask, a burst of stars hit behind his eyes and raced through his mind, each containing a simple image of Seren or a girl who looked eerily similar. The burst of stars was followed by a flood of information that took Idris's breath away. He saw their 'creation', felt the urgency for them, their birth and growth. They were treated as gods, expected to save the crumbling world from self-destruction, but their 'creation' had come too late. He saw a boy of thirteen and a girl of the same age put in living tombs and sealed away before the world *did* implode. The Destruction. It hurt him to see that, to feel the pain of the *planet,* forcing him to cry out as he fell.

Seren caught him. Idris felt his chest tighten and the world constrict around his head.

Breathe, Idris. Breathe, my angel.

The intensity popped like a bubble, leaving Idris gasping for air in Seren's arms; in the arms of a god.

"You…" Idris tried, but he was still shaking too much to speak.

"I am Seren. That is all."

Oddly enough, the answer worked for Idris who merely nodded as he finally let the exhaustion wash over him with the screeching call of the tea kettle to wake the others.

***

Demyan glanced toward the sound of the screaming tea kettle. His first instinct was to rise and tend to the important role of tea-making. The Kormandi did not see it as he did. As it was, even out where no one could find them, *someone* would tell him a king should not be serving tea.

"*Moy koral,*" Jax said. Demyan gave the duende man his full attention out of respect. "*We will be going today. At dusk.*"

Demyan nodded. He wanted to ask the destination but assumed if it had been important, he would have been told. His question would not have mattered. There was an odd, egg-cracking sensation inside his head followed by rapid fire images of Aeron in various forms of peril. He saw everything from an accidental fall to being stabbed to poison.

No matter what he saw, the bottom line was that Aeron was going to die.

***

Breaths came in rapid, panting bursts. Eyes rolled back into his skull, but he still Saw what was coming despite every effort to turn a blind eye to it. Seeing the future hurt, brought him pain and confusion without cause or warning.

"Uncle! Kaleo!"

Reven heard Rielle's voice It was higher in pitch than Eila's. He could feel his muscles spasming as he watched the blade slip between Aeron's ribs or at his gut. He Saw who - - all of them. It was more than one, all used as distraction for the murderer.

"Reven, look at me!" Kaleo commanded. "Papa, look at me!"

"I will go find the naked woman."

Serai. She was the naked woman but who spoke?

...eloved! Reven, breathe!

"Papa!"

Reven finally drew in a breath and let it go, feeling his whole body go slack in the process.

"I've got you," Kaleo said, rubbing Reven's back. "I've got you. Stay with me."

Kaleo kept rubbing his father's back. It helped to soothe the toll visions took on the body. People around them stared, whispering. Ettrian had his arm around Gael. Syrues Oenel was still not really up and moving, but he glanced over from where he lay near an open fire. Kaleo continued soothing the bard, silently daring someone to say something.

"Bloody hewls, now wha'?" Liam huffed. Kaleo threw a nasty glare at the thief-taker.

"Shut up, Liam," Marie said as she returned with Serai and Navid.

"Who asked ya?" Liam hissed back.

"No one had to ask, *idiote*. But everyone knows not to let Liam Roe talk, *non*? Only brings trouble."

Kaleo would have to get that story from his 'new' sister later. While she kept Liam at bay, Kaleo focused on Serai and the whimpers coming from the bard.

"Vision. Bad one by the look of it."

Serai merely nodded, taking the bard back so his head rested in her lap. Blood ran from his nose and the color was gone from his face.

"He'll be ok?" Marie asked. Kaleo didn't know but felt it was important to tell her the truth.

"I dunno. Usually I'd say yes, but… Serai will take care of him."

They both watched, both hoping. As normal, hoping only helped to a point. Reven remained a bit of a puddle, but Serai looked at Kaleo and Marie with concern creasing her freckled face.

"It was about Aeron. Something bad will happen soon."

Twenty

Kaleo's eyes popped open with an odd, inexplicable gasp. He lay still in the darkness, mentally grumbling at how little sleep he'd gotten after the odd events of the day before being dragged into Yira's Realm. Reven had four other visions following the first. A sense of dread curled itself up in the pit of Kaleo's stomach as a result, settling in like a rock. Kaleo frowned, laying as still as he could possibly be, while taking in his surroundings.

The Poppy Fields remained a shattered mess. The once-bright blue sky was a dark, dull gray. Black clouds laced with ribbons of lightning created harsh shadows against the broken landscape. A large canyon now tore the fields in half, leaving jutting pieces of earth along its edges like teeth in a skull. The poppies no longer held a vibrant red hue either. Instead, every single one of them was black oro blood red.

"Gods, what have we done…" Kaleo sighed. He didn't want to remain in the Fields. He was exhausted and stressed, so closed his eyes and forced himself to drift off to *actual* sleep.

Dreams for a Dreamer were not always better than walking through Yira's Realm. Kaleo knew this far too well. Nightmares had plagued him since he was a child, portents of things to come laid bare inside a hazy puzzle. It was no different now that he was grown. In fact, he would hazard to say it was worse - especially after days like he'd just experienced.

Kaleo's awareness of what was happening hit first. He'd seen these woods before, was familiar with the tall, boradhelix trunks of the *sephirot* trees of Asphondel. The blighted area made his stomach churn. Growls and hisses echoed all around him, in ways that made it difficult to discern direction. The exhaustion Kaleo felt earlier remained, filling him with pain and fear.

"Please, not tonight," he whimpered, doubling over with a cry when a sharp pain lanced across his stomach. He looked down on instinct, sure he would see a wound. There was nothing there, however. Everything throbbed and his neck burned.

"It's a dream," Kaleo said, breathing heavily through the pain. "It's a dream. Wake up, Kaleo. Wake up."

He didn't have the energy to wake himself. He only had the energy to breathe. Even that was a chore. The hell-blighted ground came rushing up to meet him as he crashed onto his side in a ball of pain. Everything seemed to be worse than it might in the waking world. It terrified him.

"I told you to run."

Kaleo looked up at the person who spoke. Jaysen. He recognized the boy instantly and, yet, there was something *wrong* with what he saw. Jaysen's eyes were red, his claws more wicked-looking and sharp. The tywyll boy wore only loose trews with a blood-red sash around his waist. His chest was covered in black runes that Kaleo did not recognize. Each one seemed to swirl just slightly as Kaleo looked up at his childhood friend.

"I told you to leave. You never listen."

"Jaysen..." Kaleo breathed out. Speaking caused pain. Jaysen glided to a squat in front of Kaleo.

"They're coming for you. This is what will happen," Jaysen said. "Just like it did for me. You *never* listen."

"I'm sorry," Kaleo managed, crying out when Jaysen grabbed him by the hair and yanked him up. "Jaysen, please!"

Jaysen ignored him, sniffing Kaleo like a predator sniffed at its prey. He then looked at Kaleo with murderous intent, grinning in an unsettling way. His fangs were long and sharp, dripping with something acrid.

"You brought this on yourself. If you'd only listened..." Jaysen said before moving like a viper, biting into Kaleo's neck before Kaleo could even register that he'd moved. Kaleo cried out in surprise and agony, desperately trying to push away without the energy to do so until that energy slowly left him, the life being drained away...

"Stop!" Kaleo cried, sitting up sharply in his tent, hand on his neck. He panted, unable to focus, pulling away from the first thing that touched him.

"Kaleo, wake up! It's Lara!" she begged. Kaleo gasped, tugging away from her into a tight ball until he could get his thoughts under control. "You're safe! It's ok!"

Kaleo remained in a ball until he could relax his muscles enough to throw himself at Lara, wrapping his arms around her waist as he buried his head in her lap and cried. Lara didn't complain, stroking his hair or back until he was a spent shell of exhaustion on her thighs.

"What happened?" she asked, pitching her voice low and soft.

Kaleo simply stared at nothing, unable and unwilling to answer. He didn't *want* to answer. Lara didn't press, holding him until the sun finally began its descent into the vast lavender sea.

***

Echoes carried far into the distance. Each sound rebounded off marble or sank into the soft soil beneath Alivae's feet. She worried about the ones left behind at the Necropolis like her brother, Maddox. He was the only family she had left and she'd abandoned him. She wondered if the demons had come to collect their prince (self-proclaimed as it was), or if it had all been a grand coincidence, like Cavian said.

The man prattled on about legends older than time itself. He told stories and fables that his mother fascinated him with as a child. While somewhat endearing, Alivae was more concerned with attracting unwanted attention.

"Will ya shut yer dang trap," she finally hissed, stopping long enough to throw a glare at him. Cavian smiled at her.

"Am I boring you, flower?"

"Yer ringin' the dinner bell, fool. Shut it!"

Cavian's smile broadened. "Where do you think we are, flower? Far enough from whatever that was back there?"

"No," Alivae clipped. She didn't want to think about it. It made her too guilty. Rather than continue the conversation, Alivae kept moving. She glanced around their surroundings, head on a swivel, taking note of everything. There were more and more vines and roots than catacombs. Her boots crunched along more of nature's cover, finally bringing her a sense of peace before she pitched forward and went flying.

"Careful, flower," Cavian said, catching hold of her. Alivae let her breath catch first before allowing Cavian to right her. He pulled her too close, making her frown at him. "I made a promise."

"Let go." He did so, if a bit reluctantly.

"What caught your pretty little toes?" Cavian purred instead of pursuing like she knew he must want to. She wouldn't give him the satisfaction.

"Rock," Alivae chuffed. "C'mon."

"Hang on..."

"Now. We can't be loiterin' so ya can study bloody, damned rocks."

Cavian ignored her, clearing moss and dirt, root and twig until a long narrow flagstone looked back at him.

"Have ya got a listenin' problem?" she hissed, moving back over to him.

"I think you've just become my new good luck charm," he clapped, crab walking around the flagstone until finding where he could fit his fingers beneath the marble. "Be a dear. Grab whatever's under here."

"What if it's a demon's corpse?!"

"Corpses are your hard limit, flower?" he teased. He ignored her discomfort and lifted the flagstone. Alivae had half a mind to leave him hanging, already envisioning what this hideous thing might look like. The glint of steel and sliver caught her eye, however, and finally decided her. She huffed, reached her hand in, took firm hold of the weapon, and yanked it out.

"Ok, set it down," she told him, stepping back to examine the sword. It was a longsword with beautifully intricate runes along its untarnished length.

The hilt was oiled leather wrapped in silver. It looked brand new despite being buried in the ground for who knew how long.

"Oh, flower," Cavian breathed in awe. "Do you know what you've found?"

"A sword," Alivae told him.

"Not just *a* sword. *The* sword. This is the Sword of Fate."

The name tickled Alivae's memory. It was one of the things he'd prattled on about, a Tool of Creation - or, in this instance, destruction.

"That's that sword what cuts life lines."

"You *were* listening, flower. I'm impressed. Very good."

"Plannin' on cuttin' life lines?" Alivae said, trying not to growl.

"Growing a collection, flower," he said as he removed his cloak to wrap the sword in. "just growing a collection. For now. Nothing to worry your darling head over. You were saying something about finding a way out of here, I believe?"

Alivae merely rolled her eyes and kept walking, watching this fool of a dragon-born awkwardly strap the Sword of Fate to his back with a grin on his face like one might see on a child during his nameday celebration.

***

Madhavi sighed with a vexed cluck of her tongue. Sunlight filled her new hiding spot with the brilliant rays of sunshine. Her lamb was becoming a problem that she needed to deal with. He was growing too bold away from her tutelage.

The other problem was her new, precocious pet. The woman sat across from Madhavi with lips pursed, eyebrow arched, and arms crossed. Her finger tapped in growing agitation against her upper arm. "Problem, demon?"

"Oh, don't start. I don't see *you* doing any of this work. If you're so eager to be rid of them, why don't *you* go slit their throats?"

"That wasn't the deal."

"That doesn't answer the question," Madhavi smirked, crawling to press her nose to Maeve's. How she wanted to show this woman what she was missing, to give her a taste of the glory Madhavi could give her.

"FOUND YOU!"

Both Madhavi and Maeve screeched, practically leaping into each other's arms. The warmth of their natural surroundings was quickly replaced with frigid cold and the playfulness with annoyance. Before Madhavi could express that annoyance, she felt herself hauled up from the ground by her hair, kicking at the fool who held her. He growled in her face, baring teeth without speaking a word.

"Roth! Unhand me!"

"*You* are not my Moppet," he hissed. She heard Maeve scream, then heard nothing more from the woman as the temperature dropped further. "Where have you put him!"

"Ah!" Madhavi cried. She had to be careful. The cold meant Ghost was near and no longer under her sway. She had both to contend with. "I haven't! An avian has him. A Powerful one. Daemodan wants them both."

"Why?" Roth growled.

"I don't know!" Madhavi screeched as he tightened his hold on her hair - - then dropped her.

"Show us, or join your friend. Ghost."

The man nodded and encased her hands in ice. Madhavi barely got a glimpse of what happened to her new pet as they hauled her away. The woman now existed in a solid block of ice, face contorted in rage, fear, and pain.

***

Night creatures sang their song to the moons above. A cool, crisp breeze blew through the trees, making the large fronds of the *sephirot* and leaves of the rowan sway in a light dance. Alivae watched and listened from the highest point of the trees, looking out over what remained of the Tria'ael tribe's village. Their homes no longer glowed with candlelight, no longer sang with the songs of their people. She frowned at the entire valley, feeling tears of anger well in her eyes. They'd done nothing to deserve this, nothing to earn the wrath of the demons that hunted the tirsai. They'd done horrible things, slaughtered millions in their time, and now reaped what they'd sewn. But the duende, the tywyll, they'd done nothing to deserve so much torment. They lived peaceful lives, even if the tywyll did side with the tirsai. They were artisans and craftsman, hunters, caretakers, not murderers like the olve of the white cities.

"Why us?" she asked of the wind. "What'd we do t'earn all this?"

No one answered, of course. She'd moved away from Cavian to collect her thoughts and feelings. Their homes, their forest had been protected by the Speaker of Tribes; Evanrae, her grandfather. Her mother, Eloiny, was to take his place. But that wasn't what happened. Instead, Alive watched her mother die, cut down by a demon that ravaged her body even after he'd sliced her from navel to nose. She'd watched her father take the wounds that would ensure his demise even as she cried for him to help her, cried for her brothers to run so they did not suffer the same fate as Hadrian. So many fell to the demons, so many lives snuffed out by hate and violence.

"It's their fault," Alivae continued. "They did

this to us. Their vileness made this happen and now we're payin' fer it. It's not right!"

"Talking to yourself, flower?"

Alivae gasped and frowned when Cavian sat beside her.

"Done playin' with yer sword," she grumbled. Alivae wanted the warmth of her mother, the looks of her father telling her to be careful and not to wander too far or to leave alone, not this dragon-born asshole.

Alivae's father had tried to protect her and her brothers, their mother. But he failed. He fell and left her behind. She wanted to scream, to hate him for abandoning her and leaving her in a land full of nightmares with an annoying creature beside her.

Cavian smirked. "I'm proud of you, flower. You *do* have a sense of humor."

"It's sarcasm, ya schite," she growled as she scrubbed her eyes and nose.

"Are you alright?"

Alivae snapped, rounding on Cavian so fast she was tottering on her feet over a very long fall to the ground below. "Why do ya care! Yer the one what did *all* this! Why? What the bloody fuck do ya gain by killin' us off?!"

Cavian blinked at her then frowned as he got to his feet with much more grace than she had. "*I* didn't do *anything* to you or yours. I've been cordial, and respectful and even promised you would not come to harm despite your open hatred and foul attitude toward me! *They* want something and they won't stop until they get it! Them, flower, not me!"

"Well, what the bloody fuck do they want!" she barked, tottering again so that her arms pinwheeled. Cavian steadied her, but she ripped her arms away from him.

"You!" he growled with a furious frown at her

continued hostilities. She didn't know what he was expecting from her, however. He was a demon! Yet she watched him soften after hollering at her and sigh. "They want you, flower. Or, rather, people like you."

"Me?" Alivae huffed. "I'm not-"

"True casters," Cavian cut in. Alivae felt the blood drain from her face. She kept that secret closely guarded lest she be treated differently than others, put on some strange pedestal like her mother and grandfather. That's not what she wanted. Now she didn't even have that. Cavian merely looked at her sideways. "You think I can't tell? That core of yours shines rather bright. And it's blooming, which means you'll be Claimed soon, if you haven't been already."

"I don't belong t'no one!"

Oh, but you do, my sweet beloved one, came a gentle caress to her mind that made her whirl so rapidly again she nearly fell off the branch. Cavian caught her.

"What's wrong?" he asked.

"Ya can't pretend ya didn't just hear that."

"Hear what?" he asked. Alivae wanted to slug him.

He can't hear me, my sweet beloved one. Only you can.

She crouched low, eyes adjusting to the light, narrowing as she searched for her quarry. It had to be a demon. She'd hunted demons plenty of times, kept her family safe. They'd all run, run at her grandfather's behest. He'd known, known the demons were coming to wipe them out in numbers they would not be able to fight off. It was still not enough. Only half of her tribe survived, the rest slaughtered in front of her eyes. She knew their tricks, throwing voices or sounds to draw out their prey. She would not be caught up in it; not this time!

"I don't hear anything, flower. What-"

"Shut up," she hissed, grabbing at her temples. Her head throbbed and her chest hurt. She choked on a gasp, sending shivers down her spine with an odd warmth that followed. She became aware of being dragged back to a safe spot, nestled against something warm and firm that smelled of pine and wood smoke. Her mind was flooded with images of the past, of things so far gone, it was impossible to think of them now. She saw her grandfather, her mother, her siblings and father - - her half-brother. Seeing Gannon's face shook her. He stood among the precipice of bright blue like she did, only his bright blue was cracked and broken with dark blue veins that made the silver seem brighter.

Alivae whimpered as things became a jumble of images and thoughts, of sensation that quickly overwhelmed her in a crashing tidal wave.

It's all right, my sweet beloved one. I'm here. Understand and accept what is given to you by right of blood.

"Right of blood?" she asked in a breathy whisper.

"Who are you talking to, flower?" Cavian whispered to her, stroking her cheek or hair. "Please tell me so I can help you."

Your blood is strong with the Power that flows in the Earth. You've been Claimed for Rhyanna who once Claimed Evanrae; who Called to Eloiny before her death. Rhyanna now Claims you.

"Claims... but..." Alivae began, then stopped as the Power coursed through her, making her scream as Cavian held her.

Chapter Twenty-one

Kaleo flopped to the soft, cool sand beside Reven in a huff. The bard watched his urchin drape his arms lazily over his knees, wings wilted, head hanging low to his chest. Reven arched a brow. He said nothing, simply watched the troubled young avian. Reven didn't need Kaleo to say anything, anyway. The boy had been walking through the entire grove, radiating angst, as only a young man of his age could do. There was too much happening for one person to handle, let alone a *young* person. Hellfires, *Reven* was too young to handle what was happening.

"You're radiating," Reven said with a nudge to Kaleo's shoulder. "What's wrong?"

"Nothing, I'm fine," Kaleo nearly growled, then sighed and let his knees drop to the sand, feet pressed together. "Ever regretted the things you've said to someone?"

"Once or twice. I usually don't have the wherewithal to care much about what I say to people. They either like it or they don't."

Kaleo snorted, throwing himself back on the sand. His hair was growing longer, at a stage where it was unruly, even tied back. Reven's hair was doing much the same. He hated it. But, on Kaleo, it almost seemed to work for him. It fanned out behind him on the sand in a halo. The child was far from angelic, yet easily gave the appearance of one; like his sisters.

"Is it Jaysen still or have you done something to upset Lara too?" Reven asked as he leaned back onto the sand beside his son. Kaleo looked over at him. Reven merely smirked. "So Lara too."

"How do you do that? I didn't even say anything," Kaleo complained. The smirk on Reven's lips broadened to a full smile.

"I told you, you're radiating."

Silence fell between them after that as Kaleo gathered his grumpy, youngling thoughts. Reven heard all of them but didn't let on, focusing on the sound of the ocean lapping up onto the shore. It brought a coolness to the evening, and a tickle of icy cold spray to the bottoms of his feet. Reven equated the sweet, heady smell brought in by the sea to a deadly flower. Nothing about the sea was safe. The smell, alone, had intoxicated desperate sailors for time eternal, promising salvation when the winds abandoned them to starve and die of thirst. Stories from all over the world told of the dangers held in the depths of the lavender-tinted sea. They fascinated Reven, engaged his mind with what-ifs and curiosities. He craved the thrill of learning new lore, of exploring new reaches and finding things long forgotten by mortal men.

The heavy sigh of the person beside him pulled Reven away from that fantasy, however. It put a small pit of sadness in Reven's gut to know he would never satisfy the itch to know *more*. It was simply not something he could do with a child - let alone four and a kingdom. He still felt uncertain about the latter, but was coming to terms with the former fairly well, all things considered. Besides, Kaleo was fretting over every little thing. Reven didn't know what to do with a fretting child.

"Stop fretting," Reven advised, letting out a slow, long breath as he stared at the stars overhead. "Start with the easiest of the two."

"Lara's pissed because I ... bartered with someone for the castle the Baron's scouts found," he blurted. Reven looked at him, desperately hiding a laugh. "Well, *Aeron* wasn't going to do it. The idiot is the *worst* negotiator I've ever met. *Liam* is better than Aeron."

Reven winced, turning his gaze back to the stars. "When did you two decide to barter for the castle? Isn't it haunted or something?"

"We figured that would be something in its favor in your eyes. And we bartered - - *I* bartered yesterday while you were recovering from your visions."

Reven nodded. He'd had five in rapid succession, all pertaining to someone's death. Each showed him a different person: Aeron, Kaleo, Demyan, Ajana, and the Baron.

"Did your step-mother use your bartering to abscond with my daughter too? I notice she's not here today."

"She did. Says you're not stable. Kal is trying to talk her down; Tondra says she should have you sacrificed to the ancestors."

"Charming woman," Reven smirked. "I'm going to guess the bartering was of a private nature?"

Kaleo colored and grew uncomfortably silent, as if Reven was not acutely aware of the kind of bartering it would take to claim a whole castle no matter how haunted it was.

"Is that what Lara's upset about, or is it the

who?"

The red in Kaleo's cheeks deepened.

"If Lara's going to be involved with a *bard* - - or even someone with as much Power as you have - - she's going to have to learn to share, no matter the whom. Is she more upset by whom or because you didn't ask her to join?"

"Papa!" Kaleo screeched in shock, even going so far as to prop himself up on an elbow to throw a scandalized look down at the bard. Reven remained a placid pool of composure.

"What? It's an honest question. *You* specifically have a great deal of Power and you study under a *bard*. Does she really believe that private performances and personal bartering involve *music*? If she does, then she's more naïve than I gave her credit for. There's nothing wrong with what you did. Stop pretending that there is. Because of you, these people have a chance to rebuild in a place *not* composed of cloth and stick."

Now Kaleo looked at him. Reven knew how such things as what Kaleo had done could be viewed. Many cultures found it to be disgusting, even taboo, while others openly welcomed it. Reven had seen every wide breadth of that thought process across the whole of the planet. It was not for him to judge what others did, just as it was not for him to judge what his son did - at least, not in that sense. Running off to gods only knew where to save a centaur, Reven would judge quite harshly; but who the boy chose to share a bed with or why was not his business.

"She'll get over it," Reven assured, lying back down on the sand to stare at the stars above. "So then what's stopping you from apologizing to Jaysen."

"He's a prat," Kaleo spat. Reven snorted.

"Says the child that can be one himself," the

bard chortled. "You're children pretending to be adults. Of course he's a prat. So is Aeron. So are you. So is every young man your age. It's expected, urchin. You've been rather cross with Jaysen for some time. You're even afraid of him now. Why?"

"He led the demons to the Empire," Kaleo croaked out. Reven felt his muscles tense.

"On purpose?" Reven asked. He pointedly kept his eyes fastened on the sky and his mind focused on the sea. The sudden rage surging through him felt out of place. These were no longer his people. That was no longer his life. Yet, knowing he had a hand in saving someone who felled an entire people made him see red.

"I don't know. I honestly don't, but I don't think so. They make him do things, look for things-"

"He's blind," Reven interrupted. The boy's eyes were near-white orbs in his skull. It was unsettling to look at them for long.

"I know," Kaleo said. "But he can hear Nodes. Their songs. They use him for that."

"They?"

"He won't tell me," Kaleo sighs. "We used to trust each other, *talk* to each other. Now all we do is argue and- I dunno."

"You've known him for a while, then?" Reven asked. Kaleo nodded.

"Since I was four, I think, or five. I got lost in a Dream. He helped me. He was there too, not much older than I was. He took me somewhere safe, to a field of grass. I said it was boring and watched the entire place fill with red as poppies raced across the green. We made the Poppy Fields that day. It's where we both start now when we Dream - and now it's shattered."

Reven remained quiet, letting the rage bleed out. If the blind boy had wanted to bring harm, he would have done so by now. Instead, he sat with Fionn in a secluded cove so the refugees wouldn't become agitated with his presence. The worst Reven had heard so far was a growl of annoyance or snide clip from the pain caused by his wound. Jaysen didn't deserve any of Reven's rage.

"You should apologize," Reven finally said. "Rebuild what you had. Friendships like that are rare."

Kaleo glanced over at Reven, his thoughts screaming into Reven's mind. He doubted this bit of advice from someone that let *his* 'friend' betray him. Kaleo had no love for Liam. Not very many people did. He was a difficult man to like, let alone love.

"Jaysen isn't Liam, Kaleo," Reven finally sighed. "And when you have as few friends as I do, you do what you can to keep the ones you have."

"You have tons of friends," Kaleo snipped.

"Had," Reven corrected. "I *had* tons of friends. Just like I *had* a wife and a title and siblings. I don't have any of that anymore because I'm not that person anymore. I have a woman, an urchin, a title I *don't* want, a centaur, and two friends. That's it. That is what I *have*."

Reven finally sat up, sighing. "Apologize. You'll regret it if you don't."

Kaleo looked at him but said nothing, opting to stay quiet until finally nodding.

***

Davenport had a very different feel to it than Brecken. It was larger, with different sights and scents. So far, every city in Tierra Vida sat along the shore, each one filled with boats moored to wooden posts in the water. Serai watched them bob up and down, the wind tangling her wild red hair around her neck. She loved the sweet smell of the sea, loved the feel of the spray on her face. However, they were all things she could feel near the Grove. Her purpose in Davenport was not to feel the spray of the sea. She sought an oracle. Rumors carried out even to the Grove, where the refugees prepared to move to a new home and rebuild their lives. A learned individual lived in Davenport, one who was often struck by visions from the gods like Reven. She needed to speak with that person, to know what plagued the man who held her heart.

"Are you coming?" Reven asked, drawing her attention to him. He came into Davenport with her to find work. The castle would not stock itself with supplies. Kaleo had gone to one of the other city states in Tierra Vida for the same purpose - work. Their trade was useful even if Reven had not performed since the incident in Mahala.

"I will find you. I must speak to someone first," Serai told the waiting bard. He nodded, gave her a smile that made her stomach flip with giddy joy, and walked on. Serai waited until he disappeared over the crest of a low hill before moving on to her destination. The tiny shack she'd been directed to did not impress her. She stared at it for a long time before finally climbing the rickety stairs to pound on a door that nearly fell off its hinges. Dust came off into her face, making her cough. No one answered.

"Hello?" she said, knocking again, this time batting away the dust that came off the door. "Hello?"

The meows of wild cats and scratches of other animals drifted out from the other side of the door. She heard the curious whine of a dog as well, and smiled. Someone was home.

"Hello? I have come to speak to the oracle of Davenport," she said to the door, her face terribly close to the fractured wood. When it opened, she squeaked and stepped back. She expected to see a wrinkled old woman, even a leather-faced old man. However, the person who looked at her had features similar to Kaleo - young and curious, with large eyes the color of sun-kissed gold. He looked at her, head tilting so the loose drape over his head fell to reveal drooping ears and small antlers. A faun.

The delighted noise Serai made came from the back of the throat. She very nearly bounced on the porch where she stood. She did not believe the creatures still existed, but now she saw one in the flesh! Navid was a miracle in and of himself until they reached Tierra Vida. There were at least four large tribes of the centaur there and she'd seen a few nagas as well. The demi-human species were so few now, all of them pushed to smaller places or eradicated entirely.

"Oh!" she eked out in a pitch so high the dog behind the faun whined again and backed away. "The ancient ones live on! It is an honor to meet you, sir faun."

Serai took his hand without asking, shaking it vigorously as she had seen Reven do. "I must speak with you. I seek your wisdom and council."

He looked at her, a small smirk curling his lips while his ears twitched. He pulled his hand away and raised his hands, indicating that she should contain her excitement. Serai did the best she could to do just that. He then pointed to his twitching ears and shook his head. Serai's heart dropped, as did the smile on her face. The little faun was deaf.

"Oh…"

He smiled anyway, beckoning her inside. Serai followed him in, taking great care not to step on the animals hovering around the door. His hooves clopped against wooden boards as old as the front door. Bundles of sage and lavender hung from different parts of the open rafters above or in the window sills that let in light through imperfect glass. She followed to a small table where she sat and waited, feeling suddenly uncertain of her purpose in coming to speak with him.

"Tea?" He asked, making her jump.

"Yes," she replied, then frowned at herself for speaking to someone that could not hear. She nodded instead. He smiled again, serving tea as if he'd been expecting her. "You knew I would come?"

He nodded and pointed to his large eyes. "I saw you. Both of you."

"Both?" she asked, again feeling silly for speaking the answer. She had no other means of communication, however. The faun did not seem to mind, sitting across from her at the tiny table with his hands wrapped around his teacup as if snow fell outside. She had yet to see a part of Tierra Vida that was *cold*. Sometimes a cool wind blew in off the sea, but that was as 'cold' as it got on the patchwork island. His small, black nose wiggled as he inhaled the scent of the tea, his senses savoring every part of it, as Reven might say, like a fine wine. She still did not know what that meant. Most wine was dry and bitter to her tastes.

"You and the one you've come to speak about," the faun said after sipping his tea. Serai looked at her cup and sipped it as well, so she would not seem rude. It did not clarify the statement the faun made. It must have shown on her face, for the faun reached across the table to tap her hand.

I won't bite you. If this is easier, I don't mind.

Serai's jaw dropped. While she was familiar with the creatures, she'd never heard of them having Power. Usually, such things belonged to the humanoid species or the fey. The faun was neither. He smiled.

Surprised, your grace? Things have changed. I am Rhys.

Serai gaped even more, absently pulling away to drink her tea. "How are you doing this?"

Speaking to you? Rhys shrugged. *I have always spoken with my mind. Most don't like it, so I just stay quiet. Mother provides for her children in mysterious ways. The gods took my hearing, but Doranelle has given me other gifts to compensate as she does with others like me, I'm sure.*

"But, I do not know anyone-"

Don't you? You came to ask me about him, didn't you? He cannot remember, but he can See. And, there is the one who can't see as well.

Serai's jaw shut with a click this time. Rhys grinned and sipped his tea.

Have you spoken to him? The boy who cannot see.

"No. He will not allow it. Only Kaleo or Eila speak to him," Serai said. Rhys nodded as if pondering the dilemma that Serai did not have the words to describe.

He hears the Songs of the Nodes.

"Yes, he is a Speaker. This is why I wish to help-" Rhys shook his head. "No?"

*He hears **all** the Songs, your grace. Every single one. They sing to him, show him the world in vibration and smell, in the music they create because he was given a gift to compensate for what the gods took away.*

Serai felt herself inch forward as if to contradict, but, instead, sat back and thought about the knowledge Rhys imparted. It made her frown more. All the horrible things done to something so beautiful. For what purpose? Who would want to destroy something so pure?

"I need to know who has done this. I must make it right," she said, still frowning. Rhys shook his head.

His path is different from yours.

"But-"

*Your path is not to fix what has already been done, but to prevent what is to come. That **is** why you came here* *today, isn't it? Because your Heart has Seen what is coming.*

Serai sighed, frowning slightly. Her Heart. She liked the sound of that. Reven had certainly become her Heart. She worried about what he'd Seen, what the visions had done to him.

Five deaths, all of people Reven cared about - Kaleo especially. Each vision had been the same except for the individual involved. Each had wracked Reven with tremors, left him disoriented at best, unconscious at worst.

He will need to learn to let go, Rhys said. *The stars are shifting and the embers are creating smoke that will hide dangerous flames. Help him see that to keep what he loves, he must first learn to let it go.*

Serai listened. She glanced at the cats and dog, at the tuft of hair at the end of Rhys's long tail. The cats batted at it when it moved.

"Does he know?" Rhys asked aloud, startling Serai.

"Who? Know what?" she blurted. Rhys smiled. Serai blushed and shook her head.

"Tell him. Soon. It will matter."

Serai's only response was to press a hand to her belly and let out a shaky, breathy laugh.

***

"Have fun in town?" Reven asked later that evening once they'd returned to the Grove. They came with trunks full of supplies, and a wagon full of rugs and mismatched furniture that would all fit nicely in the castle. The rugs of their tent were as threadbare as the ones they purchased, but they were *theirs*. Serai nodded mutely, thinking about what that meant, what the faun had imparted to her. She needed to clear her head more, to focus on the immediate instead of letting her mind drift back to the things Rhys had told her.

"Tell me what, love?" Reven asked, latching on

to that thought like a magnet. Her face turned red as an apple.

"N-nothing," she stammered. Reven chortled, glancing at her then giving her a look of disbelief.

"Come on, you don't expect me to believe that, do you? You even stammered. What's wrong? Did your oracle tell you something you didn't like?" Serai frowned at him. He smiled again. "It didn't take much to figure out where you were going. You don't really shop and you don't strike me as the 'drinking with the fishermen' type."

"How many children do you have?"

Now Reven blinked at her and grinned in suspicion. "Serai, you know how many children I have. Honestly... unless I missed something else while I was in and out of consciousness, all but one are on this island, aren't they?"

"Reven, that is not the point," she sighed, raking a hand through her frizzy red curls only to get it caught. "UGH!"

"Hold still," Reven chuckled as he gently untangled her. "Why are you asking about my children?" She remained stubbornly silent while staring at the rugs beneath her feet. "Serai?"

"They are important to you," she said, still looking down. He nodded and shrugged.

"Yes. I don't know why that would upset you."

Serai scrubbed her arm across her nose, conscious to not tangle her fingers in her hair again even as she twisted the ends up until they created natural tubes little by little. "If there was another, would it be important to you, too?"

"Would... I would imagine, but I'd have to remember or *know* them first. That sort of matters in all things qualifying importance."

Again, Serai nodded, still looking down at the

rugs. Reven frowned at her, lifting her chin so she was forced to look at him. She saw the concern in his hazel blue eyes, the worry that he'd done something wrong, something to drive her away - to change how she felt about him. He didn't have to speak to her for her to know these things. She felt it in his touch, the way he looked at her. Rhys was right. The connections he'd made since the Fall, since becoming Reven instead of the man he had been, held him aloft on such breakable, thin threads. It hurt her heart to see it.

"It," she began. "It is important for you to know your children. They are part of you. Part of who you were and who you are," Serai said. "And who you will be."

That made Reven's frown deepen. "Who I will be?"

Serai merely looked at him, her rapidly swelling and watering eyes pleading with him to understand so she did not have to speak the thing that was upsetting her the most. It didn't take long for him to catch on. It never did.

"Serai, are you -" he started. She nodded vigorously. Reven's jaw hit the ground.

She was pregnant. Reven was the father.

Chapter Twenty-Two

The sky twinkled in the darkness. Reven watched Azure circle above the tent. The little orange-blue phoenix circled higher and higher until winking out, on the hunt for his evening dinner. All around the Grove, evening fires dwindled. The refugees - now referring to themselves as Embers of the Phoenix thanks to the Baron - settled into their evening routines, ready for the rest of the weary. After a little nudge, Kaleo agreed to speak to Jaysen *and* Lara with what little direction Reven could give on the matter. Reven had not seen the boy or Lara since late afternoon, but smiled to himself. They were quite taken with each other despite their recent spat. Reven was positive there would be *another* surprise soon.

He let his mind process what Serai had told him. Or, rather, what he'd inferred from her guided silence. She hadn't said much since telling him he was to be a father - again - nor had she stayed in the tent, claiming *she* needed time to meditate and process and something else that made very little sense to Reven.

Rather than go far, he sat just outside the tent, and enjoyed the stars above, waiting for her.

A noise behind him made the bard turn to look over his shoulders. Only the shadows moved. He felt his brow twitch and the hairs on his neck stand on end, forcing his eyes to look deep into the wandering gray and black that surrounded his tent.

"Serai?" he asked, peeking into the tent, frowning when he didn't see her. She'd gone down to the beach with Malek.

The red-haired woman was in as much need of hunting as her *audeas*. For her, it was the time spent with the drake more than the actual hunt, but Reven was learning the importance of being near one's *audeas* regularly. Azure remained with him all day, hunting at night when Reven slept.

The sensation of being watched became overwhelming, along with a sudden tightening of Reven's gut that told him to move.

Just as his muscles registered the thought, a flash of silver sparked in front of his eyes, dropping him to his rear just outside the tent, but close enough to the fire for it to burn the backs of his arms. He hissed, pulling his arms around in front of him, flinching again when something popped above his head and sizzled its way down his spine.

Power.

"Move!" someone said. They stood in front of Reven, blocking him from an attack. "Now!"

Reven scrambled back to his feet, ready to run, only to come face to face with two shadowed and dazed figures that blocked his momentum. The cries and screams of others echoed to his ears as these same shadowed figures tore through the refugees.

Stop it, Reven thought, growing angry, Power filling his veins. *Stop it!*

"Leave them alone!" Reven roared. The entire Grove went still and silent as a graveyard. Children cried as they ran to their parents, the sound of their feet in the sandy grass breaking the tense silence. Reven's command was obeyed, but the shadows suddenly focused on him instead. "Drop your weapons!"

A clatter of steel and wood followed. The loud thud of a body dropping took Reven's attention for a moment as he stepped up against the winged back of his savior. His first thought was of Kaleo, but the coloring was wrong. The wings were a dark russet brown tipped with gold; an aurum.

"Th'bloody fuck…" Liam grumbled, coming out of his tent armed but only partially dressed. Reven tried to glower, but found he did not have the energy for it. He felt weak and fell back, surprised when he did not hit the ground.

"Crawlin' from your rock, Master Roe? I'd start tyin' people up before his hold is lost. Fast."

"Oh, ya've gotta be kiddin' me," Liam grumbled. Ajana popped out of the tent then, dressed in Liam's tunic with pistols at the ready. "Oi! Get movin', yeah!"

Ajana shoved the thief-taker for speaking to her that way, but helped all the same. Beyond that, Reven did not see much as his vision tunneled and muscles liquified.

"I have you," the same individual said to his ear. "Where is Kaleo? Or the Baron?"

The question made Reven frown and force himself to stay conscious with a need to protect his son. He even tried to stand again, but failed miserably in that regard.

"They are sleeping. The people; they are asleep," Ajana said, coming to stand beside Reven. Her presence soothed him, gave him peace of mind even if her words didn't.

The one who held Reven glided down to the grass with Reven's head lolling on his shoulder. "Do you know Kaleo Oenel?"

"Kaleo?" Ajana asked, just as Reven heard Serai's voice calling his name. She relieved the newcomer of his duty immediately thereafter, looking Reven over like a worried hen over a chick. Reven could hear Malek growling in the background too.

"Someone's doin' this and if it ain't Kaleo, then we got another problem," Reven's savior said, a Damaskhan by the casual drawl on his tongue.

"Who are you?" Serai asked. Reven could kiss her.

"Idris has worked with us before, Serai," Ajana explained. "We can trust him."

"Like Reven trusted Liam," Serai pointed out. Ajana remained quiet, but Reven knew the name. Idris was his son.

"Oh-ho, there's a story there, *non*?" Idris said. "Maybe for later. We need to-"

Howls cut off Idris's thought. They curdled Reven's blood. It radiated across the land and chilled him to his core. No, it was not the screams, it was the land itself that grew cold.

"Kaleo," he groaned, forcing himself to his feet. "Kaleo!"

Beloved! Fionn is injured!

"Gods no..." Reven breathed out, tripping as he forced his legs to run.

***

Demyan sat on a smooth stone that sat on one side of a great big 'stitch' in the land. On the opposing side of that 'stitch' was a stream that carried fresh water down into the sea beyond. Fish that glowed in the light of the moons above swam in the crystal clear water. It was like nothing Demyan had ever seen.

"Spook fish."

The voice of the other young man with him startled Demyan so much that he brought a hand up to his chest as if to keep his heart inside his ribcage. Seren was a very quiet creature. Idris asked for them to wait while he and Jax made sure this encampment they'd heard about was safe. Demyan wasn't sure he appreciated being left out like he was incapable of defending himself, but he could understand the caution as well.

"*Nani?*" Demyan asked, absently falling back to the language of the *youkai*.

"The fish. It is what they are called. Spook fish. Like spectres in the water."

Demyan nodded, understanding Seren's meaning now. He looked at the fish again and grinned. They did look like spectres.

"Do you think they are ok?" Demyan asked. Seren nodded. Demyan waited a minute before adding. "Do you think *she* is ok?"

Seren looked at him, studied him closely, then grinned and finally nodded. Demyan could not get Kendal out of his mind. He didn't want to. He wanted things to work with his wife, the woman with the drawling accent that was so close to a Damaskhan's it was sometimes difficult to tell the difference. She had stood so bravely at his side, taken the worst news anyone could ever take about her own people and still supported him rather than damning him as a madman. Demyan wanted her to be safe, to be happy, wanted to be the one to give her those things.

Which was when the echoing howls of others reached their ears. Demyan was on his feet in an instant, looking in the direction of the howls. Seren stood beside him, hand on Demyan's forearm as if to stop him from going toward the danger.

"I am no coward, Seren-san," Demyan said. "And she is there."

"No, you are no coward," Seren agreed, making Demyan feel a little better. "But we will go together. *Ah?*"

Demyan looked at his new friend and gave a curt nod. Seren never let go, letting Demyan focus until he could Travel directly to his wife.

***

Aeron was dragged from dozing sleep by the high-pitched squeal of Kendal Ovet's voice. His eyes popped open to see a man atop her, another atop Nadya and felt the sharp slice of a dagger slip between his ribs. He didn't even fully react to all that was happening before an explosion of Power ricocheted around the tent where he and the two women were sleeping. Kendal sobbed, scrambling back away from the man that fell face-first to the rugs on the floor. Nadya came to Aeron, making him wince when she touched him.

"You're injured."

"I'm fine," Aeron forced out, ripping a dagger out of his side with a strangled cry. He spun that dagger in his palm when a new tingle of Power brought two new people into the tent. It was still dark, making it difficult to see the newcomers. One had blonde hair, the other red. That was the best, Aeron could do but he held that dagger and absently placed Nadya behind him even if *she'd* been the one to save *him* just now. It was a thing with her. She kept saving him.

"Demyan!" Kendal screeched, throwing her arms around the young man's neck. He held her tight, burying his face into her neck.

"Are you hurt?" the man with red hair said. Aeron had to blink and shake himself, certain he was looking at Serai, rather than a man. The hair and freckles were the same.

"He is. Who are you?" Nadya asked. The man reached over to heal Aeron, smiling.

"You Speak for the shadow one," he said. "I am Seren."

"He's a friend. Jax is here too," Demyan said while still holding Kendal who sobbed and sobbed with joy, with fear, with a whole new set of worries barreling down on their heads.

***

Lara picked her way through the trees at the far end of the beach that surrounded the Grove until coming upon a small clearing that cradled a large chimera and a wounded tywyll. She watched them for a time, observing how Jaysen shifted uncomfortably or how Fionn huffed into the grass in boredom. She went down to a squat, feeling the grass beneath her as she observed this creature that Kaleo was so taken with.

She knew Kaleo cared for her, but also knew how much he cared for Jaysen. Fionn raised his head once the wind took her scent toward him. Jaysen did much the same, inclining his head in her direction.

"Who's there?" Jaysen rasped. Lara stood, then walked toward him until she was only a foot from where he sat. "Go away."

"It's Lara," Eila said, coming around Fionn. The girl spent more and more time with the Corrupted tywyll. He sneered at Lara, shifting so he could roll into Fionn's side and avoid her, then shifted again when Eila sat beside him as if unable to decide who annoyed him more. Perhaps he couldn't decide.

"Go away," he repeated. Lara stood her ground, gliding back down to a comfortable squat. She remained quiet again, watching him. Her mind wandered to an adventure with Kaleo, to the warm cave beneath the Temple and what they did after. He'd shown her Nevaeh. Her cheeks filled with warmth, but she remained silent, watching Jaysen's reaction. He said nothing, but he snarled under his breath. Lara smirked.

"Do you really want me to go away or are you just worried I will take Kaleo from you?" she finally asked. Jaysen remained sullenly silent. "He loves you, you know."

Jaysen scoffed. Eila listened.

"I see it in how he worries for you. He worries almost as much as he worries for the bard. You're special to him."

"Jealous?" Jaysen snarled. Lara remained placid.

"No," she said, surprised to know that she meant it. The love Kaleo had for Jaysen was different than anything romantic he might feel for her. Thinking about him put butterflies in her stomach. She hoped the same was true for Kaleo, but she knew there were no butterflies when he thought about Jaysen, only knots and fear.

"What do you want, Lara?" Jaysen finally asked over his shoulder.

"Nothing," Lara said. "You needed to know that he loves you. That you are not alone. That you can trust him to take care of you."

"I don't need someone to take care of me," he hissed. Lara arched a brow that she knew he could not see, but it was habit to express herself silently. So, she sighed instead, loudly, so he could hear and feel it while looking at Eila. The girl merely rolled her eyes in understanding and sympathy. "This is different. I don't normally let someone run me through with a sword."

"That's good. I don't think it's good for your health. Or his."

"Ah," Jaysen snorted. "That's what this is about. You're worried I'll do something to get him killed. Well, he did that on his own as soon as he rushed in to help me."

Lara's eyes narrowed, waiting for Jaysen to continue.

"They know now," Jaysen sighed. "*She* knows. She'll find him. She'll find both of us."

Jaysen's response made Lara frown. She could see the shift in how he slumped into Fionn, no longer just annoyed with her presence, but trying to hide in Fionn's side. Without thinking, she reached for him, her fingers barely brushing his shoulder.

"DON'T!" he growled, moving like a viper to face her before doubling over in pain. He continued to growl even through his agony. Eila helped him. *That* he allowed. Fionn let out a warning growl of his own, though Lara got the distinct feeling that the chimera growled at *Jaysen* rather than her.

"When are you going to learn that I am not going to hurt you?" she snapped back. "You are important to Kaleo and he is important to *me*. Who is coming for you, Jaysen?"

"Go away," he repeated, panting and grunting instead of growling. He held his stomach, his dirty tunic staining pink, even as Eila helped re-situate him.

"Will you let me help you first?" Lara insisted without moving away. Jaysen growled at her again. "He would miss you if you died."

Jaysen's jaw dropped. He was either not expecting her to say that or not expecting to hear that anyone would miss him. It was difficult to tell. Lara snorted and shook her head, looking down at the grass beneath her. The small clearing where the chimera slept with the wounded tywyll was open to the stars. She looked up, seeing the deep darkness that held the stars in its grasp. Each one sparkled like a diamond. Kaleo spoke of the Sea of Stars once, a place in Yira's Realm where he met Jaysen - the boy with no color. That was how Kaleo described him to her the day he told her he could walk the world of dreams.

"Is that how it looks in Yira's Realm?" Lara asked, her head still tilted up to see the stars.

"How *what* looks?" Jaysen sneered with a look of incredulity on his face. She looked at him again, seeing his ghost-white eyes searching the area, like if they moved enough, they might catch a glimpse of what he could not see.

"The Sea. The one you go to with Kaleo. Does it shine like the sky? Like diamonds?" she asked. She could tell there was a smart retort on Jaysen's tongue until he softened and angled his face down, then to Eila, who smirked. She'd asked too.

"Kaleo calls it shimmer. I don't know what that means. He says the Sea of Stars is a different color than the sky. The sky has more purple in it, he says. The Sea doesn't. It's blue. The same with the Poppy Fields. The sky above it is so … bright."

Lara watched Jaysen's eyes move back and forth as if seeing what he described. Yira's Realm was where he experienced the wonders of the world with his eyes. It made her smile and finally sit on her bottom rather than squat.

"Did Kaleo teach you what these things were? What to call them?"

Jaysen shook his head. "Madhavi did."

The way he said it made Lara frown. He did not like speaking her name, croaking it out with great caution, as if speaking the name would summon the woman to his side.

"Where is Kaleo, anyway?" Jaysen finally croaked.

"Right here," Kaleo said, looking down at Lara with a grin. "You told me you were going back to the

Grove."

"I will soon," Lara said.

That made Jaysen blink, then pause, shrugging his shoulders in a manner that Lara noticed.

"Something's wrong..." he growled, inclining his head to the left and right to hear what might be different, to smell it on the air or feel it. It was the sudden drop in temperature that made his heart sink straight down into his bowels. He was far enough away from the Grove to keep the others safe, but that also meant he was too far for anyone to offer help should he need it. And, of course, Lara was still with him.

"MOPPET!"

Roth's elated voice startled Jaysen, as it always did, while at the same time offering some odd comfort. Despite being very *ab*normal, there was something *normal* about Roth when in the presence of the others that followed in the wake of his screeching voice. And, as always, Roth rushed at him, picking him up like a rag-doll to hug and squeeze him.

"I've missed you! Did you miss me? Phier missed you too, didn't you, Phier? We were playing a game of hide-and-find to see who would find you first. I won."

"Took you long enough to find him," Madhavi hissed, her voice like sandpaper inside his ears. "Put him down, Roth."

Unfortunately, Roth complied, setting Jaysen back down into the grass beside a block of ice too close to where Fionn *had* been. He could hear Lara struggling and crying, her voice muffled.

"You're not looking so well, my lamb," Madhavi purred, coming close enough to Jaysen for him to smell her sickly sweet breath, to feel it against his face. He sneered and stepped back.

"Sod off," Jaysen snarled. Madhavi laughed, the sound sending a shiver down Jaysen's spine.

"Do you really want me to do that?" she cooed. "There's so many gloriously innocent people I smell nearby. Starting with this girl, for example."

Eila cried out. He heard Lara's muffled voice and did not hear Kaleo at all. That scared him the most. So did the terrible cold where there *should* have been warmth.

Jaysen's breath caught. He did not want to put the people of the Grove *or* Eila in harm's way. But turning Kaleo over to Madhavi was no better, condemning him to a fate worse than death if he did.

"Ghost," Madhavi said through a smile Jaysen could hear. "Tear her in half."

"No!" Jaysen barked. "No. Leave them alone. We'll go with you. Just... leave them alone."

"Ghost," Madhavi said, shifting her tone to something full of satisfaction and a teasing lilt that made Jaysen's sneer turn into a growl. "Make sure he complies."

"No! Leave him alone!" Lara hollered before screaming like the devils were taking her. Perhaps they were. Eila followed, screaming so much it hurt to hear.

"Stop it! Leave them alone!" Jaysen growled. His bravado only earned him one of Madhavi's frozen claws raking across his face, landing him hard on the equally frozen blades of grass beneath him. They dug into his palms and scratched beneath his chin and at his neck.

"You were warned, whore, not to touch *my* Moppet," Roth snarled from above Jaysen. He heard Madhavi squeal and scream in a poor attempt to fight him off and smiled to himself. She deserved every bit of hell Roth gave her.

Her squeals ceased abruptly when the girls

stopped screaming. Too much happened for Jaysen to keep track but, eventually, Madhavi stopped screeching.

"Ghost," Roth said finally, picking Jaysen up. He was aware of someone else in Roth's other arm, aware of the tickle of feathers against his arm; Kaleo. "We're leaving. The dragon bitch can find her own way home. Let *her* hunt for a change. Bring the soft ones"

And with that, they were gone in that same gut-wrenching fashion that landed him back in Madhavi's clutches.

Chapter Twenty-Three

Furious, dark clouds muted the screams pulled from Kaleo's throat. Each howl, each breath, made its way to the darkness above, swallowed in a thick vat that carried no sound at all. No one heard him, no one could hear his pleas for help. Periodically, he was allowed to breathe, to slump forward against the bonds that held him with his head hanging down to his chest. Rusted iron chains dug into the flesh of his arms and wrists. Sweat matted his hair and dripped down the sides of his temples, over the curve of his jaw and down his neck.

Others hung on the filthy walls beside him, across from him, even on the floor beneath him. None moved, each one of their lives extinguished by the agony that ripped through them. Part of Kaleo knew what he experienced only existed in the caverns of his mind, in the world of Yira's making. The goddess of dreams shifted between benign and malevolent, depending upon who wielded her power. He knew this, knew none of what he saw really existed. But the pain was real, the wounds were real. His torment existed in his mind as reality, even if the dream left much to the imagination.

Fionn...

He called for his *audeas* in a vain attempt to find help. No one answered. No one could hear him beg and plea for the pain to stop. No one even told him why the pain existed. They only wracked his mind with anguish, made his back arch, his wings curl in on themselves and his stomach clench against the inevitable.

"So much beautiful pain, my little one."

The voice made Kaleo's stomach sink. It held a sweet tone while dripping with malice at the same time. The owner reveled in causing pain; she lived for it.

"Now do you see? Now, do you understand that you will never control the world I create? How could you? You can't even stop screaming long enough to call for your pathetic little dog."

It was then Kaleo realized he was, in fact, still screaming. He stopped immediately, letting his head hang in earnest. She lifted his face at the chin, her sharp fingernail digging into the soft flesh.

"No giving up now. We have big plans for you."

Kaleo whimpered. She loved when he made those sounds. She even cooed and purred when he did it, caressing his face and neck.

"Lovely..." she murmured into his sensitive ear. "Do it again for me, my little one. Make those beautiful noises."

He refused, finding enough strength to squirm away from her. She caught his face in her hand and licked his cheek. He winced, whimpering again before he could stop the sound from emerging. She took everything she wanted from him, made him pay for his supposed crimes in flesh. The pain was not always from torture. Sometimes the pain was from pleasure - too much of it. The thought would have never occurred to him until now. How could pleasure cause pain? But it did; *she* did.

Her hand slid down his chest, sharp fingernails raking against his sensitive skin. His stomach naturally flexed against the touch, pulling back. It hurt to move. The strength to fight her - to fight anyone - vanished with the last of his non-existent voice.

"Not going to fight me this time, my little one?" she pouted, going so far as to kiss his neck and shoulders. He shut his eyes, letting it happen. The pleasure she gave him continued over and over until it became pain, until he screamed and begged for her to stop. The begging drove her desire to torment him, made her continue until he became a whimpering, bleating mess on the floor. She left him there, naked and helpless, until the clouds took him in their darkness. He let his eyes close and head fall to the grimy floor.

Get up.

Kaleo heard the command but did not truly register it.

Get up!

Kaleo heard the voice, the sound of it caressing his ear, the warm breath moving over his cheek. He flinched automatically, needing to be away from the sensation.

"Wake up!"

He frowned at the sound of the command, confused and terrified by it. No other noise existed inside his mind or in his surroundings. It was the silence of death, of perfect and absolute stillness. He didn't like it, frowning more as he groaned and shifted. He felt heavy, weighed down by an unseen force that pinned his arms above his head in contorted positions. His wings ached too long with the pressure of his back upon their joints.

"Wake up!"

He shifted again, groaning louder with a rising tightness in his chest that made breathing difficult. His stomach knotted, throat closing in anticipation of releasing a strangled scream that never came.

"WAKE UP, KALEO!"

He gasped, choking into the darkness. His head swam in undulating waves of cotton-stuffed vertigo that continued to weigh him down. He wanted to roll, to vomit, to open his eyes, but none of that happened. Instead, he coughed softly into the lightless room, freezing when he felt a hand close over his mouth and nose. The dampness of his breath ricocheted back at him as that tightness from the dream became a reality. Instinct kicked in - but there was nothing at all to pull from. A terrifying, piercing emptiness filled him. He had no Power.

"Shh. It's me."

Jaysen. That did not calm him as it should have. Jaysen was a friend - a friend that attacked him once in his sleep and did not stop either of the monsters who took them or the girls. He could only pray the girls were killed rather than being tormented like he was.

Girls...? Lara... Eila...

"Leave. Understand? You need to go, now, before she realizes you're awake."

Kaleo tried to speak against Jaysen's hand, to ask questions, to understand what was happening. The hand only tightened, digging into his cheeks like Madhavi's had. Kaleo froze, shutting his eyes tight against the horrors that flooded his mind. The lancing pain that followed pulled a cracked shout that was muffled by Jaysen's hand. His shoulder burned with fire from where Jaysen bit him! It was like Kaleo's nightmare, only more brief. There was no draining of blood, just the sensation of acid flowing along his shoulder.

"Don't fight it. I promise, this is the only way I can save you. Just remember not to fight it," Jaysen hissed. "Now, listen. Leave. Go, right now."

Jaysen shifted himself in the dark, tugging at Kaleo with more strength than the young avian amati would have given the blind boy credit for. Kaleo followed, allowing himself to be dragged away from a stiff bed to a window that allowed just enough moonlight to stream through. It illuminated a room with several beds. The sloped roof held tiny pieces of glass that glittered in the moonlight, each one shaped like a throwing star - Yira's symbol. The room was so unremarkable it seemed surreal. He knew he was not injured but he felt it in the way his arms refused to cooperate, the way his legs felt like lead, the way his wings ached with a deep soreness of the muscles.

"Run," Jaysen continued. "Into the forest. They'll hunt you, but keep running until you can't hear them anymore, until the cold creeps into your bones and the burn of acid sets in. Got it?"

Kaleo tried to look at his so-called friend, tried to ask a question, ask who would be hunting, or why it should be so cold in late spring. He didn't get the chance. The firm ground he felt beneath his feet suddenly fell away, landing him hard on his back in a mess of brambles and dried out vines. He groaned, looking up to the second-story window with incredulity, reminding himself that his friend was blind - he couldn't see *second-story* windows, only *feel* windows.

"Shit," he whispered as he forced himself to his feet, forced himself to take the first few steps, and then forced his wings to take him higher into the sky than he ever thought possible. In the dark, it was difficult to navigate through the thick trees. He flew in a disoriented line away from the house, dropping several feet and rising again as the growls and snarls followed. When he could no longer hear them, he allowed himself to drop down into a thick tree branch, several feet above the ground, and took a moment to simply breathe with terrified tears streaming down his face.

***

The rake of Madhavi's claw sent Jaysen flying against the wall with a strangled cry he'd not expected to let free. Keeping Kaleo shielded cost him. He felt weak, tired, worried. It was his fault Kaleo was in the mess he was in; his fault Madhavi found him in the first place. She had a tie to Jaysen, a way to track him no matter where he went. Usually it wasn't a problem because he rarely went far, but this time...

"Let go of me!" Jaysen heard her cry, snarling and spitting like a trapped animal.

"I told you not to touch him," Roth snarled. Despite the pain he felt in his face, Jaysen smiled. The creature was crazy, but he was Jaysen's crazy; his own personal demonic guardian angel. "He's fragile."

"I said let go, you hideous piece of shit!" Madhavi spat, then screamed. Jaysen heard her body colliding with a large piece of furniture, the wood splintering and glass breaking off inside her flesh. The scent of blood filled his nostrils, made him hungry for it. He'd already had a taste from Kaleo. He bit down on his lower lip instead.

"Are you aljright, Moppet?" Roth asked, his face uncomfortably close to Jaysen's. The touch of the Corrupted man's hand against his face made Jaysen recoil both in annoyance and pain.

"Don't!" he hissed before tempering himself. "I'm... I'm fine."

"I won't let her hurt you, Moppet. You're all I have. Just you and Phier. And Evie. Just you and Phier and Evie. And Malie. Just you and Phier and Evie and Malie."

"I know…" Jaysen continued, forcing himself up to a standing position only to feel himself fall forward into Roth's arms, too weak to stand on his own. His middle ached and felt damp, with fresh blood oozing from the wound at his navel. The fever creeping up the length of his slender neck and into his cheeks didn't help. He'd listened to Roth speak of someone called Malie. It meant 'lucky one'; Jaysen doubted Roth knew that though. He'd heard Kaleo use the word. It took a great deal of convincing to get the idiot to keep *Eila* safe, too. She was Jaysen's. Lara had to fend for herself - wherever she was. Jaysen wasn't sure. He wasn't even sure where Eila was.

"Don't worry, we're leaving," Roth said as he lifted Jaysen up. The sensation had Jaysen floating, disoriented and struggling to be away from the Corrupted Speaker while wanting nothing more than to melt into the crazy man. No, he was no longer a man, no more than Jaysen was merely a boy. They were something else entirely, caught between a nightmare and a daydream. Things shifted in odd ways as Roth Traveled from one point to the next, reemerging in a space that echoed terribly. Each sound reverberated in Jaysen's ears like a loud gong and made his head hurt. They would be punished for what they'd done. *He* would be punished. He let Kaleo go.

"Rest here, Moppet. You're safe now," Roth said in a surprisingly tender voice. It was an unusual characteristic for the Corrupted man. Normally he was bellowing at this or that, crying out for entertainment or talking incessantly about the floofs he found in random places about his person. Jaysen still didn't know what a floof was, only that it was soft and tickled when it moved.

He heard something else in the cavernous space, something with a voice in a higher, softer pitch than anyone Jaysen was used to. A child, perhaps. Maybe that's what Malie was - a child. Wouldn't that be ironic? Roth *ate* children. Babies especially. Jaysen recalled their wailing cries all too well. When his surroundings suddenly turned icy cold, Jaysen's breath caught. Ghost had followed.

"Go away!" Roth barked. "We don't want you here! Can't you see he is convalescing! You're going to make it worse!"

"Taelon is back," Ghost said. The fey prince. No wonder Madhavi was in such a horrid mood. "He has... your Evie with him. She is safe."

"My Evie? Why?" Roth clipped. Silence followed. "Keep Malie and Moppet safe. Don't let that flying cunt get near them."

That was all Jaysen heard, the silence echoing as much as the noise. Then he heard the humming - a soft, sweet noise that carried a familiar song; Argento's song.

Malie could hear the Nodes too.

Chapter Twenty-Four

A low growl erupted into the dead silence of the Black Forest. *Coedwig ddu* was what Maddox's people called it, giving it a more exotic sound than the Trade Cant could offer. He'd done some traveling in his time, seeing parts of the white cities or bartering passage to places like Mahala and Esbeth, even south to Corvis for a time before returning to the forests of his birth. Most duende of Asphondel would consider Maddox to be worldly when, really, he just had terribly itchy feet. It was those itchy feet that kept him alive when the white cities fell, kept him moving from town to town until making his way back to find his tribe, his family. By the time he reached Asphondel, however, they were already gone.

Two months through blighted woods and charred corpses, he'd seen too many skirmishes and ate too little food, living off what he found or hiding from things that *could* have been survivors but things he was too cowardly to look at. He did not want to chance a run-in with a demon. While he could defend himself, it was clear that that would not be enough against a demon. So Maddox ignored the angry growl of his stomach and picked his way forward, heading south to the shores where there were boats to take survivors - or so rumor said. Even in desolate parts of the forests, rumors spread on the lips of the dead.

He kept moving, stopping to rest for only a few hours a night in the high branches of the trees - what was left of them. Nothing moved below, no night creatures to move across the ground. The few left in the trees were as cautious as he, hiding or moving slowly to make as little noise as possible. Maddox wondered if they were as tired as he was.

The sun set with Maddox curled into the crook of an old sephirot tree that had once been someone's home. He'd climbed higher into the helix-shaped tree, nestling where there were still leaves to hide him, and watched the sun descend into the horizon. The demons hunted at night, growling and snarling as they hunted for things to tear apart. Maddox held a long dagger close to his chest, nodding off to the sounds of someone screaming far off in the distance, praying it wasn't Alivae.

***

"We need to keep movin'," Alivae pointed out. She was exhausted. Cavian saw it in her face. Her Power had changed, blossomed into something amazing. Her screams had attracted some attention that Cavian took quick care of, but she was not wrong. If they loitered too long, there was bound to be more than Cavian or his lovely flower could safely handle at once. He intended to keep his promise.

"Will you hit me again if I tell you that you need more rest?" he countered. She turned to frown at him. Her face was pale yet flushed." You've got a fever, flower."

"Azrus take me," she grumbled. "Stop callin' me that."

"What should I call you then?" he chuckled. "You never gave me your name."

"Alivae," she finally sighed after a long, sullen silence.

Cavian smiled, sticking close to Alivae, waiting for the inevitable. When she finally collapsed, he caught her, lifting her up into his arms.

"I think it's time we left this droll forest, Alivae. Don't you agree?" He directed his question to the phoenix that weighed down a nearby branch. "Don't worry, I've no intention of turning her over. My fool heart has grown too fond of her for that. We're not *all* scheming assholes."

As soon as the phoenix gave its approval, Cavian nodded, made sure the Sword was secure on his back, tightened his hold on Alivae, and took to the sky on powerful, wide wings, smiling when the phoenix followed.

***

Jaysen stopped himself from sighing heavily. It was too much to ask for any kind of normalcy to descend upon them. He was grateful to Roth for pulling him away from Madhavi, truly, but the level of annoyance that brought with it made Jaysen question quite a few things in life - like his ability to stay in it. He had no *audeas* to stop him this time, no one to tell him he was needed for some kind of hunt or search. He had enough strength for that, at least, and the only one that might actually miss him was the lunatic hollering at the mute. Roth had put Eila 'somewhere safe' but wouldn't say where. She might miss him too.

I'd miss you.

The unfamiliar voice made Jaysen's breath catch. If rolling thunder had a voice, it would be the creature that spoke to him. He was familiar enough with the sensation in his mind, the gentle caress like fire licking its way across his brain to know what it was - an *audeas*. But Tanis-

Tanis served her purpose. She gave her life for yours, as was her duty. Now it is my turn to protect you.

"Who are you?" Jaysen whispered, knowing he would not be heard over the roaring demands to leave whatever cave Roth brought them to. That much he knew just by how the Corrupted man's voice echoed back at them.

Harper. I sense your pain. Let me ease it.

Replacing Tanis seemed like an impossible task. Every ounce of love Jaysen could have possibly mustered for another living being was given to the lost chimera. To give it to another seemed traitorous somehow.

"Just go away..." Jaysen whispered. "Please, just let me go."

I can't. They need you more than you know.

A mournful sound escaped Jaysen's chest. Roth continued to argue, to growl and hiss at the other Corrupted man, the other monster. They had no place, no purpose, no one that cared - - except their *audeas*.

I'm here, Jaysen. Reach your hand out.

He hesitated a moment, feeling the sharp sting of tears at the backs of his eyes. It surprised him, for it was not a feeling he was accustomed to. He'd shed his tears long ago. But he reached out all the same, touching the warm muzzle of a chimera, feeling the breath against his palm, and finally crumbled into the creature's neck, shoulders shaking with silent sobs.

***

A deep, bone-crushing cold filled the weary chimera. It was not *just* ice. It sapped him of will, of life, of thought. He knew something was wrong but could not force enough concern to sort through the darkness, through the heaviness, and doubt to find out what that was.

Fionn!

His name rang through the thickness in which he existed, though he could not place who spoke it or why it sounded so desperate. Cotton stuffed the chimera's head, made him float through the cold. Why could he not answer?

FIONN!

His eyes rolled in his skull. He could hear the sound of his own breath from the tip of his muzzle, feel the heat of it roll up into the cold and freeze as tiny little particles of ice in the air around him.

WHERE ARE YOU! PLEASE! FIONN!

He knew the voice. It meant something to him, belonged to someone important. Why couldn't he remember!

Fionn. Listen. Hear me.

A different voice spoke now. This one held no panic, no fear, only soothing tones that cracked the ice around him. He heard it, heard it echo and winced from the pain the sound brought to his head. The sound was like a bone shattering, ringing through his skull, making his ears twitch. His wings felt sore and heavy at his sides, pinned down by the same bone-crushing cold he found himself in.

Listen to me, Fionn. Do not fight, just listen.

He wasn't fighting at all. He couldn't. Yet as soon as the words were spoken, he felt his tense muscles liquefy and let out another deep breath. The ice cracked again, creating another painful echo. It did so a few times over until that freezing cold began to melt away. It was not warm by any stretch of the word, but he did not feel as heavy. He could twitch a massive paw or lift the very end of his tail. Even an ear flicked, but that was the extent of his ability.

FIONN!

Kaleo. The voice had a name. His *audean*, his little one. His entire purpose was to protect that life, to defend it with his own. But his little one was not with him. He cried out in fear and pain with no assistance to be had. Fionn could not provide it.

Shh, we will make it right. Do not worry. Focus on me.

The soothing voice cut through the rise in panic that made his muscles tighten again and soothed him back to melted butter. Suddenly, Fionn understood. He could not panic, could not fear. That brought the cold back and muddled his mind. He forced his breath to even out. He forced the muscles of his wings to relax, one pair lying carefully over the other like a blanket.

Good, Fionn. Listen and focus. I will help you. We will make it right. We will find him. Rest. Regain strength for him.

I will...

The thought came unbidden. It was then he realized that he finally had the ability to answer. It was a weak answer, but an answer nonetheless. He also knew that he could not reach out to his *audaen*. It would cost too much. The one who spoke was closer, easier to reach. He knew that she... yes, *she* heard him.

Serai.

M'lady... please...

*I am trying, Fionn. I do not wish to harm you more. It will take time. We will find him again, I promise. Malek is hunting. We **will** find him.*

Fionn let it rest at that. His breath settled into an easy rhythm, and he waited for the cold to retreat at a glacial pace.

Oenel Family Line

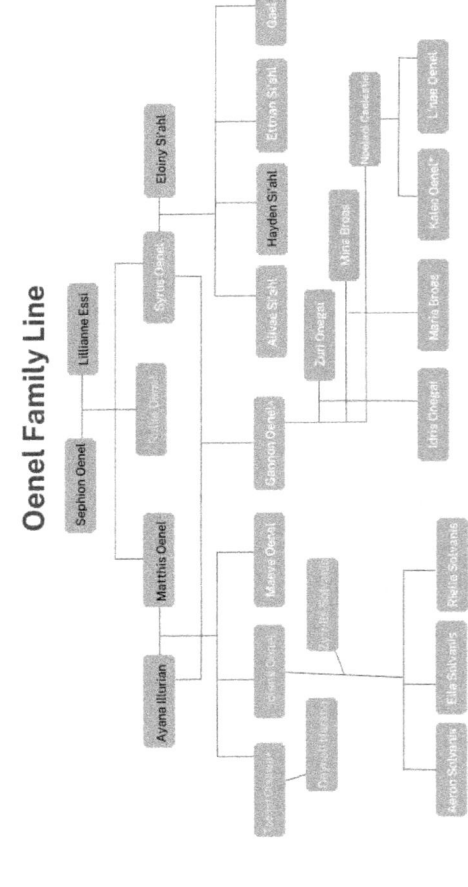

- Sephion Oenel — Lillianne Essi
  - Sallos Oenel — Syrus Oenel — Eloiny Si'ahl
    - Gannon Oenel
      - Zuri Oneiga
        - Idris Oneiga
        - Maria Broae
        - Noelani Caeasarin
          - Kaleo Oenel^
          - L'nae Oenel
      - Mina Broae
    - Alivae Si'ahl
    - Hayden Si'ahl
    - Etrian Si'ahl
    - Gael Si'ahl
- Matthlis Oenel — Avana Illurian
  - Maeve Oenel
    - Cress Oenis
      - Jaden Oneiga*
      - Freyleaf Illurian
    - Zyrielle Salvanis
      - Ella Salvanis
      - Aeron Schrevkiv
      - Rielis Salvanis

> Adopted by Emperor Matthis Oenel at the behest of the Fey God
~ Now referring to himself as Rowen Si'ahl.
* Adopted by Noelani after birth mother died during childbirth.

Black names are deceased; faded names are believed deceased but never confirmed; white names are living.

Illurian Family Line

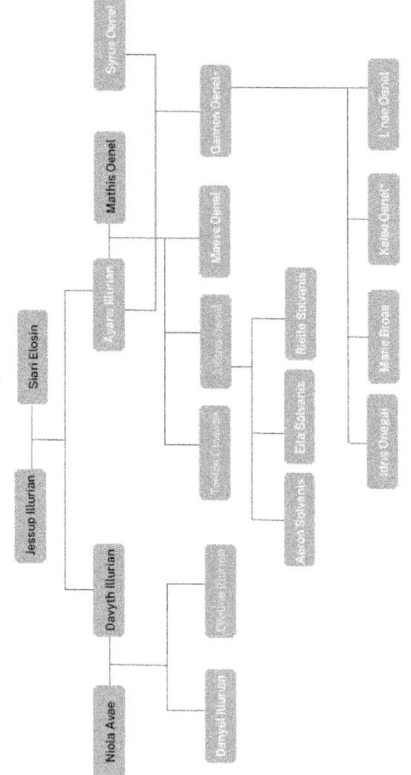

- Jessup Illurian — Siari Elosin
  - Davyth Illurian — Niola Avee
    - Danyel Illurian
    - Evelise Rachels
  - Ajaria Illurian — Mathiis Oenel — Synais Oenel
    - Maeris Oenel
    - Darren Oenel
      - Jaros Oenel
      - Mara Broze
      - Kelas Oenel
      - Lhan Oenel
    - Kaeris Oenel
      - Aeron Sovonis
      - Ella Sovonis
      - Roitte Sovonis

> Adopted by Emperor Mathiis Oenel at the behest of the Fey God.
^ Now referring to himself as Renen S'ahi.
* Adopted by Noelans after birth mother died during childbirth.

Black names are deceased; faded names are believed deceased but never confirmed; white names are living.

Dyalov Family Line

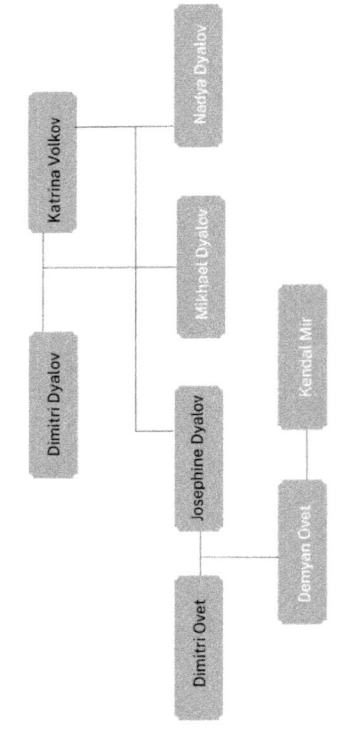

- Dimitri Dyalov — Katrina Volkov
  - Mikhael Dyalov
  - Nadya Dyalov
  - Josephine Dyalov — Dimitri Ovet
    - Kendal Mir
    - Demyan Ovet

Black names are deceased; white names are living.

Character Lexicon (By Nation)
Asphondel Forest:

Alivae Si'ahl (Duende olve) - New Speaker of Tribes. Speaker to Rhyanna Syrus and Eloiny's eldest child. Sister to Reven and Maddox.

Amber - Alivae's *audeas* (phoenix)

Eloiny Si'ahl (Duende olve) - Daughter of the Speaker of Tribes (Duende olve)

Evanrae Coryn'yl (Duendo olve) - Former Speaker of Tribes (Speaker to Rhyanna)

Ettrian Si'ahl - Syrus's third child with Eloiny, brother to Alivae and Gael.

Fallon Tria'ael - From the Dead Seer tribe. Best friend of Syrus Oenel.

Gael Si'ahl - Syrus and Eloiny's youngest child.

Maddox Si'ahl - Eloiyny's oldest child, half brother to Alivae.

Syrus Oenel - Former prince of the Phoenix Empire. Father to Gannon Oenel/Reven Si'ahl.

Cartha (formerly known as the Phoenix Empire):

Cavian (Dragon-born) - Collector and Dream Walker. Son of the Red. Twin brother to Madhavi. Younger brother to Daemodan.

Daemodan (Dragon-born) - Scientist. Son of the Red. Creator of the Corrupted Speakers. Elder brother to Cavoam amd Madhavi.

Danyel Illurian/Roth (Tirsai olve; Corrupted) - Former High Lord Speaker of the Phoenix Empire and Speaker to Sofia.

Phier - Roth's *audeas* (Corrupted phoenix).

Jaysen Daws (tywyll olve; Corrupted) - Corrupted Speaker to Eris. Friend to Kaleo.

Harper - Jaysen's *audeas* (Chimera).

Cartha (Continued)
Madhavi (Dragon-born) - Dream walker. Daughter of the Red. Younger sister to Daemodan, twin sister to Cavian.

Malie/Yulia Vi - Roth's new 'Moppet'.

Mikhael Dyalov/Ghost (Human; Kormandi; Corrupted) - Former prince of Kormaine; Corrupted Speaker to Ana. Uncle to Demyan. Elder brother to Nadya.

Havok - Ghost's *audeas* (Snow-owl gryphon).

Taelon Otsawa (Fey demi-god; Corrupted) - son of Mylan. Former High Lord General of the Phoenix Legions. Adopted elder brother to the Oenel children.

Xandrix DuAndiuin (Tywyll olve; Corrupted) - Hunter of the Speakers. Former guardian of Gannon and the members of the Phoenix Empire royal family.

Damaskha:
Idris Onegai (Aurum) - Assassin for la Maison. Son of Zuri and Gannon.

Marie Boras (Runeli) - Member of la Maison, kitchen staff of la Chateau du Soie. Daughter of Mina and Gannon.

Mama Zuri Onegai (Aurum) - Proprietor of la Chateau du Soie. Mistress to Gannon.

Mina Broas (Runeli) - Lady of la Chateau du Soie.

Esbeth:
Ayla Araceli (Avian) - Amatta (Ruling Queen) of the Esbethi Amaterasu. High Seat of Heaven. Noelani's maternal grandmother.

Iona Marca - The Amatessa's handmaiden and L'nae's caretaker.

Kalelako Anao (Avian) - Speaker to Wai. Keeper of the Ancestors.

Nessa - Kalelako's *audeas* (Chimera).

Kai Tano - Personal guard to the Amatessa.

Noelani Caelestis-Oenel (Avian) - Amatessa (crowned princess) of the Esbethi Amaterasu. Princess of the Phoenix Empire by marriage (to Gannon); step-mother to Kaleo.

L'Nae Caelestis-Oenel (Avian) - Daughter of Noelani and Gannon; Amatess (princess) of the Esbethi Amaterasu.

Rangi-Ahn Araceli (Avian) - Amat (Ruling King) of the Esbethi Amaterasu. Second Seat of Heaven. Noelani's maternal grandfather.

Tondra Caelestis (Avian) - Kenelala (General) of the Special Forces for the Protection of the Amaterasu. Cousin to Noelani.

Kormaine (Fallen):

Adrian Yerokhin (Shadow-born) - Confidante to Nadya.

Aeron Solvanis (Tirsai olve) - Heir apparent to the Phoenix Empire. Elder brother to Eila and Rielle. Advisor to Demyan.

Demyan "Shiro" Ovet (Human; Kormandi) - King of Kormaine. Speaker to Hikaru.

Aisling - Demyan's *audeas* (Snow-owl gryphon).

Gabriel D'Elian-Karov (Human; Kormandi) - Baron of the Tatengel region of Kormaine. Master of the Horse Guilds of Damaskha and Kormaine.

Jaxiam Delquire (Duende olve) - Member of the Nidoli (Kormandi thieve's guild). Best friend to Gabriel and Mikhael.

Kendal Mir Ovet (Human; Itahli) - Queen of Kormaine by marriage. High Priestess of Yira.

Nadya Dyalov (Human; Kormandi) - Princess of Kormaine. Aunt to Demyan. Younger sister to Mikhael.

Nastya Kiv (Human; Kormandi) - Friend to Nadya and Adrian.

Itahl:
Queen Isabelle Roche: Ruling monarch of Itahl.
Great Mother: Annointed by Adrastaeia as the living embodiment of Her word.
Holy Father: Annointed by Yira as the living embodiment of Her word both waking and dreaming.
Patrick Kent: Lead enforcer of the Hunters of Itahl in charge of eliminating Sinners.
Seren (Human) - Captive of the Itahli Hunters. Speaker of Speakers.

Tierra Vida Transplants from Mahala:
Ajana Dai (Half-olven; Cantari) - Thief-taker and dancer who found Reven.
Kaleo Oenel (Avian) - Reven's apprentice. Gannon's son by Inola Akau; Amatti of the Esbethi Amaterasu. Speaker to Navaeh. Elder brother to L'nae. Cousin to Aeron, Rielle, and Eila.
Fionn - Kaleo's *audeas* (Chimera).
Lara Gouveia (Runeli) - Local pick-pocket. Friend of Kaleo.
Liam Roe (Duende olve) - Thief-taker that works closely with Reven. Also known as Zorian Li'ael.
Reven Si'ahl (Tirsai olve) - Also known as the Black Bard. Mentor/father to Kaleo. Speaker to Argento. Younger brother to Maeve. Formerly known as Gannon Oenel.
Azure - Reven's *audeas* (Phoenix).
Serai (Human) - Reven's drummer. Speaker of Speakers.
Malek - Serai's *audeas* (Drake).

Tierra Vida:

Halora Golvayne (Tirsai olve) - Healer for the Tierra Vida refugee camp.

Maeve Oenel (Tirsai olve) - Lady Captain of the Illurian City Guard. Former princess of the Phoenix Empire. Elder sister to Gannon. Cousin to Danyel/Roth.

Navid Shahr (Centaur) - Former guardian to Gannon, now Guardian to Rielle and Eila.

Rhys (Faun) - Oracle of Tierra Vida.

Rielle & Eila Solvanis (Tirsai olve) - Twins. Sisters to Aeron. Cousins to Kaleo & L'nae.

Saphir Hai'lyn (Duende olve) - Scout for the Tierra Vida refugee camp.

Valance Novis (Tirsai olve) - Lieutenant of the Illurian City Guard.

World Lexicon

Audeas - Magical beast bonded to a Speaker to act as a buffer between the Node and its Vessel.

Audaen - What an audeas calls its bonded Speaker.

Corrupted - to be dammed by the fell-magic of a demon either by force or through a demon wound that has festered. The Corrupted then becomes a demon themselves.

Dragon-born - those born of the union between dragon and mortal.

Node - Magical pools of raw Power. They are a sentient network that give life to the planet of Doranelle and connect the Realms. Each Node that has Claimed a Vessel is given a name by that individual.

Shadow-born - those born of the union between Shade and mortal.

Speaker/Vessel - One who can speak for the Nodes. They are Claimed by the Node.

The Races

The Angels of Faerie - The first of the long-lived races of Doranelle. They have a natural, alluring beauty that many find entrancing and credit to the fey, whom the winged races are believed to be descendant from. Both have semi-pointed ears and a nearly ageless appearance.

Aurum - the angels of the night. They have dark olive or copper skin that seems to shimmer as if dusted by the stars. Their hair is always black, eyes in shades of brown or hazel, and wings of rich golden-brown.

Avian - the angels of heaven. They are known to have wings, hair, and eyes of matching color that can range from a muddy moss color (denoting a lower class citizen) to a bright silver (denoting a higher class citizen).

The Magical Beasts - Each of the magical beasts, with the exception of dragons, act as *audeas* to the Speakers of the world.

Chimera - large, green wolf-like creatures with two sets of wings: one feathered and one bat-like.

Dragons - also known as a Mage to the people of Doranelle. They have the ability to shift into mortal form and maintain it indefinitely.

Drake - related to the dragon but much smaller and without wings. They are more serpentine in nature and incredibly territorial with a knack for hoarding like their dragon-kin.

Gryphons - creatures that are part cat, part bird. The specific breed is determined by the region in which the gryphons live.

Phoenix - large birds made of flame. They are the only immortal magical beast.

Shigou - large mastiff-looking dogs that appear as if they are made of stone, easily blending into cavernous or mountain regions.

The Olve - The second of the long-lived races of Doranelle. Thought to be wiser than the short-lived races because of their long life spans and natural inclination towards magic. All olve have pointed ears and eternally youthful features.

Duende - the olve of nature. They have a dark tan complexion and red, auburn or brown hair. Tend to live in forests or mountains as caretakers of the land.

Cantari - the desert olve. They are copper of skin with black hair and green or gold eyes.

Tirsai - the "true" olve. They claim to be

the first of the olve and, thus, have a naturally arrogant disposition. They are fair of skin, hair and eyes.

Tywyll - the "hidden" olve. They are gray or charcoal of skin with fair hair in hues of light blue, white, or silver and lavender or green eyes. They reside, primarily, beneath the surface as caretakers of the earth.

Runeli - A creature with golden eyes and small horns at the temples. They are rumored to originate from the Ephemeral Lands (otherwise known as the Realm of Dreams) and are highly sought after as concubines for their unnatural beauty.

Shade - A human-like creature born in the Realm of Shadow.

About Doranelle

The Idea

The world of Doranelle is a very complex place that began as a story idea of a parallel planet to Earth when my oldest child was only a few months old. The first iteration of this story was... atrocious. I hid it away and didn't touch it again until my second son was born, five years later. That same year, I did NaNoWriMo for the first time. Almost two-thousand words later, I had another gods-awful piece of work that got shelved.

While I worked on other stories, raised children, worked, and did anything *but* work on Doranelle, I also played quite a bit of D&D. At the time, the *Living Greyhawk* campaign was well underway. I played a great deal with my husband, with friends, we took our children and then my oldest reached an age where he gained interest in playing a game.

It was at this time that I opted to give Doranelle a different type of life - as a campaign setting. Boom, *Ashes to Embers* was born. The characters that were finding lackluster life in a book, instead, found new vigor (and quirks)as NPCs - Non Player Characters - in a plot that began, much like this book does. My original players, however, will tell you that this book is absolutely nothing like the game, nor is it remotely related to the very first iteration of the story I wrote.

Why?

Interactive insanity.

As a GM, it is my job to provide a playground for the players to immerse themselves in. They are key players in the plot, and help direct the events that eventually culminate in a nicely wrapped up package.

Usually.

This model assumes that things always go according to plan. Do you know what I've learned? Nothing *ever* goes according to plan. Player decisions, long nights, longer weekends, and too many snacks (and probably too much alcohol) changed a lot of my best laid plans. The first campaign ran for two years. The second for a year. I've run this campaign a total of seven times over the course of ten years, currently running it's *eighth* iteration.

It is by the graces of my players that I finally sat to tell the *Ashes to Embers* after a lot of nagging to tell the grand tales of the world that had been so carefully stitched together with tears, laughter, and bellyaches.

And so, two more NaNoWriMo years, many words, many tears and achy fingers brought *Ashes to Embers* to life (finally) in the book you hold in your hands. Pieces of each campaign have found there way into the novel, the overall plot, and the outline for three more planned books. But, as with the campaign, the story in my head is ever-evolving, changing as I change. Each of these characters represent a piece of me in a way that no other piece of work I've written does. They are as precious to me as my own children. It was very difficult to let this bird fly but, in the end, I'm glad I did.

Little bastards wouldn't stop screaming otherwise.

The Characters

As previously stated, each of these people holds a piece of me. They also have a personality and voice all their own. Readers often ask how I plan my books and look quizzically as I laugh. I start with a loose outline, throw the characters in, shake it up, and see where they run.

That statement has never been more true than it is with these characters.

They are wild. They are insane. They are drunkards and whores, bastards and kings. They are the ones that control their destinies and decided where *they* wanted to go. I had no say. A few in particular screamed louder than the others while some were content to sit in the background.

Also, a few side notes:

1. No, I did not name the characters after any video games despite what some might think. While I do play, Gannon/Reven were not on my mind when I named him. Gannon actually has a meaning and Reven was just funny to me.

2. The original main character for this entire world has not actually made an appearance yet. Reven decided he wanted to be front and center sometime circa 2006ish.

3. Roth showed me his crazy long before I even wrote him down in a story. He still shows me his crazy and it makes me giggle every time.

4. Yes, he hates butterflies and rocks. Yes, there is a reason. No, you may not know it. As the great Robert Jordan used to say - RAFO!

5. Now we have new weirdos to run around wreaking havok and they are just as chaotic as their predecssors. May they leave your minds intact.

The Universe

Doranelle is but one of a vast network of planets in a solar system that is entirely unlike our own. Isn't that great! Doranelle's sun is larger than ours thus, Doranelle is further out from it's sun than we are. I distinctly recall an argument with my beloved when I first ran the campaign that my laws of physics were entirely off as I initially had the planet in a system with three suns. Eventually, I changed it to appease him, then very proudly declared that it could have worked when we saw such things on the Science Channel. It was a great day in Michelle's world.

Not only is the universe full of various planets, both with and without life, but it is also part of a larger network of Planes and Realms that overlap each other. Each of these ideas were pulled from various religious and scientific texts that tickled my fancy at the time.

And, admittedly, yes, my grasp on simple physics is not the best which is why I lean heavily on magic. Even that, however, is unlike what most would consider 'normal' for a fantasy world. I abhor normal.

The more you read, the more you will learn. There is much to come for Doranelle, it's people, and it's universe. I'm so glad you've come back for more and hope you keep doing so in the future!

About The Author

Michelle Schad is a short story author and novelist of various genres. She has work appearing in Bards and Sages online fiction magazine and all of Corrugated Sky's current anthologies, either as herself or under her pen name, Noa Rose. Her debut novel, Hellfire, was originally published in 2018 with a new rebranding in 2021.

When not entertaining others with words, she is a tamer of the chaos created by her husband, four children, mother, mother-in-law, and too many pets. She is a game master of Pathfinder, D&D, and FATE campaigns, a lifetime Supernatural fan, lover of all things Eeyore, and purveyor of all things alcoholic and/or caffeinated.

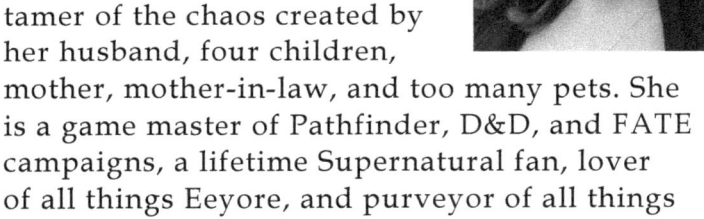

You can keep up with what she does at www.tamingchaos.net, follow her on Facebook and Instagram at @michelleschadwriter, or stay in touch via Twitter and TikTok at @ChelleSchad.

CPSIA information can be obtained
at www.ICGtesting.com
Printed in the USA
JSHW011225020423
39766JS00005B/29

9 781954 413108